HARD
TRAIL
TO FOLLOW

Elmer Kelton

HARD

TRAIL

TO FOLLOW

A Tom Doherty Associates Book
New York

HARD TRAIL TO FOLLOW

Copyright © 2007 by Elmer Kelton

A Forge Book
Published by Tom Doherty Associates, LLC
175 Fifth Avenue
New York, NY 10010

www.tor-forge.com

Forge® is a registered trademark of Tom Doherty Associates, LLC.

Library of Congress Cataloging-in-Publication Data

Kelton, Elmer.
    Hard trail to follow / Elmer Kelton.—1st ed.
        p. cm.
    "A Tom Doherty Associates Book."
    ISBN-13: 978-0-7653-1522-9
    ISBN-10: 0-7653-1522-X
1. Texas—Fiction. I. Title.
    PS3561.E3975H37 2008
    813'.54—dc22

                                                    2007035338

First Edition: January 2008

Printed in the United States of America

0 9 8 7 6 5 4 3 2 1

Dedicated to two retired Texas Ranger friends,
Joaquin Jackson and Bob Favor

HARD
TRAIL
TO FOLLOW

CHAPTER

1

Andy Pickard knew that sooner or later he might have to whip his future brother-in-law.

He had sensed Farley Brackett's dark presence before he saw him, sitting on a roan horse where the rows ended almost at the bank of the Colorado River. Farley's erect posture in the saddle indicated that he was not in a good humor. He seldom was.

Andy had walked a thousand miles up and down this fallow field, guiding a plow point through the mellow earth and staring at the rump end of a brown mule. At least, it seemed like a thousand miles. He leaned back to exert pressure on the leather reins tied together and looped behind his neck. The mule stopped in its tracks, always more willing to answer to "Whoa" than to "Giddyup." It slumped immediately into a position of rest, flicking long ears to ward off a bothersome horsefly. Andy slipped a red bandanna from his neck and wiped his sweaty face while he waited to hear the latest complaint.

Farley's voice was laced with sarcasm. "What's that you're leavin' behind you, a furrow or a snake track?"

Farley's attitude grated like a boil on Andy's backside. The furrow was not as straight as it should be, but he had never claimed he was a good farmer. He tried to match

Farley's sarcasm. "A crooked row don't mean a thing to a cornstalk. It'll grow just the same."

"You ought to've stuck to bein' a Ranger. You'll never make a farmer if you live to be a hundred and six."

"I'd gladly swap you this mule for that roan. You can push the plow awhile, and I can laze around over the country like a property owner."

Farley had spent little time behind a plow, leaving that to Andy and a couple of black laborers. As a prospective Brackett-in-law, it looked as if Andy was about to marry into a life long on hard work and short on appreciation, at least from Farley.

Farley said, "If it wasn't for Bethel, I'd fire you."

"If it wasn't for her, I'd've done quit."

He had thought a lot about leaving. Were it not for Bethel, he would have put this farm behind him months ago. He felt sure the Texas Rangers would be pleased to take him back. They had tried to persuade him not to resign in the first place. The things a man would do for a woman . . .

It was a big farm and a good one, something to take strong pride in if he had been born with hands that fit a plow handle. But of late he had revisited an old dream of going back west, perhaps to the hill country where he had spent a long stretch with the Rangers. It was still but sparsely settled. Land was easy to come by in comparison to this well-populated region of southeastern Texas. Some country out there was so far from the state land office in Austin that a man could squat on it free, at least for a few years, until he could build up his net worth. Another possibility was the rolling plains far to the northwest. There he had friends who would ride to hell's rimrock with him if necessary. They had done it more than once.

When Bethel had accepted his marriage proposal, the couple planned such a move. She had been as eager as he was. Then her mother fell ill and deeded the farm to her son and daughter in anticipation of death. The wedding and other plans were deferred because Bethel was reluctant to leave her dying mother. This was home. She had grown up here. Her father was buried in this ground, and it was likely that her mother soon would be. Now that Bethel owned half interest in the place, she no longer discussed leaving.

That her cross-grained brother shared ownership was Andy's hard luck.

At the time, Farley was recuperating from a wound suffered in Ranger service on the border, so Andy had agreed to stay and help. He worked for foreman's wages, hopeful that Bethel would sooner or later come back around to his way of thinking. Lately that hope was wearing thin.

Farley seemed now to have recovered from the latest of many injuries, major and minor, to which he seemed especially prone. He had reverted to the same cranky misfit he had been before. Andy told him, "We'd get the plantin' done faster if you'd pitch in and help. You could take the east field."

Farley shook his head. "Can't. Got to go to town and get some stuff for Teresa."

"Write me a list, and I'll go in your place," Andy said.

"I ain't sure you can read any better than you can plow a

straight row. Never did see an Indian that could be taught how to farm."

There he goes with that Indian thing again, Andy thought. He was not an Indian, but Comanches had captured him when he was a small boy and kept him several years. Farley harbored a strong dislike for Indians. Frequently he threw Andy's old Comanche name up to him. "You're lettin' that mule get almost as lazy as you are, Badger Boy. Him and you had better get back to work."

Andy prided himself on being able to get along with most people, but for years his relationship with Farley Brackett had swung back and forth between uneasy tolerance and outright hostility. Necessity had forced them to ride together as Rangers. Andy's betrothal to Farley's sister had joined them again, however reluctantly, on the Brackett farm. He had wanted to show her he could be a responsible husband and settle down to the tranquil life of a farmer. By now he had concluded that it would never be tranquil so long as he had to deal with Farley.

Turning the mule around, he roughly pushed the plow point into the ground and started another row. Farley was still talking, but Andy let the words drift away unanswered on the wind. He was saying a few words of his own.

He had often wondered why a woman so pretty and so gentle in nature should be saddled with such a brother. He tried to take into account that Farley had endured hardships enough to sour any man. He bore a war scar on his face and hidden scars deep within. His brothers had died fighting the Yankees. He and Bethel had lost their father to partisan violence that continued after the war. Farley had made himself a scourge to Union Reconstruction authorities and to state police who tried to enforce their edicts. His wildness had been both asset and liability during his later service as a Ranger.

Andy had long tried to accord him the benefit of the doubt. He realized Farley had abundant reason for being angry at most of the world, but sympathetic understanding was hard to maintain when he made himself so damned disagreeable.

The sun sank behind clouds low in the west, turning them to orange flame. The last few rows were no straighter than those before, but the hell with it. Farley could do them over if he was dissatisfied. Andy wearily laid the plow on its side and unhitched the mule. The lagging animal picked up new energy when it realized it was going to the barn for feed and rest.

Andy laid up the leather harness in the barn and fed the mule in a trough hewn from the trunk of a tree. Farley was brushing the roan. He offered no conversation, but his eyes smoldered. Anything Andy said would draw a barbed response, so he kept his silence. His feet dragged in fatigue as he walked toward the big house Bethel's father had built in prosperous times before war tore his family apart. Bethel waited on the front porch, youthful and slender and pretty enough to make a man want to hug her to death. She stood on tiptoes and invited a kiss. "You're tired," she said. "You should've quit earlier."

Looking into her welcoming eyes, he felt warm as sunshine. He embraced her so hard she gasped for breath. He said, "Didn't want to waste any daylight."

That was something he had often heard Rusty Shannon say. Rusty had more or less adopted him after his return from life with the Indians. He had managed to keep his patience during Andy's difficult adjustment to the white man's road. Though Rusty had carried a gun many years in the Ranger service, he had remained a farmer at heart, content now to work his own land a few miles from here. Andy had hoped he might be able to do the same, but now he dreaded the thought of following a mule up and down these fields the rest of his life. He had never lost the Comanche instinct for freedom, for drifting with the seasons and yearning to see the yonder side of the hill.

Bethel said, "You'll feel better when you've washed up. Teresa and me will have supper ready pretty soon. Have you seen Farley?"

"Seen and heard him. He's out at the barn."

Bethel caught the sarcasm. "I wish you'd find a way to get along with him. He's had a hellish life. And he *is* my brother."

"That's hard to forget. He keeps remindin' me that I'm just a hired hand, and you're the only reason he lets me stay here."

"You're a lot more than a hired hand. What's mine is yours, or will be when we're married."

"Ain't nothin' really mine here except a couple of horses. Your old daddy built this place. I didn't."

Bethel's eyes pinched. "Get ready for supper."

Bethel's father had made a modest fortune steamboating on the Brazos River before buying a large block of land and turning it into a prosperous farm. Carpetbaggers had stolen half of it after the war, but it was still a substantial enterprise.

Andy had barely finished drying his face on a towel when Farley stalked onto the back porch, pitched Andy's wash water into the yard, and poured a fresh panful from a bucket. He said, "Badger Boy, about what I said out yonder . . ."

Andy hoped he was on the verge of an apology, but he should have known better. Farley said, "I meant every damned word of it."

Andy's face burned. No appropriate retort came to him. He clenched his teeth and went back into the house.

Teresa Brackett was placing food on the long dining table that had once served a large family. She smiled, but her dark eyes betrayed uneasiness. New to the family, she had become painfully aware of the strained relationship between her husband and Andy. She took pains to speak gently, trying to make up for Farley's abrasiveness.

"There will come a better day," she said.

It couldn't get much worse, he thought. He had too much respect for her feelings to say it aloud.

In the past, Farley had often voiced a prejudice against Mexicans, but despite himself he had fallen in love with Teresa, the half-Mexican daughter of a border rancher. If there was anything consistent about Farley, it was his inconsistency. Now and again he acted almost human, but he usually got over it before it could become a habit.

Andy suspected that Teresa was already with child, though nothing had been said. It had been only a few months since she and Farley had married. If she delivered a son, the poor kid was in for a hard upbringing, Andy thought. Farley would work him like a mule.

Damned if I want to be around here to see it, he thought.

Farley's boots clomped heavily as he entered the dining room. He dropped into a chair at the head of the table, reaching immediately for a steaming biscuit without waiting for the two women to seat themselves. He quickly dropped it onto his plate and blew on his burned fingers. Teresa placed her hand on his shoulder for a fleeting moment. Farley's only response was a curt "You ought to've told me it was so hot."

She seated herself in a corner chair that gave her a view of his profile. She said just as curtly, "You should've known. It came right out of the oven."

Andy took satisfaction from her retort. Teresa was not letting Farley run over her. She had some snap, that little olive-skinned woman. It would serve Farley right if she bit his head off.

Teresa asked, "Did you bring me the things I asked for?"

Farley speared a slice of roast beef with his fork and plopped it into his plate. "Never quite got to town. Lost too much time makin' sure Andy didn't plow that field crossways."

Bethel's voice had the same snap as Teresa's. "He works harder than anybody around here."

"I could do better with my eyes shut."

Andy withheld comment, though he pictured himself shutting Farley's eyes with his fists. The image brought him pleasure.

Bethel said, "Teresa, you and me will go to town together tomorrow, and you can pick out just what you want.
When it comes to buying something for a woman, Farley
has no more taste than a one-eyed burro."

Farley snorted. "I had pretty good taste when it came to
pickin' a wife. Better than you've got in pickin' a husband."

Andy said, "I don't think either one of them has won a
jackpot."

Farley asked about his mother. Bethel said she did not
feel strong enough to come to the table. She would take
her supper in bed. Farley ate the rest of his meal in silence,
then shoved his plate away. "You women may hear a rumor
in town tomorrow, so I'd just as well tell you now."

Bethel tensed. "Tell us what?"

"I've been askin' around for opinions. I've about decided to run for sheriff."

Disturbed, Andy let his fork drop noisily upon the table.
"Against Tom Blessing? But he's held that office for years."

"Too many years. Tom's gettin' to be an old man. He's
earned the right to sit and rock on his front porch. The
county needs a younger man to take over that job. I'm also
thinkin' of the salary and the rewards. We could stand
some more cash income on this place. It's a long time between crops."

Andy had not thought of Tom as an old man, though he
had grandchildren old enough to help him on his farm. He
argued, "Me and you have both worked with Tom on
Ranger business. He's a good man, and he's given this
community a lot more than he ever got from it."

"It's time he had a chance to rest." Farley's brow furrowed, his eyes boring into Andy's. "You ain't goin' to oppose me on this, are you?"

Andy did not waste much time thinking about it. "I will if Tom runs for reelection."

Farley's face colored, the scar on his cheek darker than the rest. "For somebody who's anglin' to be part of this family, you show damned little loyalty."

"I've known Tom Blessing a lot longer than I've known you. He's been a friend to me and Rusty and everybody else around here."

Farley pushed his chair back. "Bethel, you could've had any man you wanted. Why in the hell did you pick *him*?"

Bethel spoke a couple of sharp words, then choked off the rest as Farley got up and left the room. She turned her gaze to Andy. He saw silent rebuke in her narrowed eyes.

He said, "He asked me, so I told him. If he didn't want an honest answer, he oughtn't to've asked me."

"You've got to give him more time. You just don't understand him." Bethel sounded hurt.

"But I do. I understand him too damned well."

Teresa looked down at her plate, her face flushed.

Andy saw that further discussion would lead to an even more heated argument. He stood away from the table. "I'd best let the air clear a little." He walked out onto the front porch. Farley stood there, smoking a newly rolled cigarette. His angry gaze touched Andy, but he said nothing. Andy went on to the barn, where a tack room had been converted into small but comfortable sleeping quarters for him. The arrangement had originally been meant to be temporary, until he and Bethel married. There were times, like now, when he wondered if they would ever stand before a preacher.

He sat on a hay bale and began sharpening a hoe to give his hands something to do. A shadow fell against the door. Bethel stood there, frowning at him. She asked, "Are you in a mood to talk?"

Andy laid the hoe aside. It had not really needed sharpening anyway. "I'm always in a mood to talk to you. But if it's about your brother, I doubt there's any use. He's what he is, and I'm what I am. I don't see either one of us changin'."

"You could if you'd both have patience."

"I *had* patience, once. Farley has worn it down to a nub."

"This farm has been a heavy load for him. He's never had this kind of responsibility before. Once he knows he can handle it, maybe he'll settle down and be easier to get along with."

"He's *never* been easy to get along with. If it wasn't for you, I'd've already quit tryin'."

"Try a little longer. We don't want our marriage to start with you and my brother fighting over every little thing that comes up."

"He's the one you should talk to. It's him that's always raisin' hell about somethin'."

She shook her head. "It looks like I can't talk to either one of you." She left the barn, leaving Andy wondering if he could have said something differently. He didn't know what it might be.

*   *   *

Late the next afternoon he was slipping the harness from the mule when he saw two riders approaching the barn. He tensed until he realized neither was Farley. He didn't know anybody who would willingly ride with Farley anyway. His future brother-in-law was not adept at making friends. Andy's spirit lifted as he recognized Rusty Shannon. Beside him rode Sheriff Tom Blessing, still straight-backed in the saddle despite his years, and broad-shouldered as a blacksmith. In fact, he *was* a blacksmith, and a farmer, and a carpenter as well as a peace officer. He could do just about anything he put his mind and hands to. Serious, self-sufficient men like him had brought Texas up from the struggling, poverty days of the republic to where it was today.

They dismounted, and Andy eagerly shook hands with both men. He considered them the best friends he had, along with a Ranger named Len Tanner and an old black farmer named Shanty.

Rusty's hair remained the same dull reddish color as when Andy had first seen him, though it had begun to show strands of gray. His years as a farmer had given him a muscular build and calloused hands. His eyes were still as keen as during the many years he had been a Ranger. They took in the whole farmstead in a sweeping glance. If anything had been amiss, he would have seen it.

He said, "Been a while since you've been over to visit with me and Alice, or to play with the young'un."

Andy nodded in regret. "I've been meanin' to, but workin' this farm has been like swimmin' in water over my head." He removed the last of the harness and slapped the mule on the rump. It moved eagerly toward the feed trough.

"You-all come on up to the house. The womenfolks keep the coffeepot on, and they'll have supper ready directly."

Tom asked uneasily, "You reckon Farley's there?"

"I expect so. He's got a habit of quittin' early. New wife, you know."

Rusty said, "We don't care to run into Farley, not just yet. We've come to ask you if it's a fact that he's fixin' to run for sheriff."

Andy looked upon Rusty as a foster brother and Tom as something of a foster father. He studied the older man with misgivings. "That's what he told me. I tried to talk him out of it, but I'd just as well argue with a fencepost."

Tom asked, "Is he mad at me about somethin'?"

"No more than at anybody else. He doesn't need a reason to get mad. It comes on him natural, like rheumatism."

Tom's eyes showed concern. "I've been sheriff a long time. I hadn't thought about puttin' away my badge."

"Anybody who knows Farley is goin' to think hard before they vote for him. He's not a man they'd want to have authority over them. Especially packin' a gun."

Rusty said, "That's what I've been tellin' you, Tom. You've got lots of friends. How many has Farley got?"

Andy said, "You could crowd them all into a small outhouse and have room left for a plow horse."

Tom frowned in thought while Rusty and Andy continued to present their case. Rusty said, "If you was to quit, that'd leave the county in Farley's hands. You wouldn't want to do that to the folks who've always supported you."

Andy said, "I've put up with Farley a long time, and I guarantee that there ain't no pleasure in it."

Tom said, "I suppose you're right."

Andy said, "Sure we're right. You've been here since they dug the river, and we need you. Everybody needs you."

The sheriff unconsciously rubbed his hand over the badge on his vest. "I'll talk it over with the missus."

Andy said, "I'd bet you a box of cigars that she'll tell you to give Farley the lickin' of his life."

Tom seemed almost convinced.

Rusty said, "That's settled." He gave Andy a critical study. "Speakin' of Farley, I've wondered why you've stayed on here like a hired hand, puttin' up with his ill temper. There's other things you could do instead."

"But I'd have to leave Bethel. She's tied down here till her mother either gets well or dies."

Rusty did not appear satisfied with the answer. "If she's really the woman for you, she'll understand. If she's not, she won't. Should you change your mind, you're always welcome over at my place. I can find plenty for you to do."

Tom said, "Same goes for me. I could use a better deputy. The county judge saddled me with a sleepy-eyed kid who doesn't know which end of the broom to sweep with. You'd be natural for the job on account of your Ranger service."

Andy said, "I'll keep it in mind. You're sure about not stayin' for supper?"

Tom said, "I need to go back to town. I've got a bad one locked up, waitin' for the Rangers to come and get him."

Andy asked, "Anybody I'd know?"

"Name's Luther Cordell. Him and his bunch held up a

bank over in Galveston. Wounded the banker." Tom's eyes went hopeful. "I'd like to hire you as a special deputy to help me watch Cordell till they take him off of my hands."

Andy did not consider long. "I've got too much responsibility here."

Tom turned toward his horse. "It never hurts to ask."

Andy watched both men remount. He said, "Tom, don't you be worryin' none about Farley. He couldn't win that election if he was runnin' against a dead man."

"I'm just worried about the cost of electioneerin'. Cigars don't come cheap."

As the two men rode away, a black farmhand came out of the cowshed carrying a bucket of fresh milk in each hand. Andy asked, "Want me to tote one of them up to the big house for you, Tobe?"

"I'd be obliged, Mr. Andy." The black workers called him *Mister,* though they used his given name. Tobe handed over one of the buckets. "That old brindle cow ain't givin' milk like she ought to. I'm afraid if Mr. Farley sees the bucket ain't full, he'll accuse me of quittin' too quick."

"I'll tell him she's dryin' up. She'll freshen when she has her calf."

It pleased him that some things were beyond Farley's control, like the succession of the seasons and life cycles of the animals.

Farley sat in a rocking chair on the porch. He did not even glance at the milk bucket. His voice was sharp. "I seen Tom Blessing and Rusty out there talkin' to you. What did they want?"

Andy considered not telling him anything, but he decided perversely that Farley needed more to worry about. "They asked me if you're really figurin' to run for sheriff. I told them you are."

"What did they say?"

"Tom thought about quittin' at the end of this term." Andy waited for Farley's satisfied smile, then added, "Me and Rusty talked him out of it. We told him he'll win the race right handy."

Farley's smile vanished like the blowing out of a lamp. "Damn you, Badger Boy." He jumped up so quickly that the chair tipped and almost turned over on its side. One rocker thumped solidly upon the porch as it came back down.

Andy saw the fist but could not dodge it. He staggered backward, dropping the bucket. Milk splashed across the porch and spilled down the steps. For a moment Andy saw only sparkling lights. Then Farley's scarred face showed through them. Andy swung at it with all the force he could bring to bear. Farley fell back against the rocking chair, knocking it over with a loud clatter. Farley bawled in rage and rushed at Andy, swinging his fists like a windmill. One drove breath from Andy's lungs, but he managed to land a fist solidly against Farley's nose. Blood ran down Farley's lips and off his chin.

Andy heard a woman's anguished cry. He did not know whether it came from Bethel or Teresa. He struck Farley again and saw his brother-in-law sprawl backward on the porch.

Both young women stepped between them. Bethel

grabbed Andy's arms. Farley struggled to gain his feet. Teresa knelt over him, pushing against his shoulders to keep him down. Bethel scolded, "Back off, Andy. What do you think you're doing?"

Andy fought for breath. "Tryin' to show your brother . . . there's some things I won't take."

"But he's not a well man. That wound—"

"That wound is all healed up. He just leans on it like it was a crutch."

Teresa scolded her husband with the same sharpness Bethel had used. "Fighting like a schoolboy. Look at you, your face all bloody. Who struck first? No, don't tell me. I don't want to know."

Bethel said, "It makes no difference who struck first. It takes two to make a fight. Either one of you could have backed off."

Andy said, "I've been backin' off too long. I'm tired of it."

Bethel's eyes cut him like a blade. "And maybe you're tired of me, too."

Andy sobered quickly under the lash of her anger. "You know better than that. But some things get to be more than a man can stand still for."

Teresa let Farley get to his feet. He swayed like a cornstalk in the wind. She took his arm and led him toward the door. She said, "We're going out to the back porch and wash your face. Look at your knuckles, all skinned and bleeding."

Farley submitted to her will but gave Andy a smoldering glance before going inside. "This ain't over with."

Bethel forcibly guided Andy backward into the rocking chair. Her voice still crackled. "What am I going to do with you?"

"What are you goin' to do with your brother?"

Shaking her head, she went to the door. She paused long enough to say, "Give Farley time to get washed, then you come in and do the same. We'll have supper on the table pretty soon."

Andy was too angry to eat.

Fighting was more strenuous than plowing. By bedtime he was sore in muscles he did not know he had. He had skipped supper, fearing that anything he ate would probably come back up. Anyway, he did not care to sit at the same table as Farley. His stomach still churned after his temper had cooled. He sat rocking on the porch, listening to night birds chirping in the live-oak trees. He wished his life could be as simple as theirs seemed to be.

Bethel came out and sat on the edge of the porch, near enough for him to touch. He did not try, for he sensed that she was still provoked at him. The two sat in silence, close together, yet far apart. He wanted to speak to her, to say something that might quiet her overcharged emotions, but he could think of nothing that would not sound hollow. He had no intention of backing down.

Finally she said, "Maybe it'd be better if you left here awhile."

That surprised him, but he knew it should not. "Been thinkin' the same thing. I don't want to go by myself, though. I'd want you to go with me."

"You know I can't. There's Mother, and there's Farley."

"Yes, there's Farley. There'll always be Farley." Andy wished he could keep the sharpness from his voice, but he was not good at hiding what he felt.

"What can we do, then?"

"Nothin' much we *can* do. We're boxed into a corner. Farley's not fixin' to change, and I can't abide him ridin' me all the time. Looks like I'd best do what you said and leave."

She reached up and took his hands. "I didn't mean what I said. I don't want you to go."

"But you don't want me to stay either. If I do, there's bound to be another fight. Maybe several. Looks like there's no choice for me, but you've got one. You can go with me."

"You know the answer to that."

Andy felt an ache deep inside. "Then don't set a place for me at the breakfast table. I'll be gone by daylight."

She arose and sat in his lap, her arms around him. He felt her tears wet against his cheek. She whispered, "I love you, Andy."

"And I love you. But . . ." There was no point in repeating what he had already said. Though regret slashed him like a knife, he realized that neither could back away. Each had taken a stand. Pride demanded that both stay with it.

CHAPTER

2

Neither Rusty nor Alice Shannon had made any comment about the bruise on Andy's cheek or the cut on his chin, but they must have seen them. Andy watched Alice rocking her baby boy in a cradle on the Shannon cabin's open dog run, where a gentle breeze toyed with the corner of the infant's blanket. Rusty and Andy sat on a hand-hewn bench against the log wall. Idly whittling on a stick and dropping thin shavings on the ground, Rusty said, "Old Shanty made that cradle. Said he built it to last for at least a dozen young'uns. Looks like me and Alice have got our work cut out for us." He glanced up at her with a shy grin.

Smiling, Alice scolded gently, "Rusty! We don't talk about such as that."

The smile caused Andy a fresh ache, for it was like Bethel's. He covered up by saying, "I've been too busy to go over and see about Shanty. How's he doin'?"

Shanty was a black farmer who had inherited a small piece of land between Rusty's place and the settlement.

Rusty said, "Pretty good, for his age. I go over and help him now and again when somethin' heavy comes up. And to make sure old Fowler Gaskin doesn't steal him blind. Shanty ain't forgotten that he was once a slave. He won't hardly speak up for himself against a white man. Not even a sorry reprobate like Fowler."

Gaskin was another neighbor. Any time he dropped by a farm, it behooved the owner to count his chickens and inventory his toolshed. He believed in the adage that God helps those who help themselves, and he frequently helped himself to whatever was not nailed down.

Andy said, "Ain't it about time Fowler died of old age?"

"I've been hopin' a rattlesnake might bite him, but I suppose they recognize their kin."

Frowning, Alice said, "He's a nasty old man. He hates Rusty and me."

Rusty explained, "He came borrowin' one day when he knew I was gone. He thought Alice would be easy to buffalo, but she tickled his ribs with the muzzle of a shotgun. He ain't been back."

Andy said, "If you'd shot him, no jury around here would convict you."

Rusty replied, "You never shoot a buzzard close to the house. It stinks too much." He abruptly changed the subject. "Now that you've left the Brackett farm, what're you goin' to do, Andy?"

"I don't know for sure. Been wantin' to go back out to the hill country, get me a place and run some cattle. I've saved up a little from my Ranger wages and what I earned on the farm, but it's not enough. I've thought about goin' up to the rollin' plains and seein' if the Monahan family could use some help. Maybe in a year or two . . ."

"You're welcome to stay here with us. I'll pay you for

your help. That cabin we built for you once is still in good shape. Been usin' it for storage."

Andy knew Rusty's gesture was made out of kindness, not out of real need for help. "You've already got three mouths to feed. And there'll be more as time goes by."

Andy looked up at Alice. She said nothing, but he knew her need for that money was greater than his own. She had one baby, and there would be more. He said, "Thanks, Rusty, but I already owe you more than I could ever pay. You took me in and finished raisin' me even when my own kin turned their backs on me for my Indian ways."

"That's why I want to help. I've got a lot invested in you."

"I need to make my own way. Besides, I'm not like you. I can't see spendin' the rest of my life followin' a plow. I'd be miserable at it, and I'd make everybody around me miserable. Especially Bethel. It's better I leave her than to make her unhappy tryin' to be somethin' I'm not."

"Everybody has got to find his own road. Looks like you're meant to travel yours on horseback."

Andy nodded. "I can't help bein' what I am."

"Then live the way that fits you. There ain't money enough in the world to pay for spendin' your life at somethin' that makes you miserable." Rusty paused in his whittling. "You heard Tom say he could use another deputy."

"I appreciate his offer, but I need to get farther away, where I won't keep runnin' into Farley."

"There's always the Rangers."

"I've thought about that. I remember some good times

with them, but I also remember how much blood I saw. A little of it was mine."

Rusty took a big slice from the stick he was whittling. "Well, if you ever need a place to come back to for a while, it's here."

Leading a pack mule, Andy rode to Shanty York's. A lanky, baying hound greeted him a couple of hundred yards out and escorted him in, announcing him all the way. Andy found the old man taking his ease in an ancient rocking chair beneath a brush arbor beside his one-room cabin. Andy had helped build that cabin after a mob of night riders had burned the original, trying to drive Shanty off his land. Shanty shouted at the dog, "Fowler, hush up that noise."

He was a small man, his shoulders hunched under the weight of his years. Though he addressed most white people as *Mister,* he had known Andy from the time he fell back into white hands after his years with the Comanches. Word by word, he had helped the lost and frightened boy to remember the native tongue he had almost forgotten.

"Andy! How do, boy," Shanty said, walking out and extending a wrinkled hand. To him, Andy was still a boy, though he was far into his twenties. "Been a while since you come to see this old wore-out bag of bones."

Andy said, "You know how it is for a farmer, always more to do than there's hours in the day."

Shanty studied Andy's pack mule with a critical eye. "Looks like you're fixin' to travel." He phrased it as a comment, but it was a question in disguise.

"Might be."

The old man looked thin enough for the sun to shine through him. Andy said, "You don't appear to've been eatin' regular."

"It was a long winter. Vittles got short. But I'll be pickin' stuff out of my garden patch pretty soon."

Shanty led Andy back to the shade. He motioned toward the rocking chair, but Andy took a bench instead. The old man studied him quietly, as if he were reading everything that was on Andy's mind. He said, "I'm just a wore-out farmer. Nobody ever comes to me for advice because if it was any good, I'd've took it myself and be better off."

Andy realized that Shanty was hinting for him to ask. He said, "Your advice has always been good enough for me."

"I been wonderin' how long it'd be before you and Mr. Farley come to a partin' of the ways. I hope there wasn't no shootin'."

Andy had not told him about their fight, but the bruise and cut spoke for themselves. Andy flexed a sore hand. "No shots fired. Just a little discussion."

"You love that girl enough to fight for her?"

"I did. That's how I came by these marks."

Shanty became pensive. "I had me a girl once, when I was young back in slave times. Trouble was, the field boss wanted her, too. He was bigger than an ox and meaner than a boar hog, but I fought him just the same."

"Whip him?"

"No, he gave me the beatin' of my life. But my girl felt sorry for me, and we jumped over the broomstick together. We had us a good life till they sold her down the river."

Old memories brought sadness to his eyes. "Never seen her again, nor our child neither."

Andy wished he had something comforting to say, but nothing came. Feeling that his visit had only served to stir up painful old feelings for Shanty, he turned down an invitation to stay. Shanty had little enough for himself, much less food to share. Andy gave as an excuse that he needed to get on into town. He took the road that veered off to the river. He had gone but a mile or so when he heard a sudden snorting and shuffling of tiny hooves just ahead. Brush crackled as half a dozen wild hogs broke out of its cover.

Once this had been prime country for a deer hunter, but most of the larger wildlife had been killed out or driven farther away as the area settled up. Feral hogs, descended from strays lost by early farmers, still ranged along the river, unmarked and unclaimed. People around here routinely killed them for meat, but this was something Shanty could not or would not do. He feared someone would claim ownership and put up a holler. A few among his neighbors still resented that he was a black landowner and felt he was not entitled to share in the land's bounty. One was Fowler Gaskin.

Andy dropped the rope that led the pack animal. He drew his pistol and spurred his horse into a run, circling to get in front of the fleeing animals. He brought the horse to a quick stop, leaned down, and aimed almost point-blank at a fat shoat.

Squealing, it stumbled but did not fall immediately. It ran beneath Andy's horse, setting it into a nervous frenzy and forcing Andy to pull hard on the reins. The wounded pig followed the others for several yards before it went

down. When he brought his mount under control, Andy
rode up close and put another bullet behind the pig's ear to
make certain.

The horse's nervousness was compounded by the smell
of blood and gunpowder. Andy waited until the other hogs
had clattered off out of sight before he rode back to pick
up the pack animal. He looked in all directions before he
dismounted. Now and again wild hogs went on the offen-
sive. They could do serious damage, especially boars with
long tusks. He gutted the shoat, then lifted it up onto the
pack animal. The mule resisted the new burden.

"Hold still, damn it," Andy said as he tied the pig into
place. "You'll carry it if I have to kill you."

He rode back to Shanty's and reined up in front of a
small smokehouse behind the cabin. He said, "Look what I
found a little ways down the river."

Shanty worried, "I hope it wasn't wearin' no mark.
Somebody might come lookin' for a piece of my hide."

"No mark. If anybody asks you about it, tell them to
come talk to me."

Once they finished cutting up the shoat, Andy said,
"Better nail your smokehouse door shut. Fowler Gaskin
may come callin'."

The hound whimpered and begged until Shanty fed him
a strip of fat. Andy said, "Did I hear you call that dog
Fowler?"

"They's some resemblance. Fool dog is always nosin'
around where he's got no business, and he'll steal if you
take your eyes off of him. If I had the heart to do it, I'd
shoot him."

"The man, or the dog?"

"The dog. It's the Lord's business what happens to the man. I always pray for them that torments me. I pray that the Lord will turn Mr. Gaskin from his sinnin' ways and help him find peace when he gets to heaven."

"The sooner he leaves on that trip, the better. Except I doubt heaven is anxious to see him. He's more apt to go the other direction."

"The Lord must have some purpose for the wicked, or else he wouldn't have made so many of them." The dog showed continued interest in the pig. Shanty shooed it away, though it did not retreat far. "Late as it is, you'd just as well stay and share supper with me. After all, you brung the meat."

The sun was already half-hidden behind timber to the west. Andy said, "I guess there's no need ridin' to town in the dark."

Shanty smiled. "We'll have us a time, talkin' about the good old days."

"They weren't all good."

"We don't have to talk about the bad ones. They's past and gone."

"Not all of them."

Andy saw no purpose in burdening Shanty with his problems, but the old man saw through his evasion. He said, "Maybe if you'd try again, you and that little woman could patch things up."

"I didn't say I was leavin' her."

"You got a powerful lot of stuff tied on that pack mule."

"I'm not goin' for good. At least, I don't mean to be. I've just got to put some miles between me and Farley

Brackett for a while. Else they'll be huntin' one of us down for a killin'."

"Good Book says to turn the other cheek."

"I tried that. I only got two."

The cabin was too small for Andy to sleep on the floor, and he declined an offer of Shanty's cot. He spread his blankets beneath the brush arbor, but he did not go to sleep at first. He kept seeing Bethel and hearing her voice. He was tempted to get up and go back to her. But he kept hearing and seeing Farley Brackett, too. And he kept feeling his hands cramp on the plow handles.

Sometime during the night the hound's barking awakened him. Andy thought some varmint was probably after Shanty's chickens, a fox maybe, or a coon. He lifted the pistol from the holster lying by his head. He discerned that the dog was near the chicken house, telling the news in full voice. In the moonlight Andy saw the outline of a man fumbling with the door that led in to the roosts. He doubted it was Shanty.

"What you doin' out there?" he shouted.

Startled, the man froze for a second, then hunched over and set off in a run. His movement reminded Andy of a spider. Almost certain who it was, Andy squeezed off one shot into the air. In a moment he heard a horse galloping away. The direction told him he had identified the man correctly.

Shanty came out of the cabin barefoot and in his underwear. "What kind of a varmint was it, Andy?"

"A two-legged one by the name of Fowler Gaskin. Figured on havin' him a chicken dinner."

"I reckon his cupboard is most as empty as mine. He

comes borrowin' from time to time, in the dark. He's got eyes like a cat."

"Or a skunk." Andy's initial anger drained slowly as he contemplated the scare he had given the old scoundrel. "He's liable to have to wash his britches when he gets home."

Shanty said, "The only time his clothes gets washed is when he gets caught in the rain."

Sheriff Tom Blessing listened with a poorly disguised smile as Andy told about the nocturnal prowler. "Sounds like Fowler, all right. Did he get away with anything?"

"I didn't give him the chance."

"Best I could do is charge him with trespass, and you'd have to prove it was really him. Even if he'd got away with a chicken, Shanty'd have to prove it was his. Nobody brands chickens."

"Fowler could have plenty of meat without havin' to steal it. He could go out and hunt wild hogs if he wasn't too low-down lazy."

"Shanty would say that the Lord puts people like Fowler here to test our religion, same as he gives us flies and ticks and scorpions." Tom shrugged off the subject. "I hope you've come to ask me about that deputy job."

"No. It'd be somethin' to do for a while, but I need to get farther away."

"It'd look tame compared to the time you spent with the Rangers, and it'd pay about as well. I'd be pleased for you to sleep in the jailhouse if you ain't particular about the company."

Andy was weakening. "Couldn't be worse than Farley."

Tom frowned. "You ain't met my newest guest. Come and let me introduce you to Luther Cordell."

The jail had only a few small cells, for this was mostly a law-abiding farm community. Hunched on the edge of a steel cot, Cordell reminded Andy of a large, shaggy bear. He looked like a tramp who might have hopped from a boxcar and tumbled down the grade. His shirt was dirty and frayed at the cuffs, one elbow out. His trousers were streaked with the grime of hard travel. His hair was tangled, and his face had not felt razor or comb in weeks. A dark beard obscured most of his facial features. However, Andy was drawn by the intensity of the man's eyes. They were like large black buttons that seemed to look through Andy and focus beyond him.

Tom said, "You'd think a man that robs banks could dress better and get himself a haircut."

Cordell's voice was like a dry cowhide dragged over gravel. "Can't afford to. I invested most of my money in whiskey and sweet-smellin' women. What went with the rest of it, I don't know. Just frittered it away, I suppose."

Tom said, "When the Rangers come for you, the state'll give you a haircut and a brand-new set of clothes."

"That'll be nice. It ain't often anybody gives me anything without I persuade them first."

"At the point of a gun?"

"That cuts down on conversation. Most people talk too much." Cordell's gaze drifted to Andy. "That's a likely lookin' young feller. What's he in for?"

Tom said, "He's an old friend of mine. I'm tryin' to talk him into bein' a deputy."

"He couldn't be sorrier than the one you've got. A lot of the time he snores so loud I can't even talk to myself. You'd best get a better guard if you don't want me to sneak out of here."

Andy imagined how it would be to fight hand to hand with Cordell. The man must outweigh him by fifty pounds, most of it muscle and bone. Very little was fat. Cordell was larger than the sheriff and appeared solid as an oak.

Andy said, "I hope you didn't have to fight with him, Tom."

"No, caught him by blind luck. I rode out to talk to Fowler Gaskin about a complaint. Cordell and Fowler had emptied a bottle together and was both sleepin' it off. Took him without a struggle."

Cordell grumbled, "I've always been cursed by a streak of kindness. I felt sorry for that poor old man and shared my whiskey with him."

Tom said, "We know that *poor old man*. He would've stole it off of you if he could. Folks around here quit feelin' sorry for Fowler Gaskin a long time ago."

"I'll remember that the next time my kind streak starts actin' up." Cordell belched. "Damn beans. You need a new cook as much as you need a new deputy. Next jail I'm in, I hope it'll serve better groceries."

"I eat the same grub when I can't go home."

"You get paid for it."

"Not enough. But at least this jail is new. Our old jail burned down."

"I may set a match to this one, too, when I leave."

Tom said, "You're not goin' anyplace, not till the Rangers come for you."

"At least I like the company here. For a sheriff, you're a pretty good feller."

Tom led Andy back out of hearing range. He said, "I like Cordell in spite of myself. He's more pleasure to talk to than most of the people I lock up in here. I just wish he wasn't a bank robber."

Tom himself was one of the most likable men Andy had ever known. He probably gave away half of his salary to people he saw in need.

Andy said, "Everybody has got some weakness. I guess Cordell's is banks. But you don't need me to help you guard him. An elephant couldn't bust out of here. They built this jail stout enough to stand up under a Galveston hurricane."

"He's busted out of others. Got a reputation for bein' hard to keep in a coop." Tom rummaged in a desk drawer and brought out a badge. "I wish you'd take this." He handed it to Andy. Tarnished, it said *City of San Antonio*. Andy figured the county was saving money by reusing what someone else had discarded.

"Sorry, Tom." He handed back the badge.

Tom argued, "I'd see to it that the commissioners' court treats you right when it comes to pay. I've got a little dirt on most of them."

Andy said, "I appreciate the offer just the same."

"I done it for me more than for you. I ain't spent a night at the farm since I've had Cordell behind these bars. He talks pleasant, but I know he's slippery."

"Not too slippery for you to catch him."

"He was drunk."

A skinny young man with sleepy eyes walked through the door. He seemed momentarily startled at seeing the sheriff. "Tom. I wasn't gone but just a minute. Thought I heard a noise and stepped out to see."

Tom retorted, "That was your snorin'." To Andy he said, "This is Speck Munson. Speck, meet Andy Pickard. I was just offerin' him a job as a deputy."

Munson's thin face fell. "Does this mean I'm fired?"

"Not yet, but it means I'm thinkin' about it, so watch you don't aggravate me. Looks like Cordell's slop jar needs emptyin'."

Munson said a reluctant "Yes, sir" and fetched a set of keys from the sheriff's desk. He walked to Cordell's cell door.

Tom demanded, "What the hell do you think you're doin'?"

"You told me to empty the slop jar."

"Not till you've handcuffed him. I've told you a dozen times. Make him slip his hands through the bars first."

Cordell extended his arms, one hand on either side of a bar. Munson locked the handcuffs over his wrists, securing the prisoner to the cell door.

Tom muttered to Andy, "See the kind of help I been gettin'?"

"He's not used to workin' with men of Cordell's caliber."

"He just ain't used to *workin'*."

Andy watched Munson carry the jar, holding it at arm's

length and turning his head away from the smell. Munson complained, "Tom, we're feedin' him way too much."

He returned in a while. He locked the cell door, then unlocked the handcuffs. Cordell faked a quick grab at him through the bars. Munson jumped as if a rattlesnake had struck. He dropped the cuffs.

Cordell's black eyes danced with laughter. "Like to've got you that time."

Munson was shaking as he laid the cuffs on Tom's desk. Tom said, "He's baitin' you for fun, but maybe that'll teach you to keep both eyes open. When he sees a real chance, he won't be funnin'."

Andy said, "When I was a Ranger, I used to study criminals and try to decide what makes them that way."

"Ever figure it out?"

"Never did."

"Some people are natural sons of bitches from the day they're born. Others learn it along the way. As far as we know, Cordell has never killed anybody. He probably carried flowers home to his mama."

Andy leaned against the bars across the aisle from Cordell and gave the man a long, silent study. Cordell stood it for a while, but Andy's staring finally got to him. He asked, "What's so interestin'?"

"You. I was wonderin' what you'd look like with a shave and a haircut and the dirt washed off."

Cordell grunted. "I've got a face that'd break a mirror. I keep it covered up with whiskers so as to not shock the public."

Andy spent the night on a hard cot in an empty cell. It would have cost him four bits to sleep in the wagon yard, a privilege he denied himself but allowed for his horse and pack mule. Tom had a cot near the jail's front door, but his sleepy eyes indicated that he had not slept much. He took out his pocket watch and frowned at it. "High time Speck was here to take over and let us go for some breakfast."

It was a while before Speck Munson showed up at the door, carrying a tray with the prisoner's morning meal.

Tom said, "I was about to send out a posse for you."

"The rooster slept late."

The smell of coffee made Andy realize he was hungry. "Still takin' your meals across the street?"

Tom nodded. "When I have to stay in town of a night. Once I get Cordell off of my hands, I'm goin' out to the farm and stayin' for a week. I intend to debauch myself on my wife's peach preserves."

"Maybe it's time you *did* retire. You could stay out there from now on."

"Don't think it ain't been on my mind, but I don't like leavin' the office in Farley Brackett's hands. I ain't sure he's the man for it."

Andy could not argue that point.

The restaurant's biscuits had been baked an hour or more already and kept in a warming oven long enough to dry them out. The eggs were burned along the edges, and the bacon had been fried to tastelessness. The kitchen badly needed a woman's influence. Andy pitied Tom, having to put up with this day after day.

He had finished his eggs and was sipping his bitter black

coffee when a farmer rushed into the restaurant. "Sheriff, somethin' don't look right over at the jailhouse."

Tom was instantly on his feet. "What?"

"I seen a man go in the door. Another is waitin' outside with some horses. Acts nervous, like he's standin' watch."

Tom exclaimed, "Speck wasn't supposed to let anybody in there." He was out the door before Andy could free himself from the table. He started to run after Tom but realized he had left his pistol in his bedroll to avoid carrying it into the jail. He sprinted to the wagon yard, past a startled hostler, and found his saddle on a rack where he had left it. He jerked his rifle from its scabbard and set off in a fast trot.

He heard gunfire from inside the jail. Two men burst through the door. One he recognized instantly as Cordell. The other man snapped a quick shot at Andy, kicking up dust. Andy dropped to one knee and brought up the rifle. He sighted on Cordell, but a horseman hurried up, leading two riderless mounts. He moved in the way of Andy's bullet and almost fell from the saddle before regaining his balance. Cordell shouted something Andy could not understand. The three set their mounts into a hard run, rounding the corner of the jail, putting it between themselves and Andy. He had no chance for another shot.

Holding his breath, Andy rushed into the jail. Speck Munson lay curled in a heap, an ugly bruise on the side of his head. In the center of the room, Tom was sprawled on his stomach, a pool of blood spreading around him. Calling his name in a choking voice, Andy grasped the sheriff's shoulder and turned him over. A bullet had nicked the badge on its way in.

Tom was in a bad way.

The wooden floor shook as other men came pounding into the room, shouting questions. Andy did not look up at them. Tears blinded him, burning his eyes.

"Damn it, Tom," he murmured. "Damn it."

The wagon-yard hostler said, "I'll go for the doctor."

Andy tried to get a grip on his surging emotions. "I'm goin' after Cordell and whoever's with him."

Several men indicated they intended to join him. Andy said, "Anybody who wants to go with me, meet me at the wagon yard."

He picked up his rifle and rushed out to saddle his horse.

CHAPTER

3

Luther Cordell should have been grateful for his release, but instead he showed a crackling anger. "Damn you, Milt, you didn't have to shoot that sheriff. You could've just clubbed him like you done the deputy."

Milt Hayward was a large man like Cordell, broad shoulders hunched a little, his heavy-featured face flushed in defensive response. "He was blockin' the door. I didn't have all day to make up my mind. How come you didn't holler about me shootin' that Galveston banker?"

"You nicked him just enough to make him mad. Anyway, nobody's goin' to miss a banker much, or a lawyer. But kill a lawman and you've got every Ranger and two-bit local sheriff in the state gettin' a rope ready for you. For all three of us."

Irony edged Milt's voice. "Maybe you want to go back and apologize."

"I doubt them folks are in a listenin' frame of mind." Cordell turned to the kid who trailed behind them. "How bad are you hit, Buster?"

Buster Jones wasn't his real name, but it served as a convenient substitute for the name his mother had given him. He was bent over his saddlehorn, arms tight against his body as if holding in the pain. "Not bad enough for you-all to go off and leave me."

"Only a rattlesnake would do that. Hang on till we're in the clear. Then we'll stop and look at that wound."

They pushed their horses hard, bent on putting as much distance behind them as possible in the first minutes. They had little chance to hide their tracks, but they were on a well-beaten trail where the dirt was soft. Perhaps their tracks would be hard to differentiate from the many others already there.

They had covered three miles. Cordell saw nobody coming up behind them. "We better stop and take care of Buster."

Milt objected, "Them people are bound to be after us by now. That kid'll get us caught sure as hell."

"The kid didn't need to've got shot at all. It was a hare-brained idea, breakin' me out. You know I always manage to bust loose by myself. I was just bidin' time till that sleepy-headed deputy got careless."

"Then you'd've snuck back and dug up the bank money. You'd've kept it all for yourself and cut me plumb out."

Cordell grunted. "You don't trust me much."

"I ain't trusted anybody since I was six, and my old daddy whipped me with the buckle end of his belt. Soon as I get my share, I'm gone. Then you can ride to hell and out the far side as far as I'm concerned."

Cordell had never understood the greed that led a man to put money ahead of loyalty to those who rode with him. In this case he attributed it to a poor upbringing. Milt's sour manner kept him from cultivating friends. Associates in crime, but not friends.

Got weaned from his mama's milk too early, Cordell thought. *Probably brought up on poke salad and clabber.*

They stopped in the shade of a live-oak tree. Cordell and Buster dismounted. Milt remained in the saddle, where he had a better view of their back trail. Buster was a freckle-faced, gap-toothed kid of nineteen or twenty with a better upbringing than Milt's. The wound was low in his shoulder. A little farther over and the bullet would have hit him in the heart.

His face was drained from shock, making his freckles stand out like speckles of brown paint. His voice was anxious. "Is it goin' to hurt much, Luther?"

"Naw, I got a touch lighter than ary woman's." He opened Buster's shirt and pulled it down off his shoulder. He poked around the wound while Buster flinched and made hissing sounds. Cordell said, "Bullet's still in there, and it looks like it busted the bone. This ain't the time or place to try and dig it out. Wisht I had some whiskey to pour in that hole."

Milt reached in his saddlebag. He pitched a pint bottle to Cordell. "I paid dear for this stuff. Don't waste it."

"I won't." Cordell took a long drink and handed it to Buster so he could do the same. "This might smart a little," he said, and poured most of the remaining whiskey into the wound. Buster shouted loudly enough to be heard back in town. The bottle was nearly empty when Cordell pitched it back. Milt looked as if he had just bitten into a buzzard's supper. "Damn you, Luther, I told you this stuff was hard to come by."

Taking a sweat-stained silk neckerchief from his neck,

Cordell tied it around Buster's shoulder and under his arm. "I ain't one to shovel out a lot of advice, boy, but this ought to make you think about findin' a better way to make a livin'."

Buster groaned.

Cordell continued the lecture. "For every night I've slept in a bed, I've laid on the ground a hundred times. Right now I ain't got twenty dollars in my pocket, hardly. You-all busted in before I finished breakfast, and I ain't likely to get dinner or supper either. Yes, sir, this kind of life has sure been good to me. I'd trade it in a minute for forty acres and a mule."

Milt demanded, "Are we goin' to talk all day, or are we travelin'?"

Cordell frowned. "Nobody likes a grouch."

"And I don't like the idea of a rope necktie. Let's go pick up that money and get the hell away from here."

Cordell's goal was a badly deteriorated log cabin that appeared almost ready to slump to the ground. Pressed by a posse, the three had split up after visiting the bank in Galveston. Cordell had been carrying the money. The day had been late and the clouds threatening rain the evening he had come across the cabin by chance. He had confronted a wizened old man who called himself Gaskin. At first he had all the charm of a snake with its rattles pinched off, but he had softened when Cordell offered to share a bottle of whiskey in return for a night's shelter from the rain.

While Gaskin was immersed in whiskey, Cordell had hidden his saddlebags in the bottom of the old man's woodbox, along with the proceeds from his latest venture into banking. He had figured on being up and gone the next morning before Gaskin woke up.

That farmer sheriff ought to have been out feeding his chickens or plowing his field. Instead, he had shown up while Cordell was fighting the worst hangover he had suffered in a long time. He had no chance to retrieve the bags or find a better hiding place. Perhaps Gaskin had not discovered them yet. The old reprobate had struck Cordell as one who did not cook much for himself but lived mostly on whiskey and tobacco. Maybe he had not dug out enough firewood yet to expose the treasure.

He said, "Ain't nobody but an old man where I left the saddlebags. I doubt he'll give us much trouble. Even if he does, Milt, I don't want you shootin' him. One man today is enough."

"What have you got to bitch about? We broke you out of jail."

"I kind of liked that sheriff. Them people back there thought a right smart of him, too."

"Maybe he ain't dead."

"You'd better be prayin' that he's not."

"I tried prayin' when I was a young'un. Nobody answered. Get me my share of that money and I won't need God or the devil either one."

Getting shed of Milt could not come soon enough for Cordell. The last thing a man needed in this line of business was to ride with such a reckless misfit. The only reason they were together was that he thought he needed someone with more maturity than Buster. But Milt had not grown up; he had just grown older.

As best Cordell remembered, Gaskin's shack should be a little way ahead. He had purposely avoided describing the place or the man for fear that Milt would decide to try taking all the money. That would be three times better than a one-third cut.

Milt shouted a curse. "Damn the luck, here they come!"

Cordell twisted in the saddle. He saw seven or eight riders a few hundred yards behind, pushing hard to catch up. For a moment he considered making a try for the bank loot in spite of the odds. He gave up the notion with reluctance. "We can't stop for that money now."

Buster lagged behind. Milt cursed again. "We'd've had time if you hadn't farted around patchin' up that kid. He's goin' to die anyway. I can tell by lookin' at him. I say we go off and leave him."

"You don't quit a partner."

"You do when it's your neck. I ain't gettin' hung for him nor anybody else." Milt broke away and turned south, quirting his horse at every stride.

Cordell ground his teeth in frustration but decided Milt's desertion was probably for the best. Cordell had had to do most of the thinking for this outfit anyway. And Milt's defection meant a larger split for himself. "Hang on tight, Buster. We'll head for the river. Maybe we can lose them in the brush."

He heard a pistol shot from behind. *Some chuckleheaded farmer,* he thought, *wasting lead.* The range was too great for accuracy, but the sound encouraged him to spur harder. Somebody back there might have a rifle and the presence of mind to dismount and take good aim. Firing from a running horse was about as useless as teats on a boar hog. He had run from enough hastily formed citizen posses to know that most gave up when they found themselves getting far from home. With a little luck he and Buster should outlast this one.

They reached the river at a point where the timber was thick, heavily choked with underbrush. He considered swimming across, but the river looked wide and deep. The pursuers might catch up while the horses were swimming. He and Buster would be easy targets. Chances were, he thought, that the posse would expect him to keep going west, upriver, the direction he had been running. He cut back to the east, into the heaviest underbrush he could find. He helped Buster down from the saddle and held his hands over the two horses' noses to keep them from nickering at those of the posse.

Buster groaned. Cordell said, "Quiet. Don't even breathe heavy."

He could see little through the brush, but he heard the riders talking, shouting, crashing through the thick undergrowth. For a time they seemed to be coming toward Cordell and Buster, then they turned away. Cordell had had no chance to conceal the trail. He hoped there was not a good tracker in the bunch.

He whispered, "Sounds like they're goin' off from us, but we'd better stay put for a while. How you makin' out?"

Buster was not making out well at all. Ashen-faced and trembling, he whimpered, "Oh, God, I didn't know it'd hurt like this." Cordell knew that sometimes a bullet could do a lot of damage even without striking a vital spot. Shock alone could kill.

He had nearly ten thousand dollars hidden away, and right now there was not a thing it could do to help this boy.

Andy was angry with himself. Many people assumed that because of the years he had lived among the Comanches, he should be a good tracker. The men who rode with him had tacitly delegated the tracking to him. The truth was that he had no particular skill at it. He had known Indians who could track an eagle's flight across the water, but that knack had always eluded him. Farley Brackett had once told him he couldn't track an elephant through a cornfield.

He could no longer find the trail of the fugitives. He had seen where one split off. A couple of possemen followed those tracks. Andy and three others tried to follow the two men who had remained together. Andy lost the trail when it led into timber along the river.

He said, "Too much vegetation. And hogs've rooted through here. They've torn up the ground."

Joe Yates was a blacksmith by trade, not a lawman. He had hurriedly saddled a horse he had just shod and had not even taken time to hunt for his hat. Sweat rolled down from the top of his balding head. He suggested, "Maybe somebody livin' around here saw them."

Andy had a nagging feeling that the fugitives were close by, but these thickets could hide the elephant Farley had talked about. He said, "Shanty York's cabin is a little ways up yonder. He might be able to tell us somethin'."

Yates said, "That darky's gettin' so old he probably can't tell a horse from a cow at thirty yards."

"There's a lot of life in him yet."

Shanty came out of the cabin, pressing one hand against the small of his back to lessen the pain of his rheumatism. He listened to Andy's description of the men, then shook his head. "I done all my doin' in the cool of the mornin'. Been laid up since dinner with this misery along my ribs. Ain't seen nobody."

Andy was disappointed but not surprised. It stood to reason that Cordell would avoid dwellings where some-body might see him. Andy said, "If they come around, tell them what they want to hear and give them whatever they want. They're too dangerous for you to mess with."

"I'll be meek as a lamb. I already inherited my piece of the earth. I aim to keep livin' on it as long as the Lord lets me."

Riding away, Yates said, "How would he know about the meek inheritin' the earth? That's out of the Bible. He can't read."

"I doubt there's a page in the Book that somebody like old Preacher Webb ain't read to him. He don't forget much."

Biscuits Vanderpool operated the restaurant where Andy had almost had breakfast. He had been squirming for a while, a sign that the saddle was chapping his rump. He said, "My horse is about give out. And I got to get back and start fixin' supper for my customers."

Andy looked toward the lowering sun and shrugged. "I reckon we've all run our horses farther than we ought to. I'll make a fresh start in the mornin' and see if I can cut their trail someplace."

Yates said, "You're not a Ranger anymore. You've got no authority to arrest anybody."

"A six-shooter has authority of its own, and any citizen can make an arrest."

"Think you have a chance of catchin' them?"

"Not much. They'll likely be halfway across the next county before daylight."

Vanderpool said, "That's what the telegraph is for. I expect by now the word has gone out to every lawman in a hundred miles."

The telegraph had become a valuable asset to law enforcement. Andy had read about a new gadget supposed to allow people actually to talk to someone miles away instead of sending out written messages by code. He would have to see one to believe it. There had to be a limit to how many more new things inventors could think up. There wasn't room for them, and most people couldn't afford them anyway.

Even in the heat of the chase, there had seldom been a minute that he had not thought about Tom Blessing. Now, returning to town empty-handed, he could think of little else. "I feel like I've let Tom down."

Yates said, "It wasn't any more your responsibility than it was ours. Ain't none of us really lawmen."

"Tom tried to hire me as a deputy. Maybe if I'd agreed, things would've turned out different."

Vanderpool said, "A man can drive himself crazy thinkin' about what might have been. You've got to live with what was and is."

CHAPTER

4

Cordell moved nearer to the edge of the thicket so he could observe the open ground beyond. He saw horsemen a couple of times, probably part of the posse that had chased him. Not until dusk did he help Buster onto his horse and venture out of the brush. Even then he held close to it in case they had to make a hasty retreat. After riding a mile or so he saw a cabin. At first he thought it might be Gaskin's, but he realized that the old man's place was farther from the river.

No telling who lives there, he thought, *but I've got no choice.* Buster stood a strong chance of dying on him if they kept riding. He drew back into the timber as he saw four horsemen leave the cabin. He watched tensely, hoping they had not seen him. The men kept riding in the general direction of town. He expelled a pent-up breath. That had been too close.

He saw a positive side, however. What better place to seek refuge than where the posse had just been?

He said, "Hang on, Buster. Maybe we can pass the night here, at least."

It was a simple one-room log cabin, with a smokehouse, chicken house, a couple of log corrals, and a long shed off to one side. A garden showed evidence of hard work, its rows neatly hoed. Plants of several kinds were showing themselves, though none were yet mature enough to yield.

Cordell had always respected good farmers, though boyhood on a hardscrabble Louisiana cotton farm had left him looking for a life without all that sweat and heavy lifting. He had thought there must be an easier way to make a living. There might be, but this was not it. That old cotton farm looked a lot better in hindsight.

Smoke rose from the rock chimney, a sign somebody was fixing supper. The thought made his stomach rumble. A dog came out, wagging its tail and barking a greeting. Cordell drew a pistol he had grabbed as he left the jail. It was not his own, but with the other offenses he had committed, theft of a firearm seemed no more than a misdemeanor. He hollered, "Hello the house."

The door opened inward. An old black man peered out. He said, "You-all a little late. The rest of the posse done been and gone."

A darky! Cordell grimaced in disappointment. He had assumed from the well-kept appearance of the place that its owner was white. "This your farm?" he asked, doubting that it was.

"Yes, sir. It ain't a whole lot, but it's mine."

Cordell briefly considered moving on, but Buster badly needed to stop. He asked, "You got a name?"

"Yes, sir, it's Shanty. Shanty York."

"Me and the boy here, we need shelter for the night. And somethin' to eat."

He thought he saw realization come into the old man's eyes. The posse had probably described the fugitives enough that he recognized the pair. Shanty said, "They's just the two of you?"

"Just us. You got anybody else in there with you?"

"Ain't nobody here but me." Despite obvious misgivings, the old man opened the door wider. "You-all come on in. I'll put your horses in the pen yonder."

"I'll take care of them myself." It struck him that Shanty might get on one of the horses and run after the posse.

Cordell was strong, known to bend horseshoes. He eased Buster down from the saddle by himself. "The boy's hurt. Help me get him inside."

Shanty looked too frail to be of much help, but he lent what support he could. "All I got is that old cot yonder."

"That'll have to do. Find me some clean cloth in place of this dirty neckerchief. Got any whiskey?"

"No, sir, I don't hold with it."

"I thought all darkies loved whiskey."

"Not this one. A man never knows when his time might come. I don't want Saint Peter to smell whiskey on my breath."

"I wasn't thinkin' about drinkin' it. I need to wash Buster's wound, then see if I can dig the bullet out."

"I got somethin' the doctor give me a while back when I cut myself with the carvin' knife." Shanty fetched a dark bottle from an open cupboard shelf. Cordell pulled Buster's shirt down and removed the bloodied neckerchief with which he had wrapped the wound. The bullet hole was red and inflamed around the edges. Buster cried out as the disinfectant set fire to him. Cordell had to hold him down.

Shanty said, "Looks bad."

"He needs a doctor."

"There's Dr. Smith in town. I could go fetch him."

"And fetch the law while you're at it? You know who we are, don't you?"

Shanty was hesitant in answering. "I figure you're the ones Andy and them are lookin' for. They say you-all shot Sheriff Blessing. I wisht you hadn't. He's a fine man."

Shanty had a small fire going. Cordell opened the blade of his pocketknife and held it over the flames until the burning was too much for him to stand. He smelled the hair singe on the back of his hand. "You hold him down the best you can." To Buster he said, "Grit your teeth. This ain't goin' to be no Saturday-night dance."

Buster cried out as Cordell probed for the bullet. The boy lunged forward, almost breaking free of Shanty's weak grip. Sweat broke out on Cordell's forehead and ran down to sting his eyes. Buster continued to cry. Blood welled up and spilled from the wound.

Shanty said, "You ain't no doctor. You're fixin' to kill him."

Cordell withdrew the blade. His hands were trembling. He realized he was doing more harm than good. He wiped a sleeve across his forehead and felt his throat tighten. "You're right. This ain't no good." In helpless frustration he threw the open knife across the room and clenched his fists.

Shanty stanched the blood flow with a folded cloth. He said, "That bullet'll kill him if it stays in there. You'd ought to take him to Dr. Smith."

Cordell snapped, "I can't do it, old man, don't you see? They're liable to hang him." He immediately regretted the outburst. None of this was Shanty's fault. It was Milt's, and it was Cordell's for allowing himself to be caught and jailed like a Saturday-night drunk. He could not fault Buster, for the kid was too green to have realized the possible consequences.

Shanty said, "Maybe they wouldn't hang him, not if he wasn't the one done the shootin'."

Cordell rubbed a huge, bloody hand across his whiskered face. "God, if I could just turn back the time. I ought to've made him go home, even if I'd had to take a whip to him."

"Boys his age can be mighty willful. Might be he'd've just gone off with somebody else and done the same thing."

"But he didn't. He went with *me*."

Carefully Shanty wrapped Buster's wound.

Cordell said, "We didn't mean for nobody to get hurt. The fool that did the shootin' ain't with us no more." He wondered why he felt compelled to explain anything to an old black man who was almost certainly at the bottom of the community's social ladder. "Did they say the sheriff is dead?"

"No, sir, all they knowed was that he was hurt plenty bad. He might've gone to glory by now, though."

"That sure would be tough luck for me." Without consciously willing it, Cordell reached up and touched his throat. He imagined the feel of a rope around it. "Are you a prayin' man, Shanty?"

"I thank the Lord every mornin' that I can wake up and get out of bed."

"Him and me ain't well acquainted. I hope you'll pray for that sheriff. And this boy, too."

"Done done it. But I'll do it some more."

They left Buster lying on the cot. Shanty fried up some pork. Buster could not eat, so Cordell finished it. The old man's wrinkled black hands shook with nervousness. Cordell assured him, "We don't mean you no harm. We'll be gone come daylight."

"You're goin' on, then? With the boy in this shape?"

"Nothin' else we can do."

Cordell figured Shanty was likely to take advantage of any opportunity to get out of the cabin and run. He spread a blanket on the floor against the door so Shanty could not slip out. He dozed off and on but did not let himself fall into deep sleep. In dawn's pale light Buster's wound looked worse.

Cordell asked him, "Think you'll be able to ride today?"

Buster nodded. His voice was so weak that Cordell heard the sound, but not the words. He said, "We've got to move. Somebody's liable to show up."

Shanty said, "He don't look like he's got much breath left in him. He'd ought to stay here."

It crossed Cordell's mind that the old man might be thinking of a potential reward. But he reconsidered, for Shanty seemed genuinely concerned. Cordell stepped through the door and looked into the sunrise. He saw no one. "I believe you mean well, but there's too many people lookin' for us that don't have good intentions. Soon as we've et some breakfast, me and Buster will be on our way."

He saddled the horses and led them to the cabin. He helped Buster to his feet, but the youth could not stand alone. He slumped back onto the cot.

Shanty said, "He'll die if you make him ride."

"Them people from town are liable to kill him if he doesn't."

Shanty argued, "I don't think so. They're good folks, most of them. Leave him here with me. Soon's you've got away, I'll go and fetch the doctor."

Cordell was slow in making up his mind. Either choice tore at his conscience. To keep riding might kill Buster. On the other hand, angry posses had been known to exact summary justice at the end of a rope. Cordell had had a couple of close calls of that sort himself. Buster was too young to have his life snatched away from him in such a sudden and brutal manner. He had not had time to sample many of the world's pleasures. So far as Cordell knew, the boy had not even known the wonder of being with a warm and willing girl.

Guilt lay heavy on Cordell's conscience. He had seen something of his own younger self in the misguided kid. After the first time he had reluctantly allowed Buster to go along on a foray, it had been increasingly easy to keep saying yes.

Staring down into the fevered face, he made his decision. "I'll leave him with you for now, but don't send for the doctor yet. I'll be back."

"If the posse comes again, they'll see his horse. Everybody knows I ain't got one."

"I'll lead him down to the river and stake him on grass where nobody is apt to spot him."

Mounted, Cordell took the second horse's reins. To Shanty he said, "You're a good and decent man. I wish I had some money to give you, but I don't right now."

"You don't owe me nothin'. I just don't want to think about that boy dyin' out on the trail. It ain't a fit way to meet his maker."

Cordell turned in the saddle. "One last thing. Do you know an old man named Gaskin?"

"Yes, sir, I'm afraid I know the gentleman."

"Whichaway is his place from here?"

Shanty pointed. "Was I you, I'd pass him by."

"How come?"

"I was taught not to speak bad about folks, but Mr. Gaskin is a sinful man. If he thought there was any reward out on you, he'd turn you in for two dollars."

"Would *you* turn me in? Or Buster?"

"If they was to come right out and ask me, I couldn't lie. It'd be against the Book. But if they don't ask me, I don't see where I got to tell them anything."

"That's good enough."

As Cordell rode away, it crossed his mind that once he got hold of that money, he ought to leave Shanty a few dollars for his trouble. Sure, the old man *was* black, and black folks were used to working for nothing. Cordell had been brought up to believe that was what they were put on this earth for. But he appreciated the old man's kindness toward Buster.

*   *   *

Even after leaving Shanty's cabin, he continued to wrestle with his conscience. He had been forced to choose between two equally onerous actions. He unsaddled Buster's horse and staked him on a long rope in the timber by the river. He hung the bridle on a branch where he could retrieve it after he recovered his hidden money. He would prefer to stay in the timber where he could not be seen, but much of the land was open, either in pasture or in plowed fields. He had to trust to luck. On occasion it had been known to let him down, as when Sheriff Blessing had caught him handicapped by a hangover.

In a while he saw the cabin. It was as he remembered it, making a last stand against inevitable collapse. He stopped two hundred yards away and scrutinized the place for a while. He saw no movement, no smoke coming from the chimney. He did not see Gaskin working in his field or the neglected little weed patch that passed for a garden. Even this late in the morning, there was a chance he was still asleep. Cordell doubted that he often watched the sun rise.

He checked the back side of the cabin on the slim chance that Gaskin might be at his woodpile, chopping fuel for the fireplace. He was not. If he was here at all, he must be inside. Cordell tied his horse well clear of the cabin in case it should fall down while he was here. It looked as if all it needed was a strong west wind.

He walked around to the front, grasped the wooden door handle, and pushed. The door dragged the floor. Pistol in his hand, he quickly stepped inside.

Gaskin was not there. Cordell saw several pieces of fire-wood lying where they had carelessly been dropped on the floor. He took three long strides toward the woodbox and stopped cold. The box was almost empty. The saddlebags were gone.

His first reaction was stunned disbelief. Trembling with a rising anger, he picked up a piece of firewood and hurled it through the glass window. Though he was alone, he shouted, "You miserable thievin' son of a bitch. You've stolen my money!"

It did not seem fair, after all the risk he had endured to take that money, the days he had spent in jail, the wound Buster had suffered in freeing him, only to have a low-down, sneaking thief steal it all.

He tore the cabin apart in a desperate search, thinking Gaskin might have hidden the loot somewhere inside. It was a futile effort.

His indignation gradually cooled enough that he could think with some rationality. He asked himself what a mis-erable reprobate like Gaskin might likely do first if he sud-denly came into such a windfall. He would go to town, of course. He would start spending it the same way Cordell had intended to when he had traveled far enough to feel safe, on good Kentucky whiskey and fiddle music and sweet-smelling women.

He had seldom felt so frustrated. He had partially de-stroyed Gaskin's cabin in a search that turned up nothing. He found a shovel and dug in several likely places where the ground looked to have been disturbed. It was a fruitless effort. He considered burning the place out of spite, but the money might still be there, hidden too well for him to find it. Its ashes would do him no good.

He considered the possibility that Gaskin had taken it with him to town, though that would be risky. The farmer had not struck him as being particularly smart, but maybe the old rascal had sense enough to understand that the law would take the money away from him. That being so, he had probably left most of it hidden. It must be around here somewhere.

Cordell could not risk going to town to search for Gaskin. He decided his best choice, though a poor one, was to hide out and wait for Gaskin to return home. If he could get his hands on the old fart, he would turn him inside out until he got his money back. Then he just might break him into little pieces and leave him for the wild hogs he had seen ranging along the river.

He felt a heavy weight of responsibilty for Buster. He should not have left him in the hands of a poor, old darky who had little to offer except good intentions, but he had seen no better choice. It was Cordell's intention, when he recovered his money, to take him far from here, perhaps back to the home from which he had come. They would hide out in some thinly populated area while Buster recuperated. This region along the lower Colorado River was among the oldest settled parts of the state. Anywhere a man turned, there were people—too many people—and they showed little tolerance for those in Cordell's chosen occupation.

Off to the southwest stretched a considerable thicket where Cordell thought he could hide while keeping an eye out for Gaskin's return. He had no provisions. He had not wanted to take the little that Shanty had, and he found nothing in Gaskin's cabin beyond some coffee and tobacco and moonshine whiskey. Gaskin had several chickens, which evidently had to scratch for their living. He managed to catch one and tie its legs together while it squawked and flapped its wings. It would taste good tonight, roasted over a hidden campfire, with some moonshine to help it go down.

Andy knocked on the doctor's front door, dreading what he might be told. The doctor's wife parted a lace curtain and peered out through the oval glass. She did not immediately recognize him.

"I'm Andy Pickard, ma'am. I've come to ask about Tom."

Her solemn expression did not ease his anxiety. She swung the door inward and said, "Dr. Smith can tell you better than I can. Come on in."

A strong medicine smell assaulted Andy as he entered. The woman motioned toward a chair. Andy sat but was too nervous to remain seated long. He stood up, turning his hat around and around as he stared out the window. Shortly the doctor came into the room, wiping his wet hands on a towel. His white apron was spotted with blood. He smelled of medicinal alcohol. His expression was as solemn as his wife's.

Andy asked, "How's Tom?"

"Hanging on by a toenail. He's a tough old rooster. He has more scars on his hide than a fighting bull. But I'm afraid he doesn't have much chance."

Andy looked away. His eyes burned as if they had sand in them.

The doctor frowned. "I don't suppose you had any luck chasing the ones who did this to him."

"They got clean away."

"Maybe not. Judge Tompkins has been on the telegraph. They can't outrun that."

Mention of the judge gave Andy a new thought. "The judge ought to have the authority to appoint deputies, shouldn't he?"

"There is one deputy already, Speck Munson. But I had to give him a sedative. His head is swollen, and he took a deep cut across his temple. He won't be of use to anybody for a day or two."

He wasn't of much use before, Andy thought. "Did Speck tell you what happened?"

"He could not talk much except to say that a big man walked in and surprised him, struck him with a gun barrel. He knew nothing that happened afterward."

Andy said, "It's clear that they released Luther Cordell and shot Tom as he rushed in. But I think I managed to wound one of them. He may be layin' dead out there someplace."

"A temporary improvement at best. There always seem to be adequate replacements for those of his ilk who fall by the wayside."

Andy asked, "Could I see Tom before I go?"

"You won't be able to ask him any questions."

"I'd just like to see him."

The doctor ushered Andy into a back room. He found

Rusty there, face grim. Rusty seemed to want to say something, but nothing came. Alice sat beside Mrs. Blessing, holding her hand. The two had been close since Alice had nursed the older woman through a long illness.

Anger gripped Andy as he looked down upon the sheriff, lying with all but his pale face covered by a sheet. He said, "We've got to do somethin' about this."

Rusty nodded but said nothing.

The doctor gave Andy an intense study. "Perhaps you are the one to do it."

"Maybe I am. I'll talk to the judge."

"Tell him you have my backing for anything you intend to do. Tom Blessing has been a friend of mine for a long time."

"He's been a friend of everybody."

Gray-haired Judge Tompkins sat with his heavy horsehide chair turned at an angle from his rolltop desk. He stared solemnly out the window, his mind carrying him somewhere far away. The sound of Andy's boots thumping on the pine floor startled him. The chair groaned under his weight as he swiveled it around. "I didn't know you'd come in, Pickard. I was just thinking about Tom."

"Me, too. That's what I came to talk to you about."

"I understand your posse returned with nothing to show for their trouble."

"The spirits must've been lookin' the other way, but we're not through. Tom said yesterday that he wanted to make me a deputy. I turned him down. I wish now I'd taken him up."

The judge's eyes narrowed. "We can fix that. I could deputize you." He took a cigar from a box on his desk and offered it to Andy. Andy declined. Tompkins bit the end from it and stared absently at it for a minute. "But you know that being a deputy in this county would give you no jurisdiction if you pursued a man beyond the county line."

Andy repeated what he had told Yates, that a pistol carried authority of its own.

The judge said, "But should you arrest a man outside of your jurisdiction, it could cause the case to be thrown out of court."

"Even if the man is guilty?"

"That is one unfortunate effect of Texas law. It is often honored more in the breach than in the enforcement, but given an accomplished defense attorney . . ." He left the rest for Andy to ponder.

Andy's mouth twisted as he considered the unfairness of an acquittal based on a technicality.

The judge continued, "You may not have considered another possibility. You have been a Ranger. You know that Rangers are not encumbered by county lines." He gave Andy a moment to think about it. "I believe I have enough influence in Austin to get your Ranger commission reinstated."

Andy's spine tingled. "You'd do that?"

"With the greatest of pleasure. I'll compose a wire right now, with your consent, of course."

"You've got it, Judge. I didn't think I'd ever care to be a Ranger again. But for Tom's sake, I'm ready and rarin' to go."

It occurred to Andy that Bethel might not approve. She

had been pleased when he took his leave of the Rangers. He hoped she would understand. But if she didn't . . . well, she had endured many disappointments in the past. One more should not prove too heavy a burden.

The judge said, "Consider yourself a temporary deputy sheriff till we hear from the Rangers. That way you'll have official sanction for whatever you do, at least within county lines."

"That'll be helpful."

"You won't have to carry the full weight alone. I've sent for another man. I'm going to appoint him interim sheriff pending an election."

Andy had a sinking feeling. "Who?"

"Farley Brackett. He has had years of experience as a Ranger, and he has already filed for election as sheriff."

Andy felt as if half the air had gone out of his lungs. He considered backing out of his agreement. The last thing he wanted was close association with Farley, especially in a subordinate position.

He hoped his Ranger appointment came quickly.

He asked, "Have you got the authority to appoint a sheriff?"

"I have to have approval by the commissioners' court, but that is just a formality. They'll do what I tell them. I have something on every one of them."

Andy had heard the same thing from Tom.

The county clerk walked past the door, saw the judge, and turned back. His bow tie hanging loose and his shirttail partly out, he was laughing to himself as he entered the room.

The judge said, "Drinkin' a little early, aren't you, Bud?"

"Just one," the clerk said. "There wasn't any business in my office anyway. And I'm glad I went, because I saw something I wouldn't expect to see again in a hundred years."

The judge nodded. "And you're busting a gut to tell us about it."

"It's old Fowler Gaskin. I don't know where he got it, but he's waving a handful of money around and drinking it up as fast as he can raise a glass."

Andy's jaw dropped. "You're sure it was Fowler?"

"Nobody else looks like Fowler Gaskin."

Andy said, "Fowler never had ten dollars at one time in his life. Wherever he got it, it's a cinch he didn't break a sweat earnin' it."

It took but a moment for Andy to put the pieces together. "Tom arrested Luther Cordell out at Fowler's place. Cordell didn't have but a few dollars on him, and yet he had just robbed a bank. I'm bettin' he hid his loot somewhere at Fowler's place, and Fowler found it."

The judge saw the logic. "We'd better go talk to him."

"The damned old fool will get his head blown off. Cordell will be lookin' for that money. If he doesn't find it, he'll be lookin' for Fowler."

Tompkins said, "Perhaps we should let him. Fowler Gaskin's funeral would be regarded as community betterment."

"As much as I'd like to be one of Fowler's pallbearers, we can't just stand back and allow it to happen."

"No, but one can wish."

They walked together to the saloon. It was regarded as a social center for men of the town and countryside, a respectable place where many a bale of cotton had been sold, many a mule traded, a place where even a preacher could feel at ease, sort of. Sermons had been delivered here by itinerant ministers who had no church. The proprietor seemed pleased to see the judge walk through the door. A tall, angular man dressed in black, he looked more like an undertaker than a bartender. He was a deacon, known for delivering short but pointed sermons to patrons he thought had stayed too long.

He jerked a thumb toward the old man slumped at a table in the corner. "Judge, can you put Gaskin under arrest or somethin'? I won't sell him any more whiskey, but he won't leave. Says he'll sit there till he's sober, and then I'll have no excuse for not bringin' him a fresh bottle. I hate to just take him by the seat of the britches and throw him out. He's so spindly he's liable to break."

The judge gave Gaskin a moment's frowning study. "Fowler Gaskin, as county judge I am ordering that you be placed under arrest on a charge of being drunk and disorderly. Andy, please take him in hand."

Gaskin was too light in weight to put up an effective struggle against a husky young man in his twenties. Especially drunk. Andy said, "For a long time now I've wanted to do that."

Gaskin tried to focus his gaze, but it wavered between Andy and the judge. "Arrest me? I ain't broke no laws. I've paid good cash money for my drinks." He pulled a handful of bills from his pocket to demonstrate. "You got no call to arrest a man that's got money."

"Where did you get it?" Andy asked.

"From the Lord Hisself. Who else would've put it right there in my cabin? He takes pity on the poor and downtrodden. Ain't but few men been trod down on more than me."

"The Lord didn't have anything to do with that money. It was taken in a Galveston bank robbery."

"I found it in my cabin, right where the good Lord put it. He does work in mysterious ways."

"Do you think He intended for you to spend it on whiskey?"

"He didn't leave no instructions. He must like a little drink hisself, or why would He have put whiskey on this earth?"

Andy wrested the money from Gaskin's hands and counted while the old man spewed profanity against him and the judge and all others within hearing. The tally was far short of the amount supposed to have been taken in the robbery. Surely Gaskin hadn't been in town long enough to drink up so much. "Where's the rest of it, Fowler?"

Gaskin spat on the floor. "I hid it to where there can't nobody find it but me. Ain't no use you goin' to look."

"Maybe you're too drunk to see the mess you're in. You remember the feller you were drinkin' with, the one Tom Blessing arrested at your place?"

"Nice feller, he was. Shared his whiskey like a true Christian."

"Some Christian. He's back on the loose and no doubt

lookin' for his money. He'd skin you alive to make you tell where it is, and then hang you on a meat hook in your own smokehouse."

Gaskin's clouded mind seemed unable to grasp the full reality. "He can't afford to kill me as long as I'm the only one who knows where that money's at."

"No, but he could break you up piece by piece. An arm first, and then a leg, and then the other arm. He could start whittlin' on your ears, and maybe your privates. How long do you think you could keep a secret?"

"He wouldn't come back, not after bustin' out of jail. He's long gone." The old man rubbed his red-rimmed eyes. "You just want to steal my money for yourself. That's what it is, you're a damned thief."

"Cordell will turn this country upside down. Safest place for you right now is in jail."

Gaskin took a couple of steps backward. "I'm an innocent man. I ain't stole nothin' from nobody."

"Jail is the one place where Cordell can't come lookin'. Tell me where you hid the money and I'll put it in there, too, for safekeepin'."

"No, sir, I ain't tellin' nobody. That money's mine."

"You're a damn fool, Fowler. But you always were."

CHAPTER

5

Andy was only vaguely familiar with Tom's office, but he remembered seeing the sheriff put the keys in the desk's bottom drawer. He placed Gaskin in an inside cell that had no window through which anyone could see him from outside. He considered it unlikely that Cordell posed any real threat to Gaskin so long as he was locked in. If Cordell wanted to break into the jail, that would be fine with Andy. It would save having to go out and hunt for him.

Only one other prisoner was in jail. He had become too rowdy on moonshine and raised a ruckus in the street. Tom would probably have turned him loose by now were he able. Andy decided to release him so he would have one less problem. The bleary-eyed farmhand shuffled to the office, dragging his feet. Andy gave him back his personal belongings, but the prisoner kept waiting expectantly. He said, "Sheriff Tom always gave me a dollar or two to help me on my way."

He had claimed he slept through the jailbreak and Tom's being shot. That had been an obvious lie. He simply did not want to become involved in any repercussions. Andy said, "I'll help you on your way, all right. With a swift kick."

"Just thought I'd ask." The man left, but not in good

grace. Andy shouted an admonition that he not be found drunk in this town again anytime soon.

He did not want to leave the jail untended so long as Gaskin was in it. He did not even risk crossing the street to order supper at the restaurant. Biscuits Vanderpool took it upon himself to walk over and ask what Andy would like to have. Andy chose beefsteak, gravy, biscuits, and coffee. "As for Fowler Gaskin," he said, "anything you can scrape up will be better than what he's used to."

Gaskin hollered from his cell, "By God, I'm a taxpayer, and I deserve a good supper."

Andy doubted that Gaskin had ever coughed up enough taxes to pay for a pot of beans. "All right, bring him whatever you bring me, but we're not goin' to fatten him up at county expense."

Rusty came to the jail after Vanderpool returned. They visited about the weather and crop prospects but avoided discussing what lay heaviest on their minds. They quickly ran out of talk, and Rusty left to look in again on Tom.

Andy lay on the same hard bunk that Tom had pointed him to. The front door was locked and reinforced by a heavy bar. Only dynamite would break it down. Andy did not sleep much, partly because of Gaskin's snoring and partly because his mind would not shut down. He kept seeing Tom in his uneasy dreams.

He had just finished eating the breakfast the restaurant operator had brought over when Speck Munson walked in. His head was bandaged, and he looked to be in pain. He said, "I'm reportin' for work, if I'm still hired."

"I guess you're hired until somebody tells you otherwise. If you're worried about it, you could ask the judge."

"Long as he doesn't tell me otherwise, I won't bring it up." Speck looked ashamed. "I suppose everybody blames me for what happened."

They probably did, but Andy thought the young man looked miserable enough already. Perhaps the experience had taught him something. "I suppose it happened so fast that you didn't have time to do anything."

Munson nodded, wincing as the movement brought pain. "I barely seen the man that hit me. He was a bad-lookin' one, and big as a barn."

"How do you know if you barely saw him?"

"It don't take long to see mean, and he was mean to the bone."

"Did you hear Cordell call him by name?"

"I thought he said *milk,* but that ain't no name."

Munson collapsed into a chair. Andy knew that in his condition he could not be trusted with responsibility. He said, "Maybe you'd better go home and get some more rest."

"Better if I stay here and make a hand. Maybe the judge won't fire me if he sees me at work." Before long Speck was asleep in the chair.

He was probably still feeling effects of the sedative the doctor had administered. Andy hoped Judge Tompkins would not walk in and see Speck in this condition, but that hope fell by the wayside. Speck was the first thing Tompkins saw as he walked through the door. He said, "Doesn't that boy do anything but sleep?"

Defensively Andy said, "It's the doctor's pills, I think."

"He never was right for this job. I had Tom hire him because the boy needed a regular paycheck. But it wouldn't be right to fire him so soon after he's been injured in the line of duty. I'll wait until he's well."

"He'll still need a paycheck."

"A plow is more fitting for him than a badge. I'll give him a job on my farm. Have you seen Farley Brackett yet?"

The name made Andy frown. "He hasn't been in."

"He's due. And I got a wire back from Austin. They're taking your Ranger application under advisement, so you'll have to remain a deputy for a while."

It was a disappointment, but Andy shrugged it off.

The judge said, "A Ranger was on his way here to pick up Cordell and take him back to Galveston. Maybe he can stay and help you. If you have to cross over the county line, you can let him make the official arrest."

"Did they say who they sent?"

"No name. Till we hear about your reinstatement, you should keep the deputy's badge."

"I never had one."

The judge rummaged in a desk drawer and came up with the same San Antonio city badge that Tom had offered. He gave it a quick glance and said, "It's the man behind it that counts. Nobody is going to read the inscription anyway. Especially if you are holding a gun on him."

The judge turned toward the door. "I'm going over to see about Tom. Want to go with me?"

"I sure do." Andy awakened Speck and told him to keep

the door locked. Then Andy and Tompkins walked to the doctor's house. The doctor's wife met them at the door. Her grim expression told them what neither wanted to ask. Andy heard Mrs. Blessing sobbing in the back room. He and the judge exchanged worried glances. The doctor met them, shaking his gray head.

"I am sorry. Tom just passed."

Mrs. Blessing sat in a chair against Tom's bed, one arm lying across her husband's still form. Alice stood over her, trying to comfort her but unable to speak. Rusty stood on the other side of the bed, looking as if he had been kicked in the stomach. "Tom's gone," he said.

Andy could not reply. He turned away and crushed his hat in his hands.

Farley Brackett was waiting outside the jail when Andy and the judge returned, both badly shaken. Obeying orders, Munson had refused to let him in. Farley grumbled to the judge, "If I was the sheriff, the first thing I'd do would be to fire that dumb kid."

The judge said, "He just did what I told him to." He gave Farley the news about Tom. Farley's peevish expression shifted quickly to one of exaggerated sadness. He said, "That sure is too bad. We'll miss old Tom."

Andy suspected Farley was not grieving all that much. Tom's passing gave him a better chance to take over this office permanently in the special election that was certain to come.

Speck was up and giving the jail a listless sweeping that left no visible effect. He went off by himself and cried when told about Tom.

Tompkins administered the oath to Farley. Farley said, "Judge, I promise you I'll get the skunk that shot Tom. We all owe a big debt to that good man for the years he's served the citizens of this county."

Andy did not comment. He knew that anything he said would be bitter. Tom was not yet an hour dead, and Farley was already settling into his job.

Farley had noticed Andy's badge. He said, "I gather that I'm in charge now. Andy's got to take orders from me, right?"

The judge was momentarily surprised by the antagonistic looks that passed between Andy and Farley. He had known nothing of their conflict. He considered for a moment. "Yes, but I would expect that authority to be used judiciously." He paused, then sprang one more surprise on Farley. "Pickard's deputy status is only temporary. I have asked that he be reinstated as a Ranger. When that happens, I would consider his authority to be paramount."

Farley's face fell.

Speck had listened in puzzlement. He understood nothing of this. He asked, "What do you fellers think we ought to do now?"

Andy answered quickly, before Farley had a chance to consider. "I think the sheriff should stay and watch the jail in case Cordell tries to get at Fowler Gaskin and make him tell where he hid the money. Farley'll need help, so you'd better stay with him, Speck. Cordell has probably already been to Fowler's place huntin' for his money, but I'll go out there in case he's still hangin' around, waitin' for Fowler."

The judge voiced approval, leaving Farley no room for argument.

Farley complained, "I don't even know what Cordell looks like."

Andy said, "Speck can tell you. He saw a lot of him while he was in this jail."

Speck said, "I'd like to see him back in here again. I'd keep him in leg-irons and make him empty his own slop jar."

Andy saw that Cordell had already made a thorough search of Gaskin's cabin. The place looked even more chaotic than he had seen it before. Pots, pans, and plates were scattered across the floor, the shelves emptied. The cot and the woodbox were turned upside down. Several stones had been chiseled out of the fireplace. The wooden floor had been pried up in several places.

He recognized the possibility that Cordell had found the money and fled with it. In that case he was probably already out of the county. But Andy thought it equally possible that Cordell had not found it. Though lazy and shiftless, Gaskin was crafty as a coyote. He was unlikely to have hidden his treasure where it would easily be found. More probably he had secreted it so well that a searcher would have to make a pact with the devil to find it.

Cordell seemed the man to make such a pact.

After a perfunctory search around the outside of the cabin, Andy reasoned that Cordell had done it before him. Any further searching would be a waste of time. He decided to return to town.

At the jail, Farley looked him over with critical eyes. "You don't look to be packin' any money, so I don't reckon you found it. And Cordell has given you the slip. Ain't no tellin' where he's got to by now."

Arguing with Farley would only get Andy's blood stirred up. Instead, he agreed. "He tore Fowler's cabin half to pieces. I don't know if he found the money or not."

"You didn't trail him?"

"You know I'm not much good at trackin'."

"That's the gospel truth. All those years with the Comanches, and you didn't learn a damned thing."

Andy turned to Speck. "Has Fowler given you any trouble?"

"Cussed me up one side and down the other is all. Keeps sayin' he didn't steal anything and he don't belong in here."

"Bad as I hate to say so, he's probably right. All we've got on Fowler is that he was drunk and disorderly. We can't even prove it was bank money he was spendin'. The judge'll probably tell us to turn him loose in the mornin'."

Farley said, "That's too bad. It's warmed my heart, seein' that old sneak sittin' behind the bars."

Andy was tempted to comment about Farley's warm heart but passed up the opportunity. "You can sit up tonight and watch him if you want to. Me and Speck can use the sleep."

Andy heard Gaskin's raspy voice calling his name. The old man's knotted hands clasped the bars so tightly that the knuckles were white. He demanded, "You been out to my place?"

"Just came back."

"Find anything?"

Andy decided the old sneak needed something to worry about. "Somebody tore your cabin to pieces and dug holes everywhere."

Gaskin's face fell. "You ain't lyin'? He dug all around?"

"You could plant a garden."

For a moment Andy thought Gaskin was going to cry. He sank back onto his bunk and buried his face in his hands. "That money is rightfully mine. I found it."

"Finders don't always get to be keepers. At least you were rich for a little while." Andy turned away from the cell, leaving Gaskin to ponder the fickle nature of fate.

Gaskin called after him, "Maybe he gave up and left."

"Maybe."

Farley muttered, "Soon as we turn him loose, he'll hightail it home to see if the money's still where he hid it."

Andy said, "I doubt that it is. Cordell has likely got it and gone." He did not entirely believe that, but he did not want Farley to second-guess a half-baked idea he had been toying with.

Farley said, "You enjoy torturin' the old man. Must be the Indian in you, Badger Boy."

Speck didn't get it. "What's this about Indians? There ain't no Indians around here anymore. Are there?"

Farley said, "Get Andy to tell you the story of his life. But not where I've got to listen to it."

Gaskin ate but little supper and only dabbled at his breakfast the next morning. He trembled with anxiety. "Ain't you-all ever goin' to let me out of here?" he demanded.

Andy said, "I'll talk to the judge when he gets to his office."

"Tell him I'm figurin' on suin' the county for false arrest. Time my lawyer gets through wringin' you-all out, I'm liable to own the courthouse."

Andy knew Gaskin had no lawyer. He had dodged lawyers and courthouses all his life. They meant nothing to him but aggravation.

Andy said, "Better eat your breakfast. If the judge turns you loose, you'll have to survive on your own cookin'." It was a wonder the old man had not poisoned himself years ago.

The judge reluctantly agreed that they had little reason to hold the prisoner. "My preference would be to let him sit there and rot, but we can't keep feeding him at the county's expense. If he would just commit a murder or something else worthwhile, we could turn him over to the state."

Andy carried the ring of keys to Gaskin's cell. "Gather up your stuff, Fowler. You'll find your mule at the wagon yard."

"I ain't payin' no feed bill. I didn't tell you-all to put him up over there."

"Just go, Fowler."

Andy stood at the door and watched Gaskin hurrying across the square on wobbly legs. Farley moved up beside Andy and growled, "Once I'm full sheriff, there'll be some changes made. I'd let that old scoundrel stay in jail till he put roots down through the floor."

"That wouldn't be accordin' to law."

"Some law you've got to make up as you go along."

Farley went back into the office and began rummaging in the drawers of Tom's desk. He found a sheaf of Wanted notices and began to study them. He smiled to himself. Andy guessed he was imaginging himself catching all those criminals single-handed.

Andy remained in the doorway until he saw Gaskin riding up the street, quirting his rawboned mule. The mule flinched at the sting but did not pick up the pace. Gaskin disappeared on the wagon trail that led off in the general direction of his farm. Andy looked back to make sure Farley was not watching him, then walked to the wagon yard and saddled his bay horse. He did not want Farley going along, for one man stood a good chance of staying out of Gaskin's sight. Two men would double the likelihood of his spotting whoever followed. Andy hung back out of sight, sure where the old man was going. He did not close the distance between them until he neared Gaskin's shack. He stopped in a stand of trees where he could watch without being seen.

Gaskin was still applying the quirt with little effect. The old mule had no speed left. Gaskin was so eager that he jumped off a hundred feet short of his cabin and ran the rest of the way in the wobbly gait dictated by his stiff joints. He attacked the woodpile in back, hurling firewood aside. He picked up a shovel that was lying nearby and drove its point into the ground where the wood had been. He was so engrossed in his frantic digging that he did not see Andy ride up behind him. Andy watched him drop to his knees. With a glad shout, Gaskin pulled a set of saddlebags out of the hole. He opened them anxiously and yelped again in joy.

Andy dismounted and walked up unnoticed until he said, "I'll take those, Fowler."

Gaskin turned so quickly that he almost fell. He clutched the saddlebags to his thin chest. His eyes were desperate. "These are mine. I found them, and they're mine."

"You know that money was taken from a bank. It's got to go back."

"Like hell." Gaskin turned to run. Andy grappled with him, trying to wrest the bags from his hands. He jerked them loose but was off balance and stumbled. With a curse, Gaskin picked up a large chunk of wood and struck Andy across the head. Andy's hat sailed away. His knees buckled as Gaskin yanked the bags from his hands and shouted in triumph.

A gravelly voice said, "Don't be in such a hurry, old man. That's my property you've got your grubby hands on."

On his knees, Andy looked up through a painful haze. The black-bearded Cordell seemed to sway back and forth. The pistol in his hand looked like a cannon. Gaskin froze, clutching the bags as if they were a baby.

Cordell said, "I'd let you-all fight it out, but I'm afraid one or both of you might get killed. Naturally they'd blame me. They always do." He extended his free hand to Gaskin. "Gimme."

Gaskin backed away, frantically holding on to the bags. Cordell touched the muzzle of his pistol to the old man's Adam's apple. "I said gimme."

Gaskin yielded them up and went to his knees, sobbing. "They're mine. You got no right."

"Go rob your own bank. Any fool can do it. Just show them a gun to let them know you're serious, and they'll empty out the vault." Cordell turned to Andy, relieving him of the pistol on his hip. Andy had been too stunned to draw it. "I remember you from the jailhouse. I don't remember you wearin' a badge then."

Andy's head throbbed. "Damn you, you killed one of the best men that ever lived."

"Wasn't me. The man that done it has took off to Mexico or someplace. Mexico looks pretty good to me, too, now." Cordell balanced the saddlebags over his free arm. "Let me have that cartridge belt. And just so you don't get a notion to follow too quick, I'm takin' your horse and that mule yonder. You-all stay put and don't get in another fight. I won't be here to bust it up."

Cordell mounted a horse he had tied at the side of the cabin and rode up beside Andy's, taking the reins. "I don't want to be accused of horse thievin'. I ain't that low. I'll leave your horse and mule down the trail a ways." He rode southward. The lagging mule limited his speed, pulling back on the reins and stubbornly refusing to move beyond a trot.

Andy said grittily, "If I was him, I'd shoot that mule."

Gaskin said, "If I had my shotgun, I'd shoot *you*."

Andy ran his hand across the place where Gaskin had struck him. It burned. He felt the stickiness of blood. His head ached as if a hatchet were sunk in it to the handle. "Fowler, you like to've brained me."

"I intended to. First time in my life I ever had any real money, and you caused that thief to get away with it."

"He was layin' for you to come back. He'd've taken it whether I was here or not."

Gaskin gave Andy another sound cursing, then went into his cabin. Andy heard him cry out in rage. Gaskin staggered back outside, trembling. "He wrecked my house. Tore up everything."

The place was a wreck long before Cordell came along, Andy thought. He tried to muster a little sympathy for Gaskin, but it was not there. He said, "You ought to set fire to it and start over."

"You always hated me," Gaskin whined, "you and Rusty Shannon and all the rest of them. You got no Christian feelin's for a poor man."

Gaskin didn't have to be a poor man. He owned the makings of a good little farm. All it needed was a competent farmer, somebody who would work at it and keep leaving fresh footprints from one end to the other. Gaskin raised just enough corn to put bread on his table and make moonshine whiskey in a still down by the creek. Andy found it hard to imagine Gaskin putting out the energy to move part of his woodpile, dig a hole to hide the saddlebags, then cover them up with firewood. Only money or whiskey would provide that much motivation.

For a moment Andy pictured what he could do with this place if it were his. The thought was fleeting. The last thing he wanted was to spend the rest of his life in this older and heavily settled part of Texas, tied to a plow, though it was what Bethel wished him to do. Memory carried him back to the western hills and the rolling plains. Someday, some way . . .

Two riders approached from the direction of town. As his vision gradually improved, Andy discerned that they were Farley and Speck. He dreaded hearing what Farley would say. He took the initiative by declaring, "I didn't ask you-all to follow me."

Farley said, "No, but you should've let me in on what you were up to. I could've told you you couldn't handle the situation by yourself. Now Cordell's got the money and gone *por allá*. You'll go back to town draggin' an empty sack and lookin' like a fool." He made no effort to hide his satisfaction. "But maybe with a little luck I'll be able to pick up the pieces."

Farley did not mention Speck. Andy guessed he hoped to catch Cordell and grab some glory for himself. He said, "That's all right. I'm not runnin' for sheriff."

Farley examined the hole where Gaskin had retrieved the saddlebags. "So this is where the money was at."

Andy's eyes were still blurry, but perhaps Farley and Speck could follow the fleeing outlaw. He pointed in the direction Cordell had taken. "He hasn't been gone long. Took my horse so I couldn't follow after him."

Farley said, "You never was much of a farmer, and you ain't much of a deputy either. I swear, I don't know what you're good for, Badger Boy. Come on, Speck, let's go catch the man that Andy let get away."

They moved off in a lope.

Andy was angrier at himself than at Farley. He shouldn't have let Cordell sneak up and get the upper hand on him. It wouldn't have happened if he hadn't been wrestling with Gaskin. The old fossil wasn't worth all this grief.

Gaskin complained, "You caused me to lose my money, and on account of you I lost my mule, too."

"That mule probably didn't like it here anyway. I sure wouldn't." Large chunks had been chewed from wooden fence planks near the barn, a sign the mule had been starved for nutrients. It had to subsist on whatever native grass it could find and dry roughage that was more straw than hay. "I ought to arrest you for cruelty to an animal."

"You're hell-bent on arrestin' people. Maybe if you hadn't put me in jail, I wouldn't've lost my money."

"If you hadn't been in jail, Cordell would've caught you by yourself and nailed your hide to the cabin door."

Andy went to Gaskin's well and turned the windlass to bring up a bucket of water. He drank his fill, then poured the rest over his throbbing head. "You've got good water here, Fowler. You'd be better off if you drank more of this and less of that moonshine."

"I'll have all the whiskey I want when I get through suin' you and the county. You'll be workin' for me the rest of your life."

"You're makin' my head hurt, Fowler. Shut the hell up."

Andy considered setting out afoot for town, but he feared he did not have enough strength to get there. Besides, Farley and Speck would likely return for him sooner or later, with or without Cordell. He sat down to rest on a bench at the front of the cabin. Gaskin went inside and began rattling things around in an attempt to straighten up his damaged dwelling. Andy felt that he deserved no help, so he offered none. Gaskin kept up a constant monologue, cursing Andy and Cordell and anyone else he considered responsible for keeping him poor all his life. Every misfortune that had befallen him since childhood was someone else's fault.

It was near dark when Farley and Speck returned, leading Andy's horse and the mule. Andy's pistol and cartridge belt hung from the saddlehorn where Cordell had left them. Farley said, "You're luckier than you deserve to be, Badger Boy. He left these where we would find them. He's an honest man, for a thief."

Cordell had probably been glad to be rid of the lagging mule, Andy thought. Farley and Speck had obviously not caught up with the outlaw. "Why didn't you trail him?" Andy asked sarcastically, knowing that Farley was no better tracker than he.

Farley said, "It was like he just left the ground and flew away. Them tracks stopped dead at the edge of a creek. We couldn't find where they came out." He shook his head. "Damned poor Ranger you are, messin' around and lettin' him escape."

Andy shrugged. "When you start campaignin', you can tell everybody it was all my fault. Things would've been different if you'd been full sheriff."

He mounted his bay horse and started toward town. Maybe by tomorrow his head would stop hurting.

CHAPTER

6

Cordell had dodged a lot of lawmen in his time. He knew how. He was confident they would not expect him to turn back toward town, so that was what he did. He entered the creek and followed it downstream several hundred yards. He felt that the two horsemen he had seen trailing after him would decide he was most likely to go upstream, for his best hope of escape lay to the west. Leaving the creek, he saw no sign of pursuit. He indulged in a moment of pride for his ability to outwit the law. He speculated that perhaps in some previous life he had been a coyote. He had that devious animal's instincts.

He stayed within cover and observed Shanty's cabin for some time before he ventured into the open. He found Buster's bridle where he had left it hanging in a tree. The saddle lay across a shoulder-high branch, out of the wild hogs' reach. Buster's horse grazed where he had been staked near the edge of the river. Cordell saddled and led him to the cabin. Shanty's mule followed, braying.

Shanty came out and shaded his eyes with his hand, calling to his dog to hush up. Cordell asked him, "How's my boy? He doin' any better?"

Shanty frowned. "He's still feverish and hurtin' a right smart. Can't get him to take no nourishment."

Cordell nodded. "I'm obliged to you for seein' after him. Been anybody snoopin' around?"

"Ain't been a soul come by. Ain't many folks bothers with old Shanty."

"I'm fixin' to take him off of your hands."

Shanty was dubious. "He ought not to be ridin'."

"Wisht I could leave him longer, but there's folks in town that's anxious to see me and Buster. We ain't anxious to see them."

In the cabin, Cordell laid the palm of his hand against the wounded man's forehead. Shanty had been right. Buster was fevered more than before. Cordell said, "Ain't you ready to get out of bed and do some travelin'? Layin' around saps a man's strength."

Buster raised up on one elbow, his face twisting in pain. "I been worried . . . you wouldn't come back."

"You ought to know I wouldn't go off and leave a pardner, not when I owe him his split. I got our property back."

Buster was wearing his trousers but not his shirt and boots. Shanty brought him the shirt. He had washed the blood from it and had done a fair job of patching the hole where the bullet had gone in. He said, "I been tellin' your friend he ought to go on and let you stay here."

Buster begged, "Don't leave me. I'm afraid."

"I ain't leavin' you. Soon as it's safe, I'll get you to a sure-enough doctor. He'll fix you up better than you was before."

Cordell knew it was likely that his description had been sent out in all directions. His black beard and shaggy hair would give him away to anybody who was paying attention. He asked, "Shanty, you got some scissors and a razor? I'd like to get rid of this briar patch. I wouldn't be surprised to see a sparrow come flyin' out of it."

He trimmed off most of the beard with the scissors, then lathered and shaved the rest. He was surprised by the clean face that looked back at him from Shanty's cracked mirror. He had not seen it in a long time, but then, neither had anyone else. Years ago, women had told him he was handsome. He doubted they would say that now. His jaw seemed more square than he remembered, and the face showed lines that reminded him of an irrigation ditch. The beard had probably been an improvement.

I've gotten ugly as hell, he thought. But a man did not have to be good-looking so long as he had money.

"I'd better shed some of this long hair, too."

Shanty said, "I ain't no barber, but I'll see what I can do."

When he finished with the scissors, there seemed to be enough hair and beard on the floor to stuff a pillow. Cordell surveyed the results in the mirror. "You're right, you ain't no barber, but it sure changes my looks. We'd better be travelin', boy."

He helped Buster to his feet and supported him through the door. He gave him a boost up into the saddle. "Think you can hang on?"

"I ain't goin' to fall off." Buster steadied himself on the saddle horn. "We owe Shanty somethin'."

Cordell reached into a saddlebag and drew out several bills.

Shanty shook his head. "I ain't askin' for money. The Lord'd be ashamed of me if I didn't do all I could for a sick boy."

"This is just for the vittles me and Buster ate. And you're apt to need a new razor. I think I ruined yours." Cordell thrust the money into Shanty's hand and climbed into the saddle. "Don't worry about the Lord. He'll smile on you for what you've done."

Shanty nodded gravely. "He already has. I just hope He smiles on that boy."

"You might not want to watch us leave. If anybody asks, you can tell them it sounded like we rode south."

Cordell headed west. Buster trailed behind him, cramped in pain. Cordell regretted the necessity, but they had to keep moving. The law might not be alone in looking for them. Milt Hayward might be looking, too. It would be his style to ambush and kill the two of them, then take the money, all of it.

Still hurting, Andy had no patience for listening to Farley run him down. He trailed behind Farley and Speck as they rode into town at dusk and reined up at the jail. Speck volunteered, "I'll take the horses over to the wagon yard."

That suited Andy. More than anything else, he wanted to get to his bunk and lie down. It would feel good despite being hard as stone. He staggered inside and made his way toward the open cell in which he had slept before.

He heard a familiar voice. "Looks like you hunters came home without no quail."

A long, lanky figure unwound from the chair at the sheriff's desk.

Andy caught a quick breath. "Len? Len Tanner?"

"If you was lookin' for Sam Houston, he died. I come in his place."

Andy gladly grasped the Ranger's hand. For a man who seemed too thin to cast a shadow, Len had a grip like a blacksmith. Andy winced.

Len saw the mark on Andy's head. "Looks like somebody went and pistol-whipped you. Cordell?"

"I'm ashamed to say it was Fowler Gaskin. Hit me with a chunk of firewood."

"Ain't that old buzzard dead yet? I thought by now somebody would've put him out of his misery." Len addressed Farley for the first time and without enthusiasm. "I see you ain't got no handsomer. Ain't that little Mexican woman of yours run you off yet?"

"Half-Mexican," Farley corrected him. "Nobody's been run off except Badger Boy."

Andy would explain to Len some other time. He asked, "How come you're here?"

Len said, "Captain sent me to pick up Cordell and take him back. Seein' as he's not in the jailhouse, and you didn't bring him in, I have to figure he's on the loose."

Andy could only nod.

Len took a small book from his pocket and flipped through its pages. Andy recognized it as a Ranger's fugitive list. He had carried one himself during his time of service. Len said, "There was three of them hit that bank. Except for Cordell, we don't have enough description to find the other two in here."

Andy said, "Speck told us Cordell called out a name that sounded like *milk*."

"That don't make a lick of sense."

"It's all we've got. What about the kid that was with them?"

"Cordell probably picked him up somewhere along the way. There ain't no tellin' who he might be."

"I hit him as he was bringin' the horses up, but he managed to ride away."

No kid had been with Cordell at Gaskin's place. Andy wondered. Perhaps he had died of his wound, or perhaps Cordell had found some place to leave him. He told Len briefly about his encounter at Gaskin's. "He said it was his partner that shot Tom. I don't know whether to believe him or not."

"Cordell has got most of a page in the fugitive book. I'd put my money on him unless I heard otherwise."

Andy's voice coarsened with anger. "Whichever one pulled the trigger, they're all guilty. I'm afraid by mornin' they'll be out of the county. I've got no legal authority to go farther than that."

"Yes, you do. Judge Tompkins told me he got a wire from the state office. They approved your reinstatement. You're a Ranger again."

Farley had listened with a frown. He said, "That won't set well with Bethel. Maybe now she'll come to her senses and look for a better man."

Farley would be eager to help her do that. Andy said, "I hope she understands. But even if she doesn't, I've got to do all I can to catch the people that killed Tom."

Len said, "Damned shame about that. He was as square a man as I ever knew." He moved toward the door. "I'm about ready for some supper. Ain't et a bite since noon. The state of Texas is buyin'."

Andy removed the badge Judge Tompkins had given him. "I won't need this anymore." He handed it over to Farley.

Farley grunted, glancing at the lettering. "You'd think this county could afford its own badges." He started to pin it to his shirt but changed his mind. "I wonder where Tom's is."

Andy said, "They'll bury it with him."

"I'd rather have my own anyway." Farley tossed the deputy badge at the desk and missed. He did not stoop to pick it up.

Andy went to supper with Len, but Farley stayed back. He said, "I'll eat later. I don't aim to have Tanner talk both of my ears off."

Len had a reputation for conversation that stopped only when he went to sleep, and not always then. It had driven Farley to distraction when they worked together as Rangers.

Rusty Shannon entered the restaurant while Andy and Len awaited their supper. Face grim, he howdied and shook hands with Len but had little to say. Andy asked about Mrs. Blessing.

Rusty said, "Alice is with her. So are several of her neighbors. Doc Smith gave her somethin' to make her sleep." His face twisted in grief. "I've got to stay here and help with the funeral. Len, you and Andy go and get them."

Andy hoped everyone would understand why he could

not stay for the funeral. "We'll get them," he promised, "if we have to follow them to the moon."

Len pondered. "I wasn't authorized to go on a chase. They just told me to get Cordell and take him to Galveston. Maybe we can catch him before the main office starts worryin' about me not showin' up."

Next morning, Andy, Len, and Farley left Speck in charge of the jail. Leading a pack mule with supplies enough for several days, they were at Gaskin's cabin a while after daylight. Len had talked all the way, recounting what he had been doing since he, Andy, and Farley had served together on the Rio Grande.

The old man met them at the door, in his underwear. His droopy eyes said he was still half-asleep. He growled, "I hope you-all are here to help me straighten up my place. It's your fault it's in this shape."

Len said, "It's been in this shape ever since I first saw it." He had spent a lot of time at Rusty Shannon's between Ranger missions, so he had known Gaskin for years.

Squinting hard, Gaskin recognized Len. "Old Never Hush. You still a Ranger?"

"It's all I know to be."

"I hope you're half as good at Rangerin' as you are at jawin'."

Len said, "I don't say nothin' that ain't gospel truth. That's more than I can say for some folks."

Andy pointed in the direction Cordell had taken in leaving. Len studied the trail and gave Farley a critical look. "Don't you know better than to mess up a fugitive's tracks? I can't tell what's yours and what was left by Cordell."

Farley was defensive. "We're wastin' time here. I can show you where me and Speck lost the trail."

They pushed into an easy lope until they came to a creek. Farley said, "Here's where we found Andy's horse and Gaskin's mule. Cordell rode in, but he never rode out."

Len said, "He must've, unless he drowned. Did you follow the creek upstream?"

"A couple of miles. You wouldn't think he could come out without leavin' sign, but I guess he did."

"How far did you ride downstream?"

"A couple hundred yards. He wouldn't have gone that way. It'd take him back toward town."

"That's just what he might figure you'd figure, so like as not he figured to fool you. Let's go downstream."

They traveled more than two miles before Len found where Cordell had left the creek. He gave Farley a grin that silently said, *I told you*. He rode out onto the bank, pausing to study the tracks. "I see a cabin."

Andy was suddenly fearful. "That's Shanty's place. I hope he didn't hurt that old man." He put his horse into a long trot.

Len caught up with him. "Cordell might steal the pennies from a dead man's eyes, but I doubt he'd hurt a harmless old darky. Probably just lookin' for somethin' to eat."

"Shanty wouldn't have much to spare. It was a hard winter."

The tracks led almost directly to Shanty's, though they detoured to a thicket. They indicated that Cordell had paused there, probably watching to be sure no outsiders were around.

Shanty was near the shed, feeding grain to his small flock of chickens. He tossed handfuls onto the ground and called, "Chickie, chickie," while they pecked around his feet. He did not hear the horses until they were close by. They startled him.

Andy called anxiously, "Are you all right?"

Shanty stared in surprised silence before greeting his company. He usually glowed when anyone came to visit. He seemed ill at ease. "Andy, Mr. Farley, Mr. Len."

Andy said, "We been trailin' a wanted man. Tracks show he came this way. Have you seen anybody?"

Shanty was hesitant. "What name does he go by?"

"He answers to Cordell."

"There was a feller come by here. That might've been his name. Yes, I believe it was."

"Was he alone?"

"A young feller come with him."

Andy was puzzled by Shanty's slowness to answer. He said, "Maybe Cordell made you promise not to tell us anything, but your word to an outlaw don't count. Tom Blessing is dead on account of them."

"I didn't know Mr. Tom had died." Shanty removed his hat and bowed his head. Reluctantly he said, "The boy had a bullet in him. I done what I could for him. Mr. Cordell, he was gone a long time, then he come back for the boy. Took him away yesterday."

"The boy . . . what was his name?"

"Buster was all I heard. I told Mr. Cordell that he'd ought to leave him because the boy was awful weak. Looked fair to die. But he said there was folks in town might hang him on account of Sheriff Tom. He seemed like too nice a boy to get hung."

Farley said drily, "But not too nice to hold up a bank."

Len asked, "Which way did they go when they left?"

"Can't rightly say. Mr. Cordell told me to go inside and not watch them. Could've gone any whichaway."

Farley said accusingly, "Helpin' them makes you an accessory. You could go to jail for that."

Andy tried to put words in Shanty's mouth to counter what Farley said. "Cordell held a gun on you, didn't he? I doubt he gave you any choice."

Shanty said, "When I seen how bad off that boy was, I couldn't say no. Like the Book says, you never know when an angel may come to your door unawares."

Farley said, "If you'd been a better shot, Badger Boy, he *would've* been an angel."

Shanty said, "The Book says thou shalt not kill. Been a time or two I was tempted, but the Lord stayed my hand." He turned to look toward his cabin. "I expect they'll be buryin' Mr. Tom today. I better put on my go-to-meetin' clothes." His voice broke. "An awful good man, he was. A real friend to me."

A few in town might resent a black man's presence at the funeral, but they would not say anything aloud. His friends far outnumbered them.

Len rode a wide circle around the cabin and came back. He pointed west. "Tracks of two horses lead off yonderway."

Shanty said, "Mr. Cordell left me some money, but I can't rightfully spend it. I wish you'd give it back to them it belongs to."

Andy said, "How do you know that what he gave you was stolen? He might've won it in a card game. You ought to go to town and buy you some groceries with it."

"Them groceries would go sour in my mouth."

"Then hide it away till we come back. We'll put it with what we take from Cordell when we catch him."

Farley snorted. "*When?* Sure of yourself, ain't you, Badger Boy?"

"We'll get him. Maybe today, maybe tomorrow, maybe next week. Somebody's got to pay for Tom."

The trail was plain for a while, then became increasingly difficult to follow. Cordell had sought out places where the ground was hard or gravelly. Farley complained, "He's gainin' time. We'll lose him."

Andy's voice had a barb in it. "That wouldn't help your campaign much, would it?"

Farley flushed. "I wasn't thinkin' about the campaign."

Andy felt certain he was.

At length Farley drew up and took a sweeping look at the ground ahead. "The county line is around here somewhere." They were not on a road, where there might have been a marker. "That bein' the case, I'm at the end of my jurisdiction."

Andy asked, "You're fixin' to turn back?"

"I hate to, I purely do, but I've got to think of my responsibility as actin' sheriff of this county. Folks will expect me to be where they can reach me if I'm needed."

Andy let his sarcasm show. "Besides, if we catch Cordell outside of the county, it'll be the Rangers that get the credit."

"I never gave a minute's thought to who gets the credit."

Len offered Farley a graceful way out. "There's no tellin' how long we may be gone, and that boy Speck didn't strike me as bein' real peart."

Farley sounded reluctant but looked relieved. "Right. I wish I could go on with you, but I've got a duty here."

Len nodded solemnly. "I'm glad you see it my way."

Farley turned back in the direction of town. Len said, "I'm glad to be shed of his gripin'. I couldn't hardly get a word in edgeways."

Andy waited until Farley was well beyond earshot before he expressed his doubts. "Cordell has tried several times to make us lose his trail. He'll do it sooner or later. Probably sooner."

"All we can do is try our best."

"He's liable to spend that money before we catch him."

Len shrugged. "I don't lay awake at night worryin' about some Yankee bank. I'm mainly interested in gettin' Cordell a room and bed at the state hotel in Huntsville." Len saw several distinct tracks. He dismounted to observe them closely. "One of the horses has got an odd-shaped hoof, like his foot was twisted a little."

Andy squatted on his heels and studied the track. He was not sure he would be able to distinguish it if he saw it again, mixed up with other tracks. His Indian training had some gaps in it.

CHAPTER

7

Long hours in the saddle had worn heavily on Buster. Only his uncertain grip on the horn kept him from sliding off. The kid's horse followed Cordell's, for Buster was too weak to offer guidance. Frequently Cordell had to stop and let Buster catch up. Much of the time the kid appeared to be only half-conscious. Cordell saw a small crossroads village ahead. He needed no reminder that the two had had nothing to eat since leaving Shanty's cabin.

He said, "I don't see no telegraph line, so maybe they ain't heard about us yet. I'll leave you in that grove of trees yonder while I go in and get us somethin' to eat. Might buy me a change of clothes, too. Like as not they've put out a description on what I'm wearin'."

He knew he looked different without the beard and long hair, but his frayed homespun cotton shirt was of a kind not widely seen anymore since most men had begun turning toward store-bought clothes. It might spark recognition in someone who had a sharp eye and memory for detail. Another reason for not taking Buster, aside from the boy's weak condition, was that the notices likely described two or even three men, one of them wounded. Alone, perhaps Cordell would not draw attention.

The village probably did not rate a place on any map.

He saw one saloon, a general store, and a blacksmith shop. A small church sat off to itself far enough that it should not distract from business at the saloon. Wind lifted dust from a street pounded into powder by hooves and wagon wheels. He had to summon willpower to ride by the saloon without stopping. The fewer people who saw him, the better. Saloons produced more idle gossip than a barbershop.

The general store offered a variety of smells ranging from dried fruit to leather goods to kerosene, but no whiskey. He found only the paunchy, graying proprietor and a woman customer, who wistfully fingered a bolt of blue dress material. The proprietor called, "I'll be with you shortly, sir. Please feel free to look around while I wait on Mrs. Jones. You might find something you want."

At another time and in another place Cordell might have wanted Mrs. Jones. She was a pleasant-looking woman, possibly in her early thirties. He had always found the ladies attractive. At one time he had considered eighteen properly young. Now as his own age advanced, he was more tolerant of extra years and experience. Eighteen seemed barely out of the cradle.

He removed his hat and bowed from the waist as she glanced at him. She gave him the merest hint of a smile and quickly turned her blue eyes away. He knew it was only an acknowledgment of his courtesy. Lacking any reason to believe otherwise, he had to assume she was a churchgoing woman, a devoted wife and mother.

Bittersweet memories came in a rush, and for a moment he was caught up in a sobering sense of loss, of opportunities not taken, of happiness wasted. He felt envy for the man, whoever he might be, lucky enough to have this woman for his wife.

She said to the proprietor, "The material is pretty, but it'll have to wait, Mr. Arnold. Perhaps the crops will be better this year."

Cordell thought of the bank money, some in his pocket, the rest in his saddlebags. He was tempted to buy the bolt of cloth for the lady, but he knew pride would not allow her to accept such a gift, not even from a friend, much less from a stranger.

He watched her go out the door. "Fine-looking woman," he said.

Arnold nodded, looking over the glasses perched halfway down his nose. "For now, but a few more years of slaving on that farm and she'll be wrinkled and gray. It happens to all of them."

"Pity." Cordell thought of prairie bluebonnets, beautiful in the spring but too soon dry and wilted. He turned to the selection of groceries. "I'm needin' some coffee, some flour, some bacon." He watched the proprietor strain to reach canned sardines on a high shelf, then place them on the counter along with canned tomatoes. Cordell fished dry crackers out of a barrel. He thought of Buster. "A little candy, too."

Arnold took a pencil from its resting place over his ear and pushed his glasses up higher on his nose. As he jotted down the prices, he asked, "Anything else?"

Cordell selected an ordinary blue work shirt that would not attract attention and a pair of plain cotton trousers. With those, he thought, he would pass anywhere as a farmer.

Arnold said casually, "I don't believe I've seen you before."

Cordell was unsure whether that was innocent curiosity or if the storekeeper might have heard something. He said, "I've got kin a little ways east of here. I don't want them seein' me in these wore-out clothes. They'll think I've come beggin'."

Arnold said, "I can understand how they might. The only time I ever see or hear from most of my kin is when they want somethin'."

"Ain't it a fact?" Cordell considered a moment before saying in the most offhand manner he could, "I've been travelin' and ain't heard much news. Anything happenin' that I might've missed?"

"Not around here, but east of here there was a jailbreak. Sheriff got killed."

Cordell had feared the sheriff would die, but this was the first time he had heard confirmation. If the folks back there had been keen to capture him before, they would be far more determined now. "They catch whoever done it?"

"The laws are out lookin'. They say there was three of them to start with. One split off. The other two was a big man with a black beard and a young man carryin' a bullet wound. You might keep an eye out for them. They're liable to be dangerous."

"Them kind always are." Cordell had left his pistol and cartridge belt with Buster to avoid arousing suspicion. Most farmers didn't pack iron, not in this settled country. "Maybe I ought to've brought a gun with me, just in case."

"Best thing is to not let them get that close. Leave them to the law. That's what we pay them for."

They probably don't pay the law half enough, Cordell thought. Years ago he had considered becoming a lawman, but he had decided being on the other side of the fence paid better. Long, hungry days on the run had often given him reason to regret that decision. Even now he would quit if he thought he could. But too many people had long memories.

Cordell paid for his purchases. Arnold said, "I keep a pistol under the counter. If they come in here, I'll shoot to kill."

That was the attitude most people would take, Cordell thought. He felt a chill.

The smart thing would be to leave Buster to fare the best he could and get far away as fast as his horse could travel. For a moment he considered that option. It was what Milt had done. But Cordell lived by a different code. He was ashamed that he had entertained the thought for even a moment. One did not abandon a friend, not if he considered himself a man.

He left the village in the same direction in which he had come in. Once out of sight he circled back to the grove where he had left Buster. He found the kid lying quietly, half-asleep or half-unconscious. It was hard to tell which. Cordell set about building a small fire. He saw no water nearby, so coffee would have to wait. Creeks were plentiful in this eastern part of Texas. Surely they would come across one somewhere, and they could camp for the night.

For now, a can of tomatoes would take care of thirst. At the moment, he wanted to stop the growling of his stomach. He fried up some bacon in a little skillet he had bought.

He grunted to himself as he considered the irony of his situation. He had saddlebags full of money but could spend little of it without arousing suspicion. By some people's standards he was at this moment a wealthy man, yet he was half-starved and had nothing to eat except fat bacon, some canned sardines, and a few crackers. Besides that, he had a near-helpless kid on his hands.

It was a great life, being an outlaw.

He would give everything he owned, from the bank money down to his horse and saddle, if he could go back twenty-odd years and start over. It would be cheap at any price.

He watched as Buster's eyes fluttered, then came open. He speared a thick strip of bacon on the point of his knife and extended it toward his young companion. "Careful. It might burn you, but it'll give you the strength to keep ridin' a little longer."

Buster took the bacon and made a valiant effort toward eating it. He gave up after a minute and shook his head in futility. "We got to keep ridin'? Toward what?"

"To where it'll be safe for you to rest. Try again. You've got to eat if you're ever goin' to get well."

Buster finally managed to get the bacon down and drink juice from the tomato can. The fever had left him badly dehydrated. He lay back, exhausted.

Cordell said regretfully, "I wish we could stay here, but

there's a chance that store man will add up somethin' be-sides the bill. We got to keep travelin' awhile longer."

Buster groaned as Cordell lifted him into the saddle.

After a few more miles they made a dry camp. Next morning they were traveling by the time the sun came up. By noon Buster was talking out of his head, and his horse was beginning to limp a little. Soon after they had stolen it, Cordell had noticed that it had a misshapen foot, as if it had been injured at some time.

He watched dark clouds building in the east, and before long he could smell rain in the wind. He saw a house sur-rounded by trees and decided to make an appeal to human kindness on Buster's behalf. It had worked with Shanty. Maybe it would work here. If it didn't, he could employ persuasion with the help of Samuel Colt.

Close up, he could see that one window was broken out, and the roof needed attention. A dead garden out back in-dicated that no one had lived here in a while, though a field to the south had growing corn. Somebody was farming the land. The place had probably been bought by a neighbor trying to expand his own acreage. It was becoming harder and harder for small farmers to survive. They had to get larger or get out.

"Buster," he said, "I thought lady luck had turned her back on us, but it looks like she's smilin' again."

Buster did not reply. Cordell wondered if he even heard.

Riding into town with Len, Andy saw a wizened, gray-haired man seated on a bench in front of a store, idly whit-tling a piece of pine. Around him on the porch and beyond lay the shavings and dried and drying brown remnants of chewing tobacco. A little of it ran down his stubbled chin. He reminded Andy of Fowler Gaskin.

Andy asked, "Mister, have you seen anything of two men—a big one and a young one? They'd be ridin' a bay horse and a dun."

The idler gave Andy a dour look and spat a stream of spittle, part of which reached the street. The rest fell on the stained porch. "Stranger, half the horses that pass this way are bays, and duns ain't exactly scarce. If you'll look up the street, you'll see several of both. Take your pick."

Len said, "We're not funnin'. We're Rangers."

The man spat again. "That ain't much recommendation. Some of the sorriest people I ever knowed was Rangers." His face turned belligerent, and he pointed at Len. "I know you, Tanner. You helped lie me into the pen once. Said I'd been stealin' hogs."

"You was."

"The puny evidence you had wouldn't've held water if you hadn't brought in a pet judge."

Andy figured that even if the old man had seen Cordell and Buster, he would lie about it. "Come on, Len. Some people you just can't talk to." He moved toward the courthouse.

Len said, "We caught that old rapscallion dead to rights. It's hard to make friends of people after you've throwed them in jail. They take it personal."

Andy almost tripped on a spittoon that sat beside the door of the sheriff's office. Above it was a small sign: *Spit before you enter.*

The sheriff sat at his desk, laboriously writing with a pen that scratched as it inked a message on a white sheet of paper. He looked up with a frown as if he resented being disturbed. The pen rolled halfway across his desk, leaving a black trail. His voice was far from cordial. "Rangers. I can tell by lookin' at you."

Andy had discovered that a few law officers were jealous of the Rangers. They shouldn't be, he thought, for chances were that they were better paid than Rangers. They just didn't have the reputation or the aura that seemed to follow Rangers whether justified or not.

Sheriff Shively was a dyspeptic-looking sort with a bald head and a prickly attitude. He drew a whiskey bottle out of a drawer and took a swallow, then put it back without offering it to the visitors. He listened impatiently as Andy explained their business, then growled, "Damn Rangers always waltz in here actin' like they've just come from the right hand of God, and they know everything. Now I suspect you're fixin' to ask me for help."

Len said, "Me and Andy don't claim to know it all. Just a little here and there."

"If you Rangers were half the lawmen you claim to be, that outlaw never would've broke out of jail. In fact, you'd've shot him when you caught him, and he wouldn't've made it to jail to start with. Shoot first is my motto. Saves time and taxpayer expense."

Peeved at Shively's attitude, Andy did not bother to explain that no Ranger had been on hand when either the arrest or the break took place. Len did, however, in full detail. "Seein' as it was a sheriff like yourself that was shot, I'd think you'd want to give us all the help you can."

"I knew Tom Blessing. To my way of thinkin' he was too easy on criminals. That's what got him killed. A smart lick across the head with a gun barrel is my way of keepin' them quiet. And if they raise a ruckus, shoot them. No pettifoggin' lawyer can bail them out of the graveyard." Shively narrowed his eyes in speculation. "If I was to help you catch them, who gets the reward?"

Andy's face warmed with indignation. About now a true Comanche would be swinging his war club. But Len shrugged off any such feelings. He said, "We ought to be able to work out somethin' that'd suit everybody."

The sheriff's calculating look indicated that he was mentally counting the dollars. "Tell me what you want me to do. I'll decide if I want to do it or not."

Len said, "You know the people that belong here. Take a look at any strangers and see if they fit the description of Luther Cordell and the young feller that was with him. Me and Andy can make the arrest."

"I'll do my own arrestin', damn it. What makes you think they're here?"

Andy said, "They was headed in this direction when we lost their trail. They might've kept on goin', but there's a chance they've decided to lay up on account of one bein' wounded."

Shively muttered to himself. "I'll do some askin' around. But I don't need no Rangers gettin' in my way. I'll do this myself."

Andy was strongly inclined to tell Shively off and leave,

but Len gripped Andy's arm in silent admonition. Len said, "They may not be easy to arrest. We're here to take that job off of your hands."

The sheriff scalded the pair with his eyes. "If I want you, I'll holler. Go set yourselves down at the Lone Star Bar and wait. It always looked to me like settin' is what Rangers are best at."

A quiet deputy with nervous eyes and the beginning of a beer belly waited until Shively had gone down the hall before he spoke. "Don't pay too much mind to the way Homer talks. He's been sour on the Rangers ever since the time he spent three hard days huntin' a horse thief. Two Rangers was just loafin' in a barroom when the man come ridin' up on this stolen pony. They grabbed him before he could swaller his drink. Got a reward from the man that lost the horse. They didn't give none of it to Homer."

Andy said, "He wasn't entitled. He didn't make the arrest."

"But he'd spent three days on the hunt, while they hadn't broke a sweat. A thing like that would naturally gall a man."

"Maybe so," Andy said, "but it don't alter my first opinion, that Homer Shively is a poor excuse for a lawman."

The deputy shrugged. "I get paid to do what he tells me. Homer will still be here when you're gone, and so will I. At least till next election. He's made a lot of people sore at him, so folks may not vote for him again."

Andy said, "Even so, we don't want to take a chance on him makin' a mistake and lettin' Cordell get away."

Andy and Len made an effort to follow Shively as

he dropped in at one saloon after another as well as the barbershop and two general stores, making inquiry, giving a thorough looking over to most of the men he encountered. It became monotonous.

Finally, however, Shively devoted his attention to a man sitting in a dark rear corner of a barroom, nursing a whiskey bottle already reduced by more than half. He was a large man with a beard.

Shively approached him with pistol drawn. "All right, you, stand up and raise your hands."

The man's red-veined eyes had trouble focusing on the sheriff. He made no move to comply.

Shively repeated, "Stand up, damn you. Keep them hands where I can see them." He poked the pistol in the stranger's direction.

The man's voice was belligerent. "You ain't no general, and I ain't no soldier. Who the hell are you to be givin' me orders?"

"I'm the county sheriff, and you're under arrest for murder."

Andy saw that this man was not Cordell. He said, "Shively—"

Before he could say more, Shively brought the barrel of his pistol down on the stranger's head. The man fell across the table, tipping it over. The bottle crashed to the floor.

Andy flared. "Damn it, Shively, I tried to tell you. That is not Cordell."

Shively gave him a look of disbelief. "He's a big man with a beard. He fits the description."

"I saw Cordell close enough to know this isn't him. I hope you haven't busted this man's skull."

"He oughtn't to've sassed me. It was his own fault, not showin' respect to the badge."

"He was probably too drunk to see it."

Shively turned to his deputy. "Get somebody to help you drag him over to the jail. We'll charge him with bein' drunk and disorderly."

Andy wanted to knock Shively all the way back to the wall, but he restrained himself. Though justified, such an action would probably set off a legal confrontation between state and county jurisdictions and lead to no end of paperwork. Andy dreaded paperwork.

Len took Andy's arm and pulled him aside. "Maybe he had the right idea about us takin' a sit-down in some pleasant place. We can wait and see what he finds out."

"I don't understand how he ever got elected sheriff."

Shively heard the comment and turned angrily. "There used to be a lot of lawbreakin' riffraff in this county. The citizens got tired of it and wanted a man who would get tough. That's me. I give this kind of trash no quarter."

Sometimes the line between lawbreaker and lawbringer was too thin to define, Andy thought.

He had never developed any particular liking for liquor. He took a beer but sipped it so slowly that the glass was only half-empty after Len had finished two shots of whiskey. Len said, "Everything in this world can't be just like we'd want it. You was about to get in a tangle that I wasn't sure you could win."

"He's got a good whippin' comin' to him."

"And he'll get it sooner or later, but it ain't our place to do it. Right now we've got more important business."

Andy felt uneasy about wasting time when Cordell might be using it to get farther away. "Maybe we ought to go see if Shively has pistol-whipped anybody else," he suggested.

Len showed no sign that the whiskey had affected him. For such a skinny man, he had long demonstrated that he could put away a prodigious amount of food. He seemed to have the same high tolerance for whiskey. He said, "We'd better. He looks slippery as hog grease."

They found that Shively and his deputy had left town. The hostler at the stables said, "I told him I'd seen a couple of strangers out at the old Graham place. A big man and a smaller one. Him and his deputy rode out of here like they'd been turpentined."

While Andy and Len quickly saddled their horses, the hostler gave them directions. "Neighbor named Wilson bought the farm after old man Graham died. It's a good house. Roof don't leak, hardly."

Riding in an easy lope that would not overtax the horses, Andy said, "If it's really Cordell, he's apt to shoot Shively's head off."

Len asked, "Then what are we hurryin' for? We ought to give him time to do it."

"What happens to Shively doesn't worry me, but the idea of losin' Cordell bothers me a lot."

They could see what they took to be the Graham house a mile or so ahead. They heard a distant rattle of gunfire.

Excitement prickled Andy's skin. He said, "We'd better whip up."

They pushed their horses hard across the remaining distance. As they approached the house, they saw two men standing and two men flat on the ground. Andy halfway hoped Shively was one of those lying still, but he saw that the sheriff and his deputy remained on their feet.

Len declared in surprise, "I'll be damned! They got Cordell."

Hearing the oncoming horses, Shively whirled around, pointing his pistol toward the Rangers. Andy instinctively dropped low over the saddle horn. The sheriff might shoot first and check identities later. Shively lowered the weapon when he recognized the two. As Andy and Len reined to a stop, Shively said with pride, "Told you I didn't need no Rangers to help me. Looks like that reward is all mine."

Andy thought he should be pleased that Cordell was dead, regardless of who killed him, but he was not. "Maybe," he said.

The larger of the dead men was lying facedown. Andy dismounted and studied him for a minute, then turned him over. He felt his stomach draw into a knot. "This isn't Cordell."

Shively's chin dropped. "What do you mean it ain't Cordell? He's a big man, like you said. And he's got a beard like you said. You tryin' to slicker me out of my reward?"

"Cordell's beard was as black as a crow's wing. This one is brown, with some gray in it."

Shively began to sweat. "Then why did he draw a gun on us as we rode up?"

"What gun? I don't see one."

Andy went to look at the young man, whose lifeless eyes stared up at the bright blue sky. He had seen Cordell's companion only at considerable distance. This boy appeared somewhat heavier, though he could not be sure of that. He said, "If this is the right man, he ought to have at least two bullet holes in him. One of them was mine." Andy knelt. "I don't see a gun on him either."

Sweat rolled down Shively's reddening face. "I swear they was both armed and fixin' to shoot at us. They must've hid those guns."

Andy turned to the deputy. "Did you see them aim at you?"

The deputy trembled. "Homer said they was. I was busy duckin'."

"They never fired a shot, did they?"

The deputy did not answer, but his silence told Andy all he needed to know. Furious, he faced Shively. "You wanted so bad for it to be Cordell that you shot first and didn't ask any questions. You just killed two innocent men."

Shively stammered, "How . . . how do we know they're innocent? It's just your word that this ain't Cordell."

Andy heard hoofbeats. Turning, he saw a middle-aged farmer in overalls, riding up on a mule. The man gave Shively a quick glance and demanded, "What's happened here, Sheriff? I heard shootin'." His gaze dropped to the men on the ground. "Oh my God! George!"

He slipped down from the mule's back and dropped to his knees beside the larger of the two dead men. "Who shot him?"

Shively wiped a sleeve over his sweaty face. "You know him, Wilson?"

"My brother-in-law, George Blaine. I let him move in here to work this farm on shares. That's his boy Adam yonder." He repeated, "Who shot them?"

Shively took a step backward. "It was all a misunderstandin'. An accident. I thought they was a pair of outlaws."

"And you shot them down like dogs?" Fire leaped into Wilson's eyes. "If I had a gun, I'd kill you." He advanced on the sheriff, his fists clenched.

Shively pointed his pistol at the farmer. "Stand back, Wilson. I'll shoot you if I have to."

Andy grabbed Shively's hand and forced the pistol down, then roughly twisted it from the sheriff's grasp. "You've already killed two unarmed men and pistol-whipped another. How many more mistakes do you want to make in one day?"

Wilson demanded, "Who are you?"

Andy said, "We're Rangers. We got here too late."

Wilson's shoulders slumped. He looked again at the two men on the ground. "My wife'll near die when I tell her. She set a lot of store in her brother. That boy, too." He turned a furious gaze back upon Shively. "Since you're Rangers, I want you to arrest him for murder. He's lorded it over this county too long."

Shively's voice was hollow. "I was just tryin' to do my duty. Anybody can make a mistake."

Len said sarcastically, "And that reward never entered your mind. Me and Andy are placin' you under arrest."

Shively's voice seemed about to break. "I thought it was them. Swear to God I did."

Andy told the deputy, "You'd better stay here with the bodies. We'll send help from town."

The deputy looked queasy, but he made no protest.

Wilson declared, "You'd better not let Shively out on bail. If I see him on the street, he's a dead man."

Andy considered placing Wilson under arrest, too, for safety, but perhaps the farmer would cool down once the initial shock subsided.

They presented Shively to the county judge, who agreed that the sheriff belonged in jail for his own good as well as for justice. He said, "He's made too many enemies. Without that badge to protect him, he's a walking target."

With the sheriff in jail and the deputy still out at the farm, Andy and Len were the only lawmen in town. Andy said, "Len, you better go get you some supper while I watch the jail. I'll eat when you get back."

Len was gone long enough to have eaten two suppers. Darkness had come by the time he returned. His expression was grave. He said, "There's a lot of ugly talk goin' around. This old wooden jail looks too flimsy to stand up against a mob."

Len's uneasiness was contagious. Andy said, "We'd better slip him out of town before things come to a head."

Len said, "You need to keep huntin' Cordell. I'll take Shively back east to the next county seat and send a wire to Austin."

Andy was reluctant, but right now Cordell was more important to him than Shively. "I'll miss havin' you with me, Len."

"You've ridden by yourself many a time, and you know

your job. Besides, I'm gettin' to where I can't remember which stories I've told you and which I ain't."

"I don't mind hearin' them twice. Sometimes they're different in the second tellin'."

"I've got a creative memory."

Andy stood watch while Len brought his horse around behind the jail, leading a second for Shively. Len said, "Watch out for yourself, Badger Boy. Don't take no chances with Cordell."

Andy felt an emptiness as Len and the deposed sheriff disappeared into the darkness. He took no offense when Len called him Badger Boy. It was a different matter when Farley Brackett did it.

Andy freed the prisoner Shively had arrested in the saloon. The man was obviously hurting. Andy gave him the bottle he had seen Shively take from a desk drawer. "Don't drink it all at one time," he said.

The judge came around after a while, worried about the possibility of mob violence. Andy showed him the empty cell and explained Len's mission. The judge nodded approval. "You've already done what I was about to recommend."

Andy asked, "What do you reckon'll happen to Shively?"

"He'll stand trial before twelve good men and true, who will probably decide he deserves a stretch in the state pen at Huntsville. He'll find a number of men he sent there. They'll be glad to see him." The judge grimaced, pondering the mental image. "Now, I don't think you and I want to hang around here and face those men when they come. It could be unpleasant. I suggest that we leave the jailhouse door open for their convenience and repair to the Lone Star Bar for a quiet drink."

Andy said, "Just one beer."

After a day like this one, a beer would be worth its weight in silver.

CHAPTER

8

The remnants of a woodpile lay scattered out back. Cordell hurried in with an armload and went back out to fetch more before it got wet. He whittled shavings from a piece of broken chair to get a fire started. Buster seemed to alternate between chills and fever.

Cordell rolled Buster's blanket out on the floor near the fire. He said, "You'll feel better when I get some warm food into you."

A damp, cold wind ushered in the rain. Cordell felt a chill. He pulled Buster's blanket up to cover the boy's shoulders. "Can't have you catchin' pneumonia on top of your other troubles."

He stoked the fire in an effort to heat the room better. He brought in more wood, though it was wet now. Stacked near the fire, it might dry before he had to use it. He made coffee and fried some bacon, but Buster showed little interest in it or even in the candy Cordell had bought. He lay listless, his face hot to the touch. He occasionally murmured words Cordell could not decipher.

"Damn it, kid," Cordell said, "don't you go and die on me."

The last thing he wanted to see was visitors, but there they were, a man and a woman in a wagon. They drew up near the door. The woman climbed down and hurried into the house, out of the rain. The man drove the wagon around back. He unhooked the horses and hurriedly led them to a shed where Cordell had placed his and Buster's.

The woman was surprised and a little frightened to see Cordell. He would guess her to be a farm wife in her thirties. "We didn't know anybody was here," she said, keeping her distance. She shivered, her clothing wet.

Cordell said, "We mean you no harm, ma'am. Get over close to the fire and warm yourself. Me and the boy were just passin' by and came in out of the rain."

She complied, holding her arms tightly against her body. "A spring rain can be awfully cold."

"Yes, ma'am. Sure can."

The man entered the house with obvious apprehension. He gave Cordell an uneasy study. "I was surprised when I saw two horses in the shed. Been a while since anybody lived in this house. We tried to get here before the rain started."

"Live around here, do you?" Cordell asked.

"A few miles farther on. We didn't figure on the rain. Our name is Archer. I'm Daniel. My wife is Patience." Hesitantly he extended his hand, and Cordell took it.

The woman had glanced at Buster when she entered. Now she gave him a closer look. "I thought he was just sleeping. But now I see that he's sick."

"Got himself hurt, ma'am," Cordell said.

"Has he been to a doctor?"

"We ain't been anywhere close to one."

The man knelt beside Buster and pulled the cover back. "Burnin' up with fever. What happened to him?"

Cordell let his hand ease down toward the pistol on his hip, then caught himself. He saw no sign of a gun on this couple. They were farmers, and no immediate threat. "Got himself shot."

Archer said, "I'd better not ask you how."

"I'd as soon you didn't."

Archer's expression indicated that he was making a pretty good guess.

The woman gasped. Her hand went up to her mouth. "You two are outlaws."

"There's some would call me that, but this boy ain't one, not at heart. He just let himself get misled."

"By who?"

"Mainly me. I was raised better, but somewhere along the way I turned left when I ought to've turned right. I'm mortally ashamed for lettin' this boy follow me down the same road."

Mrs. Archer said, "I think you're the man we've heard about. They say you killed a sheriff."

"I've never killed anybody in my life, except maybe in the war, and I ain't even sure about that."

Archer's face was grim. "Looks to me like the boy's dyin'. He needs a doctor real bad."

"If I take him to one, he faces a stretch in the pen—or worse."

The woman had gotten past her fear. Severely she said, "I think he'd rather take his chances with the law than to lie here and die in this miserable old house."

"I just don't see what I can do."

Archer glanced at his wife. "There's somethin' *we* can

do. Patience and me, we can take him to town in the wagon and let you go on by yourself. You could be a good many miles on your way before the law knows anything about it."

Cordell could not understand these people. They were willing to help without even asking about payment. "You could get in trouble."

Mrs. Archer said, "We're all human beings. Anyway, the sheriff is a friend of ours."

Cordell turned to the door, working his way through a tangle of misgivings. Reluctantly he said, "You've got a deal. I'll harness that team back up for you." Hurrying outside, he saw that the rain had slackened. He hitched the team to the wagon, then saddled his horse. He decided to leave Buster's here. Buster wouldn't need him.

He carried the boy to the wagon and placed him in its bed, making sure the blanket was wrapped tightly around him. The Archers followed him out. Cordell extracted a handful of bills from a saddlebag. "This is for your trouble."

Archer shook his head, and his wife frowned disapproval. "We're not doin' this for money," Archer said.

"Then why?"

The woman said, "It's plain to see that you're not a churchgoing man. If you don't know, there's no way we can explain. You'd better be on your way, Mr. Cordell, if you intend to stay ahead of the law."

Cordell was taken aback by the use of his name. He had not told them what it was. That damned telegraph! A man couldn't ride fast enough or far enough anymore to get ahead of it.

He watched the wagon move away into a light mist that lingered after the rain had waned. He told himself this was the best thing for Buster. Maybe the law had enough mercy that it wouldn't hang a green kid, though he probably faced a stretch in Huntsville. At least he would have a chance for a better life once he served his time. Maybe he would stay on a straight road from then on, as Cordell wished *he* had.

But what if Buster didn't live? Archer had said he looked to be dying. Cordell tried to deny it to himself, but deep in his soul he knew Archer was right. It might already be too late for a doctor to save the kid. Cordell could leave here now and get away from the law, but he would never get away from Buster. He would always wonder: did the boy make it, or did he not?

Aw hell! he thought. *I never did have the sense God gave a jackrabbit.*

He set his horse into a lope to catch up to the wagon.

The Archers both looked back over their shoulders. Cordell rode up even with them. They asked no questions, and he offered no explanation. At length Archer said, "You're takin' a big chance. From what we hear, the law is lookin' for you all the way to Austin and San Antonio."

"Life is like a poker game. Sometimes you hold a good hand, and sometimes you don't. You play them as they're dealt and hope for gambler's luck."

Mrs. Archer said, "Or pray for providence to intervene."

It was midway between midnight and dawn when they reached town. Archer pulled the wagon to a stop in front of a house. A wooden sign was attached to the front gate, though Cordell could not read it in the dark. Archer knocked on the door hard enough that Cordell feared he might wake up half the town. Soon a moving lamp cast a dim light through the front window. The door opened. Out came a smallish man in long underwear, unbuttoned trousers, and no shirt. He extended the lamp toward Archer's face.

Archer said, "It's an emergency, Doctor."

"It always is when folks come in the middle of the night." The doctor carried the lamp to the wagon and peered at the blanket-wrapped figure. "Anybody I know?"

"I doubt it. The kid has got a bullet in him. He's far gone."

Cordell dismounted and lifted Buster from the wagon bed. The doctor motioned toward the house, and Cordell followed him to a back room. The doctor said, "Put him down on the bed. I'll have a look at him." He apologized to Mrs. Archer for being half-dressed. "Hold the lamp, would you, Mr. Archer?" He folded the blanket back, opened Buster's shirt, and gazed with disbelief at the wound. He demanded, "Who the hell put this bandage on him?"

Cordell said apologetically, "It's all I had."

"Damned poor job." The old bandage was stiff with dried blood. He stripped it away and said, "I hope the bullet was taken out, at least."

Cordell said, "I tried. Couldn't get it."

"How long has it been in there?"

Cordell counted. "Four days, I think. Maybe five. I lost track."

Angrily the doctor said, "You let him languish to the

point of death, then expect me to save him? He should have seen a doctor right away. That bullet has poisoned his blood."

Cordell had sensed it but had denied it to himself. "What chance has he got?"

"There's no point in lying to you. I doubt that God himself could bring him back."

Cordell slumped into a wooden chair. His throat was constricted, and his eyes burned. Must be that smoky lamp, he thought.

The doctor's tone softened. "Is he your son?"

Cordell shook his head. "I wouldn't have led my son into a mess like this. And I shouldn't have let that boy get into it, either. I'd give anything . . ." He broke off.

Mrs. Archer's eyes showed pity. "Maybe you'd better get away while you can. We'll stay here with him. He won't die alone."

"No, I'll stay. I won't blame you if you send for the law."

Archer said, "We won't do that till the boy is gone. Even then, we'll try to give you a little time."

"Why?"

"It's plain to see that you did what you could for him, except gettin' him to a doctor. A lot of men in your situation would've gone off and left him."

"I ain't so noble that it didn't cross my mind."

Patience Archer said, "That's the first step toward redemption, facing temptation without giving in to it."

"I'm afraid I'm beyond redemption."

"No man is beyond redemption until he draws his last breath."

Buster called out weakly, "Cordell. Where are you?"

Cordell left the chair and gripped Buster's hand. "I'm here. I wasn't goin' anyplace without you."

"Cordell, am I dyin'?"

Cordell swallowed, trying to think of an answer he could give without lying. He saw none. "No, kid, you're goin' to be all right."

"I heard the doctor." Buster began to weep. "I don't want to die."

Cordell was too badly choked to say anything.

Buster pleaded, "Don't tell my mother . . . I don't want her . . . to know what I done."

Cordell wanted to speak but nothing came.

Buster murmured, "God, it hurts so bad."

He drifted into sleep. Head bowed, Mrs. Archer began to pray in a whisper. She reached out to her husband, taking his hand, then reached toward Cordell. He was uncertain what was expected of him, but he bowed his head as she had and took her hand while she continued her prayer. He could not remember the last time he had heard someone pray. Though confused and ashamed for his shortcomings, he took warmth from the compassion of these strangers.

Buster slipped so quietly into death that Cordell was not sure just when the passage came. The doctor covered Buster's face with the blanket, then moved toward the window. "Sunup," he said to Cordell. "The sheriff will open his office in a little while. I'll have to tell him. If you're going to leave, you'd better get started."

Cordell struggled for control of his voice. "I'm obliged to you, ma'am, for the prayer. It's been so long since I've talked to the Lord, I guess I've forgotten how. And I'm afraid He's forgotten about me."

She said, "He never forgets anyone. If it's any comfort, your young friend is now in His care."

"It's better care than I gave him." Cordell laid his hand on the blanket that covered Buster. "I'm thankin' you both. You done more than anybody like me had a right to expect." He turned toward the doctor. "I'm leavin' you some money. I wish you'd see that he gets a decent burial with a preacher to read over him. And get him a proper headstone."

"Anything you want put on it?"

"Just that his real name was David Jackson. And that he was a good boy." Cordell blinked his burning eyes. "I've got to let his mother know somehow. I can't just let her wonder what ever became of him."

"You heard what he said."

"I can tell a good story when I have to. He was shot tryin' to protect some folks from a robber. If any of his family ever comes askin', I hope you won't tell them different."

The rising sun caught Cordell squarely in the eyes as he walked outside. It brought tears.

Riding away from town in an easy lope that he hoped would not overtax a horse already tired, Cordell felt as if a hundred-pound weight had settled in the bottom of his stomach. He kept seeing Buster's fevered face and rehashing the things he might have done differently. He had had more than one chance to take Buster to a doctor. He had told himself he held back out of fear that the boy might be hanged. Now he wondered if that had been the real reason. Maybe his stronger fear had been for himself.

It changed nothing to brood over past mistakes, but he could not help it. If thirty lashes across his back would relieve him of his guilt, he would welcome them.

He slowed to a trot to ease the stress on his horse, but he looked back often, half expecting to see someone catching up. The ground was still wet from the rain, and his tracks were more visible because of it. He would be easy to trail. He looked for a well-traveled road where his tracks might be lost among others, though this meant more people would see him. The old notices would describe him as heavily bearded and wearing different clothes, but the Archers and the doctor were sure to give the authorities a more current picture of him.

He came to a road perpendicular to the westerly direction he had been traveling. It had seen some traffic since the rain. Two freight wagons approached from the left. He turned to the right, two hundred yards ahead of the wagons, hoping the hooves and the iron rims would obliterate his tracks or at least cause confusion and lost time to anyone trying to follow.

He sensed that they might be Rangers, hard men to shake loose from. In the wild days of Reconstruction after the war, the Rangers had been disbanded. A unionist government had organized an alternative, a state police force. Most of these men could not find their butt with both hands. For someone of Cordell's persuasion, those had been good times.

Late in the morning he saw a farmer in a distant field,

working two mules to a plow, and envied him. The farmer didn't have an ill-starred kid weighing heavily on his conscience. He had probably left a comfortable house at sunup after his wife fixed him a good breakfast and perhaps a lunch to carry with him to the field. Tonight he could go home to a hot supper—maybe even pie or cake—and share a soft bed with his woman. If he ever felt compelled to look back over his shoulder, as Cordell was doing, it would only be in hope that he would see a good rain coming over the horizon.

Cordell could not remember the last time he had enjoyed pie or cake, much less a woman.

We harvest what we plant, he thought. *Sometimes wheat, sometimes weeds. Looks like all I've sowed is weeds.*

Len's never-ending talk had made the miles seem shorter. Sometimes Andy paid little attention to the words, but it had been comforting to hear the constant rise and fall of Len's voice and know he was not alone. He was alone now, and since leaving town he had seen nobody except a couple of farmers.

A house lay just off to his right. He decided to go ask a few questions. Though he had found no trail he could be certain was Cordell's, his instincts told him he was traveling in the right direction.

A window was broken out, and a few shingles were gone from the roof. The place was obviously vacant. He had a gut feeling that he should check it anyway. His Comanche hunches had a hair-raising way of being correct from time to time. A vacant house would be a good place for the fugitives to lay up.

Even if he saw Cordell, he was not certain he would recognize him. The times he had seen the man, a thick beard had covered most of his face. He might look different if he shaved it off. But a shave would not change the eyes, and Andy remembered the eagle sharpness of Cordell's.

Horse and wagon tracks were plain in the drying mud. Someone had been here recently. Dismounting, Andy looked closely at the horse tracks. He did not see the twisted hoofprint Len had shown him earlier.

A dun horse nickered and ambled out from behind the old house, curious about Andy's mount. Andy felt a tingle of excitement. This could be one of those he saw at the jailbreak. He circled around to look at the tracks the horse left. He recognized the print and drew the rifle from beneath his leg. Cordell might be in that house.

Andy's mouth went dry. He tied his horse and approached from the front, crouching to make a more difficult target. He jumped up on the small front porch and threw his back against the wall in case someone came out shooting. Nobody did. He rushed through the door, holding his pistol at a level that would take a man in the brisket. The worn pine floor creaked under the weight of his boots. He saw no one. The place was as dead as an Indian graveyard.

He saw dried mud on the floor and coals in the fireplace, still warm. He was certain the fugitives had been here, but they had been on horseback. Andy wondered about the fresh wagon tracks. One of the men was wounded. It could be that the wagon had carried him away. That would explain why his horse was still here.

Cordell had probably kidnapped whoever had happened along in the wagon. Perhaps he had killed them. He had not had time to go far. Andy hurried out toward his tied horse. The horse and wagon tracks headed westward. *Even I ought to be able to follow those,* he thought.

Cordell had the devil's own luck, but maybe this time his luck was running out.

Andy had ridden for an hour or so when he met two freight wagons coming eastward. He signaled for the lead driver to stop. The bewhiskered man first gave him a quizzical look and seemed disinclined to obey. Andy wished he had a badge to show him, but the state had not yet seen fit to issue them to the Rangers. Len had had a silversmith make his from a Mexican peso. He had paid for it himself.

"I'm a Ranger," Andy shouted. "Pull up."

The driver sawed on the lines and brought his team to a halt. "We don't stop these wagons for just anybody," he said. "I couldn't tell you was the law."

"Did you meet a wagon along the way?"

"Just one. There was a farmer and his wife on the seat and a sick man layin' behind them. They said they was takin' him to town."

"Anybody else with them?"

"Big feller on horseback. Are they charged with somethin'?"

"Two of them are. They killed a sheriff."

The driver hunched his shoulders as if he had taken a

chill. "Glad we didn't have nothin' they'd want. That big man had a dark look about him. He may not be took easy."

"I'll take him."

"Maybe. Maybe not." The driver shook his head. "It's no wonder they've buried so many of you Rangers."

Andy said, "They ain't goin' to bury this one anytime soon."

Though he burned to break into a run, he held to a moderate pace. He did not want to be set afoot, leading a wrung-out mount.

Darkness caught him soon after he left the teamsters. Clouds obscured the stars and moon. It was about to get as dark as the inside of a tar barrel. He wanted to keep riding, but he knew he was likely to lose the tracks. Moreover, he had pushed his horse hard. At least, he knew his quarry was headed for town.

He staked his mount and the pack mule. He made coffee over a small fire and tried to content himself with a strip of beef jerky. It was like chewing a dry cowhide. The only flavor came from the pepper and salt applied in the drying. To him, jerky was the next thing to nothing. But when he had nothing else to eat, jerky had its compensations.

About the middle of the next morning, the wagon tracks led him within sight of town. There they were lost amid a multitude of newer tracks. He had been here before and remembered that the town was a county seat. He saw its courthouse from half a mile away, its cupola reaching far above its second floor. From a quarter mile, Andy heard the loud strike of its clock. He recalled having been here as witness in a trial. Court had to stop and wait while the bell shook the building and made more racket than three lawyers yelling at the same time.

This was a typical farming town for its part of south-central Texas, a cotton gin standing alone and silent at the edge of the settlement. Last year's crop had been ginned, and this year's harvest was months away. Andy's fingers itched as he remembered how the dry hulls scratched when he pulled the bolls. It was another reason he had no wish to spend his life as a farmer.

He wished Len were here, though neither would know just where to start looking. He could imagine Len asking, "Ain't there some Indian spirit you can call up?"

Perhaps he could, if he could talk to a Comanche medicine man. But they were long since gone, either dead or exiled to Indian Territory. Still, he reasoned, if those people were bringing the wounded man to town, they would be looking for a medicine man, a white one.

At a loading dock on the side of a general store, a clerk wearing a tie and an apron was loading groceries into a wagon. Andy rode up to him and asked, "You got a doctor in this town?"

The clerk pointed. "Doc Satterwhite, down the street yonder on the opposite side. He's pretty good if you're not too sick."

"Much obliged."

He found the house by a sign on the yard gate. He doubted that Cordell was still there, but if he was, he would flush like a quail.

If Len were here, one could take the front door, the other the back. As it was, Andy walked up to the front door and knocked. He dropped his hand to his pistol and held his breath until a woman peered at him through a curtain. She swung the door open. Andy took a quick look inside before he moved. He saw nothing in the front room that caused alarm. He could hear a child whining and a mother's soothing voice in a back room.

The woman at the door asked, "What can we do for you?"

"I'm a Ranger, ma'am. Did somebody bring a wounded man in here last night?"

"Yes, the Archers from out on Branch Creek."

"Is he still here?"

"I'm sorry to say that he is not."

Andy heard a man's voice in the next room. "Excuse me, Mrs. Johnson. I'll be right back." A middle-aged, little man with a carefully trimmed mustache and goatee came out into the front parlor. "I'm Dr. Satterwhite. I heard you ask about a wounded man. Friend of yours?"

"He's a fugitive. I've been trailin' him and an older man for several days."

The doctor frowned. "I did what I could, but it was already too late. It always hurts to see a young man die in such a miserable way. Whoever put that bullet in him has no reason to be proud of himself."

Andy felt as if the doctor had hit him with a sledge. "It was me," he admitted. "I aimed at somebody else, but the wrong man got in the way."

The doctor's severe countenance softened as he recognized Andy's regret. "It should not have been a fatal wound. He could have lived if he had received proper attention early enough."

"I reckon we were pressin' him and Cordell too hard."

"Cordell?" The doctor said. "That's the name the sheriff and the Archers used. The sheriff said he's a bad one."

Andy said, "Bad enough."

"Funny thing, though, for a bad man. He wept when that boy died. You'd have thought he had lost his own son. He left money for a decent Christian burial and asked me to buy a headstone."

"Did he give you a name? All we know is that the boy was called Buster."

"I wrote it down. It was David Jackson."

"Did Cordell mention where he came from?"

"No. I heard the boy beg him not to let his mother know how he died. Cordell promised."

Andy considered for a moment. "The people that brought Jackson in . . . I hope Cordell didn't do them any harm."

"Quite the contrary. He thanked them for their help. Mrs. Archer told me he even tried to give them money, but they wouldn't take it."

"Odd. Most outlaws aren't much on givin' money away. But I guess he didn't put much work into gettin' it."

The doctor said, "On the contrary again, I'd say he paid a high price."

The sheriff was a portly man named Mitchell, well into middle age and walking with heavy dependence on a cane. He explained that he had suffered a broken leg a few months ago, trying to stop a runaway team of mules. He said, "I halfway been expectin' you. A wire from your state office said you might come along lookin' for Luther Cordell. They asked me to lend you any assistance."

Andy said, "A wounded kid was brought to town last night. Cordell was with him."

"I know. I talked to the Archers. They said he left about daylight. Everybody was careful not to watch which way he went. I've sent two deputies out to try and pick up his trail, but I don't hope for much. Too many roads leadin' out of here, and too much traffic."

Mitchell related the description the Archers had given. Andy was not surprised to learn that Cordell had shaved off his beard and cut his hair. Mitchell said, "Mrs. Archer told me she was scared of him at first, but she got over it when she saw how upset he was about that boy. Said a man couldn't be all bad if he had them kind of feelin's."

"Didn't seem like he had much feelin' for Tom Blessing."

"It's hard to understand the criminal class. They ain't hooked up the same as me and you."

Andy said, "I'd just as well wait and see if your deputies find anything. I could use a good meal anyway."

Mitchell opened a desk drawer and offered a drink. Andy demurred. Mitchell took a swallow and almost choked.

"Prime moonshine," he said. "A cousin of mine makes it."

Andy said, "That's illegal, isn't it?"

"There's good laws, and there's bad laws. I don't enforce the bad ones. A man ought to be able to do what he wants to with his own corn crop." Mitchell dismissed the subject. "Hadn't you better take a look at the body? Confirm that this David Jackson is the man you shot?"

"I only saw him at some distance, but I'll go see."

They walked over to the undertaker's. The kid lay covered in a coffin balanced across two sawhorses. The undertaker was finishing a wooden lid. He stopped to uncover the face.

Though Andy had not had a good look at Jackson, he studied the peaceful features and knew instinctively that this was the rider he had shot. Regret settled over him like a shroud. "He's nothin' but a kid."

Mitchell said, "You acted in the line of duty."

"He's no less dead."

"I've killed a couple of men that needed it real bad, but they still laid heavy on my conscience. You have to look at it as part of your job. When you wear the badge, you take what comes with it."

Andy tried for consolation. "I guess if I hadn't shot him, somebody else would've. He was marked when he took up with the wrong kind of company." He felt a rising of anger against Cordell. "What kind of a man would lead an innocent kid into a life that was likely to get him killed?"

Mitchell suggested, "Maybe he never was all that innocent. Some of the worst criminals I ever saw was preachers' sons."

The undertaker said, "Brother Jones will preach the funeral at two o'clock up at the burying ground. The Archers said they'll be there." He looked like a preacher himself.

Mitchell said, "Even an outlaw kid deserves a few mourners. I'll go."

Andy covered Buster's face. "Me, too. I owe him that much. And I'd like to talk to the Archers."

Standing beside the open grave, Bible in his hand, the minister delivered a fervent preachment against young men taking the wrong road in life. Andy was the only young man present to hear it. The gathering was small, just the sheriff, the Archers, and a few townspeople who came mostly out of curiosity, or perhaps for lack of anything better to do. The brief ceremony closed with each person dropping a handful of sand into the grave. It made a soft, whispering sound, falling upon the pine lid of the plain coffin.

The Archers were grim-faced as they turned away. Andy hurried to catch up to them. He identified himself as a Ranger and said, "I'd like you to tell me anything you can about Cordell."

The man and his wife glanced at one another before Archer answered, "We don't know much to tell you. We only saw him for a little while. It was not the kind of situation that calls for a lot of talk."

"What did he look like?"

Archer described him as large, muscular, clean-shaven except for a two- or three-day growth of whiskers. "He could be any farmer you'd meet travelin' down the road."

Mrs. Archer said, "He was overcome with grief and remorse. Like a father who has just lost his son."

Andy said, "You know, don't you, that he has a price on his head?"

"So we heard, but he did not strike us as the badman the sheriff described him to be. You should have seen how gentle he was with that boy. Had I not known otherwise, I could more easily have taken him for a preacher than an

outlaw." Mrs. Archer looked to her husband for confirmation, and he nodded in solemn agreement.

Archer said, "He swore to us that he never killed anybody. He acted like a man who truly wants to change his
ways. We know you consider it your duty to capture him,
but couldn't you somehow just lose his trail and let him
get out of the country? He wouldn't be the first outlaw who
ever got away."

Mrs. Archer said, "We have heard that under extreme
circumstances the Rangers have been known to act as
judge and jury. Couldn't you be a judge in this case? A le-
nient one?"

The suggestion left Andy off-balance. "That would be
against the oath I took as a Ranger. Anyway, somebody
killed one of the best friends I ever had. Maybe it was
Cordell, and maybe it wasn't. Either way, I've got to find
out for myself. That means stayin' on his trail."

Archer said, "Then I'm afraid we can't wish you luck."

Mrs. Archer added, "If you do find him, please try to
take him without bloodshed. I believe he's a better man
than you give him credit for. Perhaps better even than he
knows."

The couple walked away arm in arm, leaving Andy
shaking his head. How could a man with a record like
Cordell's so easily turn strangers into friends?

CHAPTER

9

The horse was wearying. Even at a walk, it labored to keep moving. Cordell had put many miles behind him in the days since Buster had died. They had been melancholy miles, for his burden of guilt had lost little of its weight. Again and again, memory punished him by bringing him the face of the dying kid.

Cordell was aware that carrying Buster to a doctor had exposed his whereabouts, giving the law a fresh start in its search for him. He had traveled hard to put several county lines between him and that town, pushing his mount to the edge of its endurance. Now he had to find a place to lay up, or he had to make a trade. Under the circumstances he disliked having to steal a fresh horse. It was not that he had moral objections, but he knew it would put the locals on his trail as well as possibly alerting the Rangers. Not even bank robbery stirred people's dander as violently as horse theft.

He had carefully avoided towns, so he did not know exactly where he was. He knew only that he had reached the central part of Texas. The landscape of chalky hills suggested that he was probably somewhere north of Austin. A cousin named Jedediah Fergus lived near Lampasas. Jedediah had his faults, but surely he would be willing to hide his kin a week or two while Cordell and his mount rested.

Lampasas had a rough reputation. The Rangers had been called in more than once to put down a savage feud between families and to break up gangs that made life precarious for people caught in the middle. It had been Cordell's kind of place. A man who knew his way around could profit from that sort of situation without actually being drawn up in the funnel of the cyclone. During the feud, he and Jedediah had sold horses to one side, then taken them back under cover of darkness and resold them to the other. The cousin had then branched out on his own, succumbing to an ambition that outmatched his abilities. Caught, he had served a couple of years of involuntary employment with the state down at Huntsville.

Cordell, on the other hand, had sensed that the risk had begun to outweigh the potential profit and had sought his fortune elsewhere. Though willing to take a gamble, he always made it a point to hold back some chips.

Jedediah had married a farm, the only way he would ever have acquired one. He had survived an attempted assassination only because his father-in-law was a poor shot. He had the good fortune to see the enraged old man die of a massive heart seizure immediately afterward. Sometimes, Cordell thought, it was more profitable to be lucky than to be smart.

Following a deeply rutted wagon trail, he came to a fork and was stymied. He did not know which direction to take. A farmhouse stood on a hill a quarter mile away, but he was wary about going up and asking directions. Some people in this part of the country surely remembered him and possibly knew the law was looking for him. He was about to make an arbitrary decision and hope for the best. Then he saw a young black man approaching, riding a mule. He was probably too young to remember Cordell's horse-swapping days here. Because of his color he would be out of the mainstream of local society and likely knew nothing about the current manhunt.

Cordell greeted him with a nod. "Boy, does one of these roads go to Lampasas?"

"Why, yes, sir, they both does. One sashays a little to the north and the other sashays a little to the south. But they both gets to the same place."

"Which one is the shortest?"

"I reckon they're pretty much the same."

"Which one is the best?"

The young man pondered a moment. "Neither one. Whichever you take, you'll wish you'd taken the other."

Cordell flipped the youngster a fifty-cent piece. "You've been a lot of help."

The youngster smiled as broadly as if it had been ten dollars.

Cordell remembered that his cousin's farm lay among hills more or less north of Lampasas, so he took the right-hand fork. As he had done for days, he pulled off the trail and sought cover when he saw someone coming. In due time he spotted the town ahead, on low ground along Sulphur Creek. It appeared to have grown some since he had been here last. He quit the trail and cut across country, for now he recognized landmarks. He counted more houses than he had seen before, and new fields in places where the land was flat enough to plow. Cattle grazed on the hills.

Rain had brought up more grass than he remembered, but that was likely to be temporary. From here west, dry spells outnumbered the wet ones. Prosperity was elusive.

He hoped it had touched his cousin, for Jedediah was prone to hard luck and bad times, mostly self-imposed through lack of good judgment and avoidance of sweat. He was one of those people who seemed addicted to wrong choices. One of his few good choices had been when he managed to marry a plain-looking woman whose father owned property, and whose sudden death left it in her possession.

Cordell's impression was that Irmadell never let Jedediah forget it. Whatever material benefit the marriage had brought him, he had earned it by having to live with that barren, demanding shrew.

Smoke rising from a metal chimney told him she was in the kitchen and reminded him how long it had been since he had eaten anything substantial. The thought of food tempted him to rush, but better judgment prevailed. Caution made him approach slowly from the farm's back side, keeping the large red barn between himself and the modest frame house.

He heard cursing and stepped quickly down from the horse, his hand on his pistol. He held still, listening, until he was confident the cursing was not aimed at him. The voice was Jedediah's. The comments were directed toward a brindle cow he was milking beneath a low shed. "Hold still, you damned old slut! I'll take a whip to you."

Cordell said, "Do, and you'll get clabbered milk."

Jedediah jerked around in surprise, tipping the bucket

and spilling milk on one leg of his overalls. A little brown tobacco juice trickled down his long, bewhiskered jaw. "Luther! What the hell you doin' here?"

"Just come to visit my kin."

Jedediah was large, like Cordell, except that he ran more to fat than to muscle. It took him a bit to steady down. He seemed to have lost his breath. At last he said, "Good thing you didn't come yesterday. We had John Laws goin' over this place like a swarm of bees, lookin' for you."

Cordell felt a letdown. He had hoped he was far enough west to put the excitement behind him. "Then the news has gotten here."

"And gone a lot further, I'd wager. They're sayin' you murdered a sheriff."

"They're mistaken. It wasn't me that done it."

"They say it was, and that's what counts. They got a reward out for you. Three thousand dollars, dead or alive."

"Three thousand." Cordell was surprised. "That's more than I've ever been worth." Before the bank robbery in Galveston, at least.

Jedediah went back to his milking. "There was somebody else here lookin' for you. Said you and him was partners."

"Did he give you a name?"

"Milt. I don't remember the last name."

"Hayward. Milt Hayward." Cordell cursed under his breath. He knew he should not be surprised. "We done a couple of jobs together, but he wasn't no partner of mine."

"He said you mentioned me one time as bein' kin.

Seemed anxious to find you, more anxious even than the law."

Cordell didn't need this when he already had more than enough to worry about. Milt would be looking for his share of the Galveston money. He would probably be happy to take it all if he could. Even by Cordell's liberal standards, he was a scoundrel, a criminal of the lowest degree.

Jedediah stopped milking and turned the cow's calf in with her to finish what was left in her udder. He said, "There's folks around here who don't remember you too kindly. They'd jump like a bullfrog at a chance to collect. If I was you, I'd keep ridin'." Jedediah looked hopeful.

"Been ridin' too long already. My horse is about wore out, and I ain't far behind him. I need a place where we can rest for a few days."

Jedediah declared with alarm, "Not here."

"We're kin. I figure you owe me. You made good money when we worked together."

"But then you rode off and left, and pretty soon the laws had me by the short hair. When I got out of the pen, Irmadell like to've not let me come home. She was mad at me, but she was a hell of a lot madder at you."

"Do you always let that little bitty woman tell you what to do?"

"I have to. Everything around here has got her name on it."

Jedediah never did have the backbone of a lizard, Cordell thought. He had been handy in their business transactions because he was a natural follower. He did what Cordell told him to. When he tried to do something on his own, it usually collapsed in a puff of dust.

Cordell said, "Since the law has already given this farm a goin' over, maybe they won't be back."

"Irmadell still don't like you, Luther."

"Maybe the sight of a little money would make her like me better."

Jedediah's interest perked up. "You still got what you raised in that bank robbery?"

"Ain't had a chance to spend much of it."

Jedediah began looking hungry. "I'll bet you got it right there in them saddlebags."

Cordell frowned in suspicion. They were cousins, but only by an accident of birth, not by choice. When money was involved, blood ties could easily develop a slipknot. "Never you mind where I've got it. Just tell Irmadell I'll make it worth you-all's while to put me up."

Jedediah became as friendly as a pot-licking dog. "You got me all wrong, Luther. I was just thinkin' of the danger to you. Of course we'll take you in. What're kinfolks for, anyway? The thought of you givin' us money never entered my mind."

"Of course not." Cordell led his horse into a corral next to the barn and unsaddled him. He carried the saddle into the barn and dropped it on the floor. He detached the saddlebags and hung them over his left arm. Finding a barrel of oats, he scooped up a good serving in a bucket and dumped it into a trough. Cordell listened to the horse's teeth eagerly grinding the grain and thought again of his own stomach.

"How long till Irmadell serves supper?"

Worry returned to Jedediah's face. "Maybe you better let me go in the house and talk to her first. She'll need a little softenin' up."

"Tell her about the money. That ought to smooth out her ruffles."

As Cordell remembered, Irmadell had always expressed moral opposition to his and her husband's horse dealings, though she had never shown any reservations about the money they brought in. She had grabbed Jedediah's share and held it like a miser. He would not have had whiskey money if he had not held out some.

Cordell waited outside the door, listening. He heard Irmadell's strident voice raised in indignation. He could not hear what Jedediah was saying, but Irmadell slowly calmed down. Cordell assumed the talk about money was what did it. He entered the kitchen and said, "Howdy, Irmadell. You look like you've lost some weight."

Women had usually responded with a smile when he made a comment like that, but Irmadell had no excess weight to lose. In contrast to her husband, she was short and scrawny. Dynamite sticks were small too, yet they could yield fire and brimstone. Her mouth tried to smile while her eyes stayed cold. "No more than this old place produces with Jedediah farmin' it, a body is bound to lose weight. But you can share what little we got."

He sensed that she was already counting the money.

She said, "If you was to see fit to share a few dollars, I could go fetch some extra groceries from town."

Cordell did not have to study long on that proposal. If

Irmadell showed up in town with money, the law would immediately be on the alert. It would not take much persuasion to wring the truth out of her. "We'll get by on what's here," he said. "I'll pay you for it when I leave." Maybe anticipation would keep her pacified, even if a long way short of happy.

She made a poor effort to keep her resentment from showing. "Then it'll be beans and corn bread, and little else."

"That's more than I been gettin'."

She walked to the door and looked out. "I reckon Jedediah told you, the law's been out nosin' around. They could go hard on us if they catch you here."

"They ain't goin' to catch me. And if they was to, I'd tell them I forced you to take me in."

"Then you can sleep in the barn, and burrow under the hay if they come lookin' again."

Jedediah offered, "We can hide them saddlebags under the house." He looked too eager for Cordell's taste.

Cordell said, "I'm much obliged, but I sleep better when I use them for a pillow."

Andy was stumped. He wished he still had Len at his side, not that it would make much difference in picking up Cordell's trail. It had gone as cold as January. Andy could not be sure whether the fugitive had gone north, south, east, or west. He could have gone straight up for all the trace he had left. But because his direction from the first had generally been westward, Andy took that as the highest probability. He would go that way, checking with the sheriff in each county seat he came to. Since most such towns had finally been connected by telegraph wire, perhaps some word would turn up.

Anyway, Austin would want him to keep moving. The state office did not cheerfully pay a Ranger's expenses while he sat around waiting for something to happen. He feared his superiors might decide to pull him in and let Cordell go, leaving Tom's death unpunished. They probably would anyway were they not under pressure from the Galveston bank to get its money back.

He had already sent one wire notifying Austin about David Jackson's death and asking if there might be some record of him or his family. Maybe his relatives could shed light on Cordell's possible whereabouts.

The answer had been no help. It simply said, "Too many Jacksons, need more particulars."

Now he sent another wire saying that he had accompanied sheriff's posses while they searched the county. Writing was labor for Andy. His schooling had come in fits and spurts, usually undertaken with reluctance. "No sine of fugative," he wrote, struggling over the words. The telegrapher corrected his spelling and sent the message.

The sheriff was apologetic. He swiveled around in his big wooden chair and stretched out a bad leg in an effort to find some comfort. "We done our best, but Cordell is too slippery a fish."

Andy said, "We'll land him yet. He's got a lot to answer for."

"We'd've gotten him if Doc and the Archers hadn't

waited till way up in the mornin' to tell us about him. But they're good people. I guess they had their reasons."

"Too bad they never knew Tom Blessing. They'd've felt different."

"They all took a likin' to Cordell. They were impressed with how concerned he was about that boy." The sheriff handed Andy a letter. "Stage driver brought me a message while ago. Sheriff over in San Saba County says he's got a prisoner you might want to talk to."

Andy's spine tingled. "Cordell's partner, maybe?"

"Feller claims he's ridden with Cordell in the past. Knows his habits. He may just be tryin' to buy a softer punishment, or he might be of real help to you."

Andy's spirits picked up. This might be the third man in the jailbreak. "I'm leavin' right now. If Austin sends an answer to my wire, can you forward it to me?"

"Sure. I like to play with that new telegraph." The lawman got up and reached for his cane. "Anytime you get tired of takin' orders from them state-office clerks, I could use a good deputy. I've got the goods on the county commissioners, so the pay ain't bad."

Andy had seen over the years that many Rangers grew weary of the travel and hardships and took a less demanding job in local law enforcement. It would be something for him to think about when that time came. It might ease his saddle sores, though at this point he had rather put up with saddle sores than try to convince Bethel. He feared she was still too deeply rooted to that farm.

But sooner or later she would have to leave it or else

shoot her brother Farley in exasperation. Unless somebody else did it first. Andy had rather be tied to two wild horses running in opposite directions than to try to live again with Farley, especially as his brother-in-law.

The trip carried him into the second day. The clock in the courthouse cupola struck ten times as he rode up and tied his horse to a rail in the town square. He saw what passed for a restaurant and was tempted to stop there first. He decided to postpone eating until he finished what he came for. He walked up the steps to the limestone courthouse and stopped inside to look for the sheriff's office.

The lawman recognized him as a Ranger right away. Andy wondered how some people did that. Something in the way Rangers carried themselves, he supposed. The sheriff was tall and lanky, a generation older than Andy. He said, "Old man Ames wired me that you were on your way. You want to see the prisoner now?"

Andy said, "Sure enough. I've lost a lot of time already, tryin' to follow a cold trail."

"I can't promise this'll heat it up much, but you might want to see what he can tell you about the man you're lookin' for."

The sheriff led him outside to the jail, built of the same stone as the courthouse but without the style. It was square and plain, as befitted a prison. The cells were shut off from the front office by a heavy, barred door that the sheriff unlocked with a large key. He motioned toward a cell holding a balding, forlorn-looking man well into middle age. "This here is him, Maxwell Hawkins, alias John Smith, John Jones, and other such names. He got caught breakin' into a store the other night and gatherin' up a sackful of grub. He's got a record that'd reach from here to the San Saba River, but he doesn't look very ferocious now."

The man had the subdued look of a whipped dog. Andy had to strain to hear, for the prisoner spoke barely above a whisper. "I was hungry. I've come on hard times."

Andy flipped through the pages of the Ranger fugitive book Len had left with him. "Sure enough, he's in here. Served time once for attempted bank robbery. Another time for attempted horse theft. Looks like he's good at attemptin'."

"Hard luck has followed me all of my life," the prisoner said almost apologetically.

Andy asked, "When was the last time you saw Luther Cordell?"

The prisoner considered. "Been a year, maybe a little more. I rode with him off and on till he took up with Milt Hayward. Coldest man I ever saw, Milt was. Didn't have a speck of moral character."

Milt! Tom's young deputy had said he heard a word that sounded to him like *milk.* Andy felt a stirring of excitement. He asked, "Do you have any idea where this Hayward might have gone to?"

"No notion atall. He never was one to talk much. I don't know where he come from. He might've crawled out of a rattlesnake den."

"What about Cordell?"

"He was raised in Louisiana or Mississippi or one of them other Confederate states. I got the idea some bad things had happened to him. They made him what he is now."

"A sheriff killer?"

"I never knowed of him killin' anybody. Not while I was with him, for sure. That was more Milt's style. When Luther hooked up with him, I decided to leave. Sooner or later Milt was bound to do somethin' awful and get us all caught. He's got a criminal mind."

Andy said, "We believe he was part of the jailbreak and split off from Cordell when the posse got too close. Do you know anything about the kid who was with Cordell at the time?"

"You mean Buster?"

"His real name was David Jackson."

The prisoner shook his head. "I didn't know that. Buster was all I ever heard. He showed up in camp one day, beggin' for somethin' to eat. Talked like he got tired of the farm and ran off from home. I never heard him say exactly where he came from. I did hear him say somethin' once about the Clear Fork."

Andy recounted the circumstances of the boy's wounding, and his death. Morosely the prisoner said, "That could've been me if I'd stayed with Luther. I'm sorry about the kid, but I'm glad it wasn't me."

"Too bad Cordell didn't give him a meal and send him on his way."

"You know how it is. Feed a hungry pup, and you can't get rid of him. Luther always had a weak spot for folks down on their luck. He had been there himself a lot of his life."

Andy mused, "He doesn't sound like most outlaws I ever knew. There ain't one in ten ever cares about anybody except themselves."

"Luther did. That's why I can't believe he shot that sheriff. My guess is that Milt done it. He wasn't goin' to get his share of the bank money if he didn't bust Cordell out of jail. He wasn't goin' to let no small-town law stand in his way."

Outside, the sheriff said, "Maybe you've been chasin' the wrong man. You might ought to be lookin' for Hayward."

"I don't know what he looks like, and I've got no idea where he went to. But it appears he ran off without his share of the bank loot. If I can find where Cordell is, maybe Hayward will show up. Then I can get them both."

The sheriff said, "You'd better find Cordell before Hayward does. For ten thousand dollars, I suspect Hayward would shoot him without blinkin' an eye."

The lawman accompanied Andy to the restaurant and watched him put away a hearty meal of beef stew, beans, and biscuits. The sheriff said, "The boy spoke about the Clear Fork country. You reckon Cordell might be headed that way?"

Andy said, "It's hard to guess what he might do."

"I followed a trail herd through that country once. I hear it's settled up a right smart since."

Andy had known the area a few years ago. The Clear Fork was a tributary of the Brazos River, originating in rough breaks that marked the eastern edge of the staked plains. East of the escarpment and the breaks lay a rolling country that had once teemed with buffalo and now furnished grazing for thousands of cattle. In flatter areas its deep soil offered an opportunity for farming, though it was often beset by extended periods of too little rain.

Andy said, "I'll ease up that way and take a look. I'll have to be careful not to flush the quail too quick, though. If he hears that a Ranger is askin' questions, he'll take to the tules."

"Don't tell anybody you're a Ranger. Just act like an ignorant cowboy lookin' for a job. You can look ignorant, can't you?"

"I often do. Right now, for instance."

CHAPTER

10

Cordell had never considered Irmadell much of a cook, but he was so hungry that raw prairie dog would have tasted like beefsteak. He attacked a plate of red beans, shoveling them onto his spoon with a large piece of corn bread. Jedediah and Irmadell picked at their supper and watched him with poorly concealed resentment.

"This is mighty good fixin's," he said. "A man in my business has to put up with a lot of lean days."

Irmadell said, "It's the Lord's punishment for bein' in that kind of business. You'd be way ahead today if you'd got yourself married and took up real work instead of robbin' honest people of the fruits of their labor."

"I ain't never robbed honest people, just banks and such."

"What about the horse stealin' you lured Jedediah into? It got him sent away for a couple of years."

"Them wasn't honest people. They was tryin' to kill one another. Anyway, I did get married once." He stopped there, for he didn't want to talk about it.

"I've heard. You picked the wrong woman, is all." Irmadell went silent, staring darkly at her plate.

Jedediah thought he heard something and jumped up, striding anxiously to the window. He slumped in relief.

"Wasn't nothin' but that fool tomcat. He knocked the milk bucket off of the rack."

Cordell said, "Sit down, Jedediah. You're too nervous."

"And I'll stay nervous as long as you're here. I'm sure you've got better places to go."

"I'll leave when I feel like my horse has rested enough. I don't guess you've got one you could trade me? I'd be on my way a lot sooner."

"Ain't got but one, and he's a plow horse. You'd just as well walk."

Cordell felt Irmadell's narrowed eyes burning him. She said, "Looks like your cup's empty. Want some more coffee?"

"I'd be much obliged."

She got up from the table and fetched the coffeepot from the top of the cast-iron stove. She brought it around behind him and poured coffee into his cup, then splashed it on his arm. It was scalding hot. In reflex he rose halfway to his feet, shouting in surprise and gripping the burned arm. She took advantage of the distraction and yanked his pistol from its holster. He whirled around, but not in time to catch her. She stepped back, the pistol in both hands and aimed at his nose. She had dropped the pot. Its remaining coffee spread dark across the floor.

She declared, "Now, by God, you'll raise your hands. Jedediah, come around here and take this gun."

Jedediah seemed as shocked as Cordell. He was slow in rising from the table. She spoke more sharply, "I said get yourself up here, damn you, and act like a man for a change."

Relieved of the pistol, she stood with her hands on her

narrow hips, her eyes crackling. "So you thought you'd just waltz in here and take over, did you? My old daddy didn't put up with that kind of treatment, and neither does his daughter. Put your hands flat on the table and keep them there. Else I'll tell Jedediah to shoot you. That reward is paid dead or alive."

Cordell was too taken aback to answer. He saw two possibilities. They could turn him in for the three thousand dollars, or they could kill him and bury him in secret, hoping to keep the nearly ten thousand he carried from that Galveston transaction.

Irmadell had already made her choice. "You keep him sittin' there, Jedediah. I'll saddle a horse and ride for the sheriff. That three thousand would really fix up this old place."

Jedediah said, "They claim he took ten thousand from that bank. If we was to kill him, we could keep all of it."

She shook her head. "The law would come down on us as soon as we started to spend it. This way we get it legal. Three thousand in the hand is better than ten thousand that we can't use."

Jedediah said, "Have it your way. Take our horse. Luther's is wore out."

She hurried through the door. Shortly Cordell heard the plodding hooves of a plow horse, galloping away in the direction of Lampasas.

Cordell felt like a fool, letting that witch of a woman get the better of him. He rubbed his burned arm and studied his cousin, looking for weakness. He said, "That woman of yours could make Jesus Christ use God's name in vain."

"But as long as she's got property, I've got property."

"You pay a hell of a price for it. You ought not to let a scrawny little woman like that run over you the way she does. I'll bet she don't weigh a hundred pounds."

"But it's a hundred pounds of pure hell."

Cordell looked his cousin squarely in the eyes. "She'll get you killed someday."

"Not me. I figure on outlivin' her. Then everything'll be mine."

"By that time, you'll be trippin' over a long gray beard."

"No, I won't. When she's gone, I'll sell this damned old farm and go to San Antone or someplace. Maybe even Chicago. I'll live high, wide, and handsome."

"High and wide, maybe, but you'll never be handsome." Cordell coughed. "My throat's dry, and my coffee's gettin' cold."

"Let it. Keep your hands on the table, like she said."

Cordell frowned. "She's gone now. Without her bein' here to tell you to, I don't believe you'd really shoot me."

"For three thousand dollars, I'd shoot Irmadell."

"More than likely, she'd shoot you first. Money or not, she ought to anyway, just on general principles. You ain't worth a bucket of cold spit."

"But I'll soon be worth three thousand more than I am, and you'll be sittin' behind bars. I never did like you, Luther. You always acted like you was better than the rest of us."

"Hell, I *was* better than the rest of you."

Cordell struck the coffee cup and sent it flying across the table. Instinctively Jedediah ducked. Cordell wrested the pistol from his hands before his cousin could regain his wits. He said, "Jedediah, you're too easy. A man can't take any pride in outsmartin' you." He pointed the pistol in his cousin's face.

Jedediah pushed trembling hands forward in supplication, eyes brimming with tears. "For God's sake, don't shoot me."

"I ought to, but it'd be too big a favor to Irmadell. I want her to be stuck with you till you're both shriveled and old." Cordell motioned for Jedediah to stand, then motioned again toward the door. "We're goin' out to the barn together. You got any more guns in the house?"

Jedediah stammered. "Just that shotgun over the fireplace."

Cordell retrieved it. "I wouldn't want you to shoot me as I ride off." He dropped a little money on the table. "This is for the groceries you're fixin' to sack up for me. Some coffee, some beans, all of that corn bread."

"Anything you want. Just don't keep pointin' that six-shooter at me."

Jedediah gathered up most of the food that was in the kitchen. Then Cordell marched his cousin outside. "Too bad you ain't got a decent horse. Saddle mine for me."

Jedediah complied, still trembling. Cordell checked to be certain the girth was tight enough. It would be like Jedediah to leave it loose, hoping for the saddle to slip. Mounting, Cordell said, "I'll take the shotgun with me. Tell the sheriff I'm sorry not to make his acquaintance. And if Milt Hayward comes back, tell him he ought to've gone to Mexico and stayed there. It's on account of him that they got a murder charge out on me."

Jedediah stood with shoulders drooped, his mouth sagging open. Cordell took pleasure in picturing the blistering he would get from Irmadell when she returned and found herself three thousand dollars short of expectations.

Cordell said, "I can't hardly believe we had the same granddaddy. Maybe old Granny wasn't quite the lady she made out to be."

Riding away, he was aware that the horse was still tired. "Sorry, old friend," he said. "Them people didn't give me any choice. Be glad *you've* got no relations."

Without wanting to, he began to dwell on what Irmadell had said about his not being married. The memories always brought him pain. He had married a neighbor girl named Martha back in Louisiana just prior to the war of Northern aggression. She had given him a son before he marched away with a local company of Confederate volunteers. He had never lost the memory of the boy's face, the eyes blue, sparkling with laughter.

Wounded in the last year of the conflict, he had been left behind by his retreating brothers-in-arms. He suffered through the rest of the war in a miserable prisoner of war camp, staying alive only by the force of his will. He had finally limped home, only to find he no longer had a home. Yankee troops had burned the house, and carpetbaggers had confiscated the land. His wife's family had been nervously evasive about her whereabouts. A sympathetic neighbor broke the news as gently as he could. Martha had taken up with another man. They had left with the intention of going to California, far from the war. Naturally, she had taken their son.

Cordell had followed in the vain hope of finding them, but California was far larger than he had realized. He never found any sign. For all he knew, they might not have made it that far. They might have changed their plans, or Indians might have gotten them somewhere along the way. They came close once to getting Cordell.

He had drifted back as far as Texas, bitter and disillusioned, looking for a new life. Times were hard after the war, and an honest man had a tough time making a living. So he had given up being an honest man. There was money to be made for those who were bold, and Cordell had thought he had nothing to lose.

Now he was in his fifties, weary, hungry, hounded by the law. He had close to ten thousand dollars in his saddlebags, but at this point he would trade it all for a safe place to stay.

Irmadell had been right about the wasting of his life. He *had* had something to lose, and he had lost it.

Perhaps when the heat died down, he could take a new name and start a fresh life somewhere far away, like California, where nobody knew of him. In San Francisco he had seen ships in port. He might even book passage on one and sail to the west. He had heard talk about an island named Hawaii, where a man could lie around all day on a warm and sandy beach, just waiting for coconuts to fall from a tree.

That sounded like his kind of life. It wouldn't matter whether they had banks there or not.

But first he owed Buster's family the boy's share of the ten thousand. As to telling them about Buster's death, he had plenty of time to build up a plausible story. Many miles of travel lay ahead of him before he reached the Clear Fork.

Darkness came as a friend. He let the horse slow its pace

to a walk. Even at that rate, he could make a lot of miles before daylight gave the law a chance to pick up his trail.

The Lampasas sheriff had predisposed Andy to dislike Jedediah and Irmadell Fergus on sight, and they met his expectations. Having no family himself, he put great stock in blood kinship and could not fathom how a man could betray one of his own and live with his conscience.

Stopping to consult local law enforcement officers in each county through which he rode, he had learned of Cordell's visit to the Fergus farm. The sheriff guided Andy there, giving him a lengthy and uncomplimentary history of the pair.

He said, "You remember what the Bible said about a tongue that biteth like an adder? That's Irmadell. And if ever anybody deserved her, Jedediah is that man."

Irmadell dominated the conversation. Though she weighed hardly a hundred pounds, it was easy to see that her two-hundred-pound husband was cowed by her. He stood half a pace behind her and a little to the side. If he had been a dog, he would have had his tail between his legs. Across his cheekbone he bore a severe bruise of recent origin. His eye was swollen. Andy first thought Cordell was responsible, though he soon became convinced that Irmadell was the culprit. The longer he listened to her tirade against her husband's cousin, the more she seemed capable of inflicting injuries far out of proportion to her diminutive size.

She said, "We didn't invite Luther to come here. He took advantage of our hospitality, then rode off without a word of thanks. Didn't leave us nothin' for what we was out on groceries."

Jedediah looked at the floor as if he had something to hide. She declared, "Not a widow's mite did he leave us. On top of everything, he carried off our only shotgun. Now we've got no way to guard our chickens against the varmints. I lost two hens last night."

Andy tried to look sympathetic, but it was not in him. He said, "The way I heard it, you were on your way to town to fetch the sheriff."

"Yes, I was. Luther's got a lot to answer for when he stands at them pearly gates. The sooner he gets there, the better it'll suit me."

The Lampasas sheriff had said Jedediah's past did not stand close scrutiny either.

Andy asked, "Did he give you any idea where he was goin' from here?"

She turned to her husband. Her eyes had the sting of a wasp. "Jedediah was the last one to talk to him. He played the fool and let Luther get away."

Jedediah did not look Andy in the eyes. "I was scared he was fixin' to shoot me, so I didn't ask him no foolish questions. He just cussed me out and rode off west." He pointed in that general direction.

Irmadell said, "I had him captured dead to rights, right here in my kitchen. And it was me that put the sheriff on his trail. Looks like when you catch him, I ought to be due part of the reward."

Andy figured she didn't stand a snowball's chance in hell. "You'll have to argue with the law about that."

"You bet I'll argue with them. It ain't my fault this fool sheriff couldn't follow the trail past the top of the hill." She

shifted her accusing gaze to the local lawman. His face red-
dened, but he did not waste breath trying to argue with her.

Andy had already learned that Cordell and Jedediah had
spent time together as boys and had reconnected some years
after the war. Irmadell assured him that they had nothing in
common except blood kinship. "And that ain't no way our
fault," she said. "A man can't choose his relations."

If they could, Andy thought, Cordell and Jedediah
might both have chosen different limbs on the family tree.

Leaving the house, the sheriff said, "I'm afraid you
didn't gain much by comin' out here. If they knew anything, they didn't spill it."

Andy shook his head. "Cordell would've been too
shrewd to tell them what he figured to do. He had to know
they'd go runnin' to you for the reward."

"At least you've got a fresh start. You know he was right
here a day or so ago."

Andy had been even closer when Buster died, but he saw
no reason to dwell on the negative. "He left on a tired horse,
so he can't push too hard. Thanks to you and that stableman in
town, I've got a fresh horse. And grub aplenty on my mule."

"Nothin's too good for the Rangers. I wish I could go
with you, but there's enough wild men around here to keep
me busy. Have you got any notion as to where he might be
goin'?"

"It's a thin one, but it's all I've got." Andy explained
about the kid who had ridden with Cordell, and the possibility that the outlaw might be headed toward the Clear
Fork in search of the kid's family.

Even if Andy had been an expert tracker, he would have had difficulty in following Cordell's trail. The sheriff's posse had ridden all over the place, trying to pick it up. They had ruined whatever sign Cordell might have left.

"Sorry about that," the sheriff said, "but I had to deputize anybody I could find that had a horse."

"I'm not much of a tracker anyway."

"The Clear Fork country is big, especially if you don't know just where to look."

Andy said, "I only know that the family's name is Jackson."

"The world is full of Jacksons. Even if you find the family, you can't be sure Cordell is headed that way. If I was him and had all that money, I'd light out for parts unknown."

"Cordell's a robber and a thief, but accordin' to an old partner named Hawkins, he's got his own notions about honor."

"Yeah, he probably says 'Pardon me' before he steals your money. But he takes it just the same."

The sheriff rode with him a couple of miles until they cut into a well-worn wagon road that led northwestward. He said, "You'd best watch yourself. You're in the land of the forty thieves. There's boys around here can steal your socks without takin' your boots off."

Andy nodded. "I've met some of those boys. I've still got my socks."

He suspected that Cordell might have taken the same road.

He had observed that the outlaw liked to follow well-traveled roads from time to time, which allowed his tracks to be lost among the many others. Yet nobody ever seemed to see him. He evidently saw them first.

Andy had become used to riding long distances alone, but nevertheless he wished for Len Tanner's company. Len could make a man's ears ring with all his talking. Still, his stories were entertaining if sometimes suspect. His long experience as a Ranger made him a good man to have along. He knew how to cover a partner's back.

Another reason for liking him was that Farley Brackett didn't.

The sheriff was about to ride back toward town but stopped abruptly. "Looks like somebody's comin'. I'll wait and find out if he's seen anything."

Approaching from the west, the rider proved to be an agitated man of considerable bulk. His ruddy face was flushed with stress and indignation. "Sheriff," he shouted before he was within good talking distance, "I was on my way to town to fetch you. Somebody's stole that good black stud of mine."

Andy immediately thought of Cordell. "Did you get a look at the thief?"

The rider gave Andy a suspicious frown, as if he thought he might be the sheriff's prisoner. "No, he made a swap out in my pasture. Left a horse that looked like he'd been ridden to a fare-thee-well."

"When did this happen?"

"Could've been anytime in the last day or two. I had the stud turned out with some mares." The man squinted, giving

Andy a close scrutiny. "Who are you to be askin' me questions? My business is with the sheriff."

Andy was put off by the man's belligerent attitude. The sheriff answered for him. "Andy Pickard is a Ranger. He's been trailin' a fugitive who might be your horse thief."

The red-faced man said accusingly, "The trouble with you people that work for the government is, you're always a day late. Damned pity you didn't catch your man before he stole my horse."

The sheriff said, "Just be glad you didn't run into the thief yourself, Thaddeus Hunnicutt. He's accused of killin' a sheriff."

"I wish I *had* run into him. I'd've shot him so full of holes that he couldn't hold his water."

Andy took that for idle bluster. Hunnicutt struck him as a man who talked a good game but folded quickly.

Hunnicutt declared, "I paid five hundred dollars for that stud. Best I ever owned. You'd better get him back, Sheriff, if you expect any financial support from me at the next election."

The sheriff looked as if Hunnicutt had stepped on his sore toe. "I didn't have any financial support from you in the last one. But I'll do what I can. Me and the Ranger." He looked at Andy. "Are you with me?"

Andy nodded and gave his attention to Hunnicutt. "Show us where the stud was stolen from."

Hunnicutt reined around and started back west. He grumbled, "A man pays his taxes and expects the law to protect him, but he's got to do most of it for himself." He rode on ahead, leaving Andy and the sheriff behind.

Andy said, "Except for you, everybody I've met around here so far has been about as agreeable as a badger with its foot caught. Is there somethin' wrong with the water?"

"This county has got the best folks you could ever hope to meet. It's also some that ought to've been drowned at birth like a sackful of kittens. It takes a few of those to make you appreciate the rest."

Except for the possibility that Cordell was the thief, Andy would be content to let Hunnicutt hunt his horse by himself.

They traveled several miles before coming to a barbed-wire fence that ran parallel to the wagon road. Such fences were going up in a lot of places, enclosing private property. Sometimes they illegally enclosed state land as well, leading to all manner of disputes and problems for local law enforcement. Andy saw the practical side of the fences, though he would be better suited had the wire never been invented. They went against all the free-roaming instincts fostered by his youthful years with the Comanches.

Hunnicutt said, "I spent a wagonload of money buildin' this fence so I could keep my breedin' program clean. I don't want no wild studs gettin' in amongst those good mares of mine."

Andy doubted that even barbed wire would stop a determined stallion if it saw mares on the other side.

They came to a barbed-wire gate. Hunnicutt waited as if he expected Andy or the sheriff to dismount and open it. Neither offered, so he got down and did it himself, mumbling under his breath. His temper was not improved by his having to strain to get the tight gate open, then closed again after the horses passed through. He said, "Soon as I saw a strange horse in this pasture, I had a hunch that somebody had made a trade. I wish he'd taken a mare. None of them cost me more than fifty dollars."

Andy could see horse tracks everywhere. It would be futile to try to pick out one set and follow them, even if he knew which belonged to the missing stud. "The thief wouldn't have stayed in this pasture long. Do you know where he went out?"

"He broke my fence about a mile up the way. Didn't have a proper cutter, so he twisted the wires till they busted in two. Some of my mares got out, is how I come to see I'd been robbed."

The three riders followed the fence line until they reached the place where the wires were broken. They had been patched in haste. Hunnicutt said, "If he'd only known it, there's another gate about a mile farther on. He didn't have to leave my fence in this shape."

Andy could see by the tracks that several horses had strayed out through the opening. He told the sheriff, "I hope you're a better tracker than I am."

"I couldn't track a freight wagon through a mudhole."

Hunnicutt's frustration reached a new level, his face redder than before. "You mean you're both drawin' wages from the taxpayers, and you can't do the job you're hired for?"

The sheriff said, "I know somebody who's a tracker, and he's already on your payroll. Choctaw John."

"That damned half-breed? He ain't on my payroll. I fired his insolent ass."

"Looks like you'd better hire him back if you want us to find that stud."

"I'd rather take a whippin' with a wet rope." Hunnicutt mulled the proposition awhile. "All right, but I ain't payin' that Indian more than a dollar a day. And if he gives me any of his sass, I'll fire him again."

The sheriff said, perhaps a bit too hopefully, "You won't need to go with us. Just John and me and the Ranger."

"It's my stud horse we're talkin' about. Damned right I'm goin' with you. I hope I can shoot whoever's got him."

The sheriff took his disappointment in stride. "Then you'd better plug your ears and bite your tongue where John is concerned. Lose him and you've like as not lost your horse."

Hunnicutt grumbled, "The indignities a man has to put up with just to get back what belongs to him . . ." He pointed southwestward. "He's livin' in that miserable shack he built over on the creek."

The sheriff said, "Lead off. We'll follow you."

Trailing behind the rancher, Andy asked the sheriff, "Is this John really an Indian?"

"Half of one. His old daddy was a Scotchman. He brought a Choctaw wife down from the Territory. Pleasant woman, she was, and plumb white in her ways, but folks around here didn't cotton to her much. They remembered the Comanches and couldn't see the difference. John had to whip most of the boys his age before they quit aggravatin' him about his Indian blood."

Andy could relate to that. Though he was not Indian by blood, he had lived with them as a boy captive and picked up many of their ways. As a youth returned to the white man's road, he had bruised his fists many times in defending his right to walk with shoulders straight as anyone else's.

From Hunnicutt's description, Andy had expected Choctaw John's cabin to be as dilapidated as Fowler Gaskin's. It was small, but it was sturdily built of sawmill lumber and bore a coat of white paint, a luxury many houses lacked in rural Texas. It had been set in the midst of several live-oak trees, which would help shelter it from the worst of sun and wind. Andy thought he would not mind having a house like that for himself, though Bethel would probably want its size doubled or tripled. Several varmint hides were stretched and hanging along the outside walls.

Hunnicutt said, "He was always off runnin' traplines and such when I needed him. Claimed he made more money from them than he made workin' for me. Looks to me like the man payin' the wages ought to be the one who says how much he'll give, and the workin' class ought to be grateful to get it."

Two hounds came running out from under the house to announce the visitors. A man appeared in the open door, gave them a moment's study, then stepped out onto a narrow front porch. His arms were folded, and a deep frown creased his face.

"Thaddeus Hunnicutt," he said in a deep, booming voice, "I run you off of my place ten days ago. You sure don't learn very good."

Hunnicutt sputtered something unintelligible.

The sheriff said, "Howdy, John. We need your help."

"Poor way to ask for it, the kind of company you're keepin'." John shifted his attention to Andy, his black eyes questioning.

The sheriff made the introductions. "This here is Andy

Pickard. He's a Ranger. We need your help to trail a horse thief."

"One of Thaddeus's horses? That sorry black stud of his, I hope."

Hunnicutt glowered, seeming to puff up like a prairie chicken on its stomping ground. "It wouldn't surprise me if we was to find that stud right here on this place."

John said, "Now, what use would I have for a stallion, even if it was a good one? I don't own no mares, and if I did, I'd think more of them than to turn that stumble-footed black in with them." He paused, staring hard at the rancher. "What's the pay?"

Hunnicutt said, "I'll give you seventy-five cents a day."

The sheriff put in, "You said a dollar."

Hunnicutt turned on him angrily but seemed to have second thoughts about antagonizing the lawman more than he already had. "All right, a dollar, but he furnishes his own horse."

John took his time before agreeing. "Mind you, I'm just trackin'. I ain't doin' no camp cookin'. And the first time Thaddeus raises his voice at me, my price goes to a dollar and a half."

The sheriff told Hunnicutt, "Maybe you'd better go home and leave it to us, or this trip is liable to cost you more than you'll want to pay."

Sullenly Hunnicutt said, "I'm goin' with you, but I'll try to keep my mouth shut."

The sheriff gave Andy a look that said he did not believe in miracles.

CHAPTER

11

Cordell considered himself a good judge of horses, but he had been dealt a joker on this black stallion. He had spotted it in a fenced pasture with several mares and had thought it one of the best-looking animals he had seen in a long time. He knew the risk he took in making an involuntary trade, but that was outweighed by the fact that the horse he had ridden so long was nearing the limits of its endurance. He did not want the poor animal to die beneath him.

He had had the devil's own time catching and saddling the stallion, and now he was having the devil's own time riding it. The animal had an iron jaw, an unbending neck, and a will that matched Cordell's own. It seemed well aware that it outweighed him five or six times over.

"You're a damned hoodoo," he declared. "I'd sooner ride a burro."

The black shook its head violently, as if it understood. It had stumbled more than once. It responded to the tickle of Cordell's spurs by trying to pitch him off. He had no credentials as a bronc rider, but he knew what would result if he let the animal get away from him. Afoot, he would be easy pickings for whatever lawmen were surely following him, and the money in his saddlebags would go where the stallion went. His big right hand took a death grip on the saddle horn.

I ought to've known better than to pick a stud, he thought. *They've just got their mind on one thing.*

He knew he had to make another horse trade whatever the risk. This stallion was going to get him caught.

They've probably already got a noose sized for my neck. They can't hang me any higher for stealing another horse than for stealing this one.

He and the stud feuded until they came after a time to a creek lined sporadically with pecan trees. He saw a horse standing in the shade. At the distance, he could tell little about age or conformation, but so long as it had four legs and none of them were lame, it had to be an improvement over the stallion. Riding closer, he saw that the animal was a bay, tethered on a long rope to allow it to graze. An old buggy stood idle not far away, its wheels sprung a little out of line.

He brought his hand down to his pistol, for someone was camped on the creek. The stallion began acting up, curious about the tied horse. Cordell hoped it was not another stud, for he might be caught in the middle of a vigorous horse fight. He felt some relief when he saw that the other animal was a mare. Even so, he could have trouble on his hands if she happened to be in heat.

She wasn't, for the black's interest waned. Cordell tied him some distance from the mare and moved cautiously along the creek bank. Halfway down, he saw a small canvas tent. At the water's edge, a man sat with a pole in his hand, intently studying the point where his fishing line met the river. It began bobbing up and down. He gave the pole a yank to set the hook, then swung it around, dropping a large catfish on the ground nearby. It flopped about, struggling for life.

Not until then did the fisherman notice Cordell. His eyes widened in surprise, but he offered no threat. If he had any kind of firearm, it must be in the tent or the buggy, for Cordell saw none.

He opened the conversation. "Looks like you've got the makin's of a good supper."

The fisherman looked to be seventy or more, with friendly eyes and a smiling countenance. He said, "It's big enough for both of us if you're of a mind to stay. I'd admire some company for a change."

Cordell could not remember the last time he had enjoyed a good bait of catfish. Back in Louisiana it had frequently graced the family table. And he, too, would admire some company. "Wish I could, but I've got places to go."

The fisherman shoved his hand forward. "Dobson's my name. *Son,* better known. They hung that nickname on me when I was a kid so they could tell me from my old daddy."

That must have been a long time ago, Cordell thought. He shook hands but did not offer his name. Gray whiskers and bent shoulders told him the fisherman was past being able to do heavy work. He suspected the old fellow was whiling away the twilight of his life, sustaining himself and getting by the best he could.

The old-timer said, "I had to wait a spell before he finally took the bait, but hours don't matter much to an old, wore-out farmer. It's the days that I've got to count. Sure you won't stay for supper? I'll have this fish cut up and fried in about two shakes of a lamb's tail."

Though he felt the pressure of pursuit, Cordell also felt the pressure of hunger. "I reckon I could stay for just a little while."

He dragged in some dead tree limbs to stoke up the fire while the old man gutted the fish. Soon it was sizzling in a cast-iron frying pan well greased with bacon drippings.

Cordell asked, "Doesn't it worry you, campin' out here by yourself? No tellin' who might come by."

"Nobody would want to hurt me. I'm an old man, just about useless to anybody but myself. I've got nothin' worth stealin'. Got nothin' but time."

"But what if your heart was to give out with nobody around?"

"I don't know a better way to go, or a better place to go from. I like it out here all by myself. Don't get me wrong, I love my grandkids, but damned if they can't make enough noise sometimes to wake up everybody in the cemetery. You ever have any kids?"

The question brought a stab of pain. "Just one. Lost him." Cordell saw no point in further explanation.

"Sorry. I had four kids. One boy died. Two daughters got married and went wanderin' off with their husbands, one to Arizona, one to California. Ain't seen them in years. My oldest son runs the farm now. Does a better job of it than I ever did. I ain't of much use to him anymore, so I do a lot of fishin' when the weather is favorable."

"Sounds like a good way to spend your declinin' years."

Cordell had given little thought to his own declining years. In his occupation, he had doubted he would have any.

Dobson said, "The fish is about done. I've got some cold biscuits I made in the skillet this mornin'. Help yourself to the coffee."

"Much obliged." Cordell could not remember when anything had tasted better, certainly nothing at Irmadell's table. He could have eaten the whole fish, but he did not want to deprive Dobson. It was his camp, and his catfish.

He found himself envying the farmer. He wished he could relax here on the creek bank, watching a line in the water instead of watching his back trail for evidence of pursuit. Such a worry-free life would fit him like a well-worn pair of boots, he thought. He knew he could not rob a harmless old man like this, one willing to share his supper with a stranger and wanting nothing in return but a little company. He said, "I was wonderin' what you might ask for that buggy mare. I'm pretty near afoot."

The fisherman had seen the black, tied up on top of the creek bank. "That's a right smart lookin' stud. You're a long ways from bein' afoot."

"He's got some habits that I can't abide."

"I'd swap my mare for him, but I wouldn't want to beat you. She's past her prime."

"I'd need to pay you cash. That stud ain't mine to swap. There's some question about his ownership."

The old farmer seemed to catch on. His pale eyes twinkled. "Got him kind of cheap, did you?"

"You could look at it that way. Would a hundred dollars be enough for your mare?"

"I'd be cheatin' you. I could buy me two good horses for that."

"It's worth it. I've already got enough people mad at me without you bein' another one." Cordell frowned. "There's liable to be somebody behind me, kind of anxious about that stud. If they was to ask you, you could tell them you've got no idea how he come to be here."

The farmer smiled. "I've never seen you in my life." His smile spread even wider when Cordell paid him.

Cordell said, "I hate to leave you afoot. That stud is too much horse for you to try to ride, and he'd probably tear up your buggy."

"I wasn't goin' nowhere. My son'll come to see about me when I don't show up in two or three days." The farmer watched Cordell put his saddle on the mare. "You don't look like the type to've killed somebody. Have you?"

"They claim I did, but they're wrong. I've made myself unpopular with a few moneylenders, but I ain't killed no-body."

"I've seen some outlaws in my time. Most of them didn't look any worse than the sheriffs that trailed after them. They just crossed the line somewhere."

"It's a thin line. Easy to cross over and hard to cross back."

Cordell rode the mare in a circle to be sure she was not lame.

The old man said, "She's seen better days, but ain't we all? She's still got lots of heart."

"Much obliged for the supper." Waving his hand, Cordell crossed the creek and headed westward. The stallion followed him and the mare for a hundred yards or so, then lost interest, lowered his head, and began to graze.

Cordell liked the mare from the first. She had a smoother trot than the stallion, setting a steady pace that could cover ground without pounding his rump raw. She had been worth the price, especially considering that he bought her with someone else's money. He halfway wished he had paid the old man more.

Thaddeus Hunnicutt had promised not to abuse Choctaw John, but that promise soon evaporated. John was slow and careful in picking the stallion's tracks from those of the mares that had followed him out through the opening the fugitive had left in the fence. And he lost the tracks a couple of times where the stallion had been ridden over rocky ground.

Hunnicutt said, "If you cause me to lose that black stud, I'll whip you all the way back up to Indian Territory where you belong."

John responded, "You'd better be ready to eat that whip, handle and all. Sheriff, I wish you'd send Thaddeus home before the Indian side of me decides to scalp what little hair he's still got under that hat."

Hunnicutt said, "You can't send me home. It's a free country, and I got a right to look for my horse."

The sheriff's voice was clipped. "You'll be lookin' for him all by yourself if you don't tighten the rein on that mouth of yours."

Andy had been listening without comment. His interest was not in the stallion but in the man who might be riding him. Local quarrels were none of his business. Hunnicutt and the sheriff dropped back twenty or thirty yards, giving John plenty of room. Andy was curious about the tracker and remained beside him, trying to study his method. John had picked up the tracks again.

"They're pretty old," he said. "I figure a couple of days. There ain't much left of them." He looked back at Hunnicutt. "I don't care if the old dickens never finds his stud horse, long as he pays me. And the longer we keep trackin', the longer he's got to pay me."

Now and again the tracks were plain enough that Andy could have followed them himself. Other times he wondered at John's ability to see that which was not there. For a while he suspected that John was stringing Hunnicutt along for the money. Then the tracks would show up again.

John's face showed little that seemed distinctly Indian beyond being a shade darker than average.

Andy said, "You don't look like most Indians I've known."

"I'm just half, from my mama."

"That's what I heard. Some people say I'm half-Indian, too. When I was a boy, the Comanches captured me. I lived with them for several years."

John was not impressed. "They're wild men. We ain't nothin' like them."

"You don't talk like an Indian either."

"Us Choctaws've been civilized since my great-granddaddy's time." He frowned. "I've heard Comanches talk. They're savages. I never could make any sense of what they was sayin'."

"I used to speak Comanche. I'm afraid I've forgotten some of it."

"Just as well. They ain't likely to rise again."

Andy was momentarily miffed at John's prejudice against those Andy considered his adopted people. On reflection he remembered that the Comanches regarded all others as inferior to themselves. He remembered hearing Comanche warriors boast about killing Choctaws. They regarded them as being almost white. Prejudice was not the sole property of one race.

He said, "I take it you've worked for Hunnicutt before."

"Several times. We get mad at one another, and he fires me or I quit. Then he needs me again."

"And you keep goin' back to him?"

"Money ain't overly plentiful around here."

"He's not payin' you much."

"But when I'm at his place I carry enough home out of his kitchen to make up the difference. I can still eat durin' the times I ain't got a job."

Andy considered. "If I had to be around him much, I'd sooner or later want to kill him."

"I get even in my own way, like sometimes I pee in his coffeepot. The old hayshaker never knows."

"Where's the revenge in it if he doesn't know?"

"The point is, *I* know."

Andy wished Len were here. He would appreciate John's off-center logic. Andy liked it himself.

They camped at an abandoned homesite where a dug well provided passable water. John gathered wood for a fire but did not offer to contribute to the cooking. Neither did Hunnicutt, so Andy and the sheriff took care of supper. The lawman opened a couple of airtights of tomatoes. Andy managed to burn Hunnicutt's bacon, frying it down to a shrunken and blackened sliver. He boiled a pot of coffee and kept an eye on John in case he might seek a little revenge on his employer.

The next morning John said the trail was becoming fresher. Andy had to take his word for it. John pointed to a small area where the ground was disturbed. "Looks to me like that black stud tried to pitch him off."

Hunnicutt took heart. "Maybe he got away."

John shook his head. "No, the rider managed to stay on him. Probably knew he'd be in bad trouble if he lost him. The tracks straighten out afterwards and head west like before, and a little to the north."

They came in the afternoon to a tree-lined creek, where an old buggy stood on the bank. John said, "I smell woodsmoke. Somebody's camped down yonder." He swore in surprise. "Well, I'll be damned. Yonder's that sorry black of yours." He pointed toward the stallion, which raised its head from the shin-high grass and nickered at the oncoming horses. "I guess you just owe me for two days, Thaddeus."

Hunnicutt demanded, "How do you figure two days? It's no more than a day and a half."

Andy drew his rifle. "It don't seem likely that Cordell would be layin' around in camp, but we'd better go slow. We don't know who's down there."

He remained in the saddle, keeping a tight grip on the weapon. A fishing pole was wedged between two stones.

He saw someone lying on the creek bank, evidently nap-
ping. Andy rode within touching distance before he spoke.
"Raise up easy. Don't make a move toward a gun."

An elderly man blinked the sleep from his eyes and
stared up at Andy, or more precisely at his rifle. He said in
a shaky voice, "Ain't no use pointin' that thing at me. I
ain't got a gun. And there ain't much here that's worth
stealin'."

The sheriff's tension eased. He said, "Don't worry,
Andy. This is old man Dobson. I've known him forever."

The fisherman managed a weak smile but did not look
away from Andy's rifle. "Son, better known. Howdy, Sheriff."

Hunnicutt swung his bulk down from the saddle and approached Dobson with red-faced belligerence. "What the
hell are you doin' with my stallion?"

Dobson got to his feet. The move appeared to stir up
arthritis, for he winced in pain. "I ain't doin' nothin' with
him. He just showed up here. I wish you'd take him home.
Every time he goes down to the creek for a drink, he paws
the water and scares away the fish."

Hunnicutt shook his finger in Dobson's face. "If you
was thinkin' about breedin' him to one of your mares . . ."

"I don't own but two mares, and I doubt they'd associate
with that stud horse of yours. They're too prideful for
that."

Andy pushed in front of Hunnicutt, stopping his attempt
at argument. "What're you doin' out here all by yourself,
Mr. Dobson? I see a buggy, but I don't see a buggy horse."

"Since my wife passed on to a better life, I like to get

away from my son's family once in a while and camp here on the creek, where it's quiet. Sometimes a man is his own best company. My son'll fetch me a buggy horse when I get ready to go home."

Andy thought the story plausible, as far as it went, but he suspected there was more to it. "That stud didn't just stray in here, it was ridden. We've been followin' its tracks."

John put in, "Not *we, me.* You'd just as well tell him, Son. This young man is a Ranger."

Andy could see that his three companions knew Dobson. Two had respect for him. Hunnicutt did not, but that was a point in Dobson's favor. "Tell us about the man who rode in here on the stud."

Dobson rubbed his gray-whiskered chin and looked from one visitor to the other. Reluctantly he said, "I don't want to get anybody in trouble."

Andy said, "He's already in trouble."

"Seemed like a nice feller. An outlaw, I suppose, but he was square with me. Bought my buggy mare and paid me double what she was worth."

If the fugitive was indeed Cordell, that payment was made with stolen money. Andy knew that he should by law confiscate it, but he had no intention of taking it away from this old man who did not appear to be overly endowed with the world's goods. He asked, "What did this man look like?"

"He was a big one. Not fat, mind you, just had shoulders on him like that black studhorse. Hands that looked like they could choke a mule. Black eyes, but friendly, the kind you feel like trustin'. I'd've been willin' to lend him that mare if he hadn't offered to buy her from me."

Hunnicutt said, "You'd've never got her back."

"I've lost things a lot more valuable than the mare. Anyway, *you* got your stud back."

John looked straight at Hunnicutt. "Thanks to me. You owe me for two days."

Hunnicutt shrugged. "All right, two days. But that's where it stops."

Dobson looked on quizzically, not understanding the exchange.

The sheriff said, "Here's where I have to leave you, Andy. The county line is just ahead, and my authority stops there. I'll help Thaddeus take his horse home."

Andy hated to bid the lawman good-bye. He said, "Maybe I'll see you again, next time some lawbreaker passes through your county."

"You're welcome to all you can catch. We've already got enough that we don't need any more."

Andy said to Dobson, "I don't suppose you'd want to tell us which way he went from here."

Dobson glanced at Choctaw John. "I gave him a halfway promise. Anyway, with John to do the trackin', you don't need me to tell you. He can follow a crow's shadow for ten miles."

John said modestly, "Maybe five."

Hunnicutt looked suddenly alarmed. "I ain't payin' that Indian past today. If he goes with you, it's up to the state or the county to foot the bill." He reconsidered. "Not the county either. Your fugitive did his dirty work someplace

else. I don't see why us Lampasas County taxpayers ought
to ante up for it."

Andy turned to John. "How about it? Are you goin' on
with me?"

"Trappin' season is over, so I got nothin' better to do.
The state's money is as good as his." He nodded at Hunnicutt. "Better, because I won't have to listen to the state
bellyachin' all the time."

Dobson seemed downcast. He said, "If you catch up to
him, I hope you don't shoot him. I feel like he ain't a bad
man at heart."

Andy said, "We don't shoot people for the fun of it.
Only if they force it on us." It continued to puzzle him that
almost everyone whose trail Cordell crossed bore kindly
feelings toward him. Damn it all, the man was a bank robber. And even if he might not actually have fired the shot
that killed Tom Blessing, he was partially responsible. It
happened while he was being broken out of jail. And there
was that kid, Buster. Cordell was at fault in his death as
well. He had given Andy a double load of guilt: part for
being late in coming to Tom's aid, and part for knowing
that it was his bullet that ultimately killed the youngster.

He said, "Let's go, John. We've got an outlaw to catch."

CHAPTER

12

Cordell was pleased with the bay mare. True, she was long past being a colt, but she still had enough *go* about her to carry him miles into the night without acting up as the stud had done. He made a dry and fireless camp. He would have liked some coffee, but that could wait. He would stop somewhere after daylight and boil a pot without much risk that his campfire would attract attention. He had no specific reason to believe anyone was actually on his trail, but he trusted his hunches. They told him it was likely that someone was. They just didn't tell him how far behind the pursuit might be. He had no intention of making it easy for them.

The stallion had been so feisty that it had been a constant fight to make it go where Cordell wanted it to. The mare was more pliable. He guided her onto hard, rocky ground where the terrain offered any. Unlike the stallion, she never stumbled. His snaky trail would be difficult for even an expert tracker and impossible for anyone less apt.

He had begun to notice a considerable scattering of buffalo bones bleaching on the prairie. He realized that this was all that remained of the vast shaggy herds that had once roamed the country. No one could have believed beforehand how quickly they would be decimated once a market developed for the hides.

"All wiped out," he told the mare. "Their time has come and gone."

He tried not to dwell on it, but he could not help thinking that his own time would probably soon be gone, too. With John Laws of all kinds covering Texas like horseflies, little room was left for free spirits like himself. Before long, bankers would be able to rob the public without having to worry about somebody robbing *them.* He would have no choice but to change his occupation. Maybe he could make a living gathering up buffalo bones.

In a couple of days he came to the crumbled ruins of what he took to be a frontier military fort. Partial stone walls gave him some idea of the post's original configuration. He recognized one small structure as having been a powder magazine, constructed at a distance from the other buildings as a precaution in event of an accidental explosion. Remnants of charred wood told him the fort had been burned in the distant past.

From stories he had heard, he realized this was probably what remained of Fort Phantom Hill, built as an outpost against Comanche and Kiowa, then abandoned. It would have been logical to assume that Indians had burned it, but Cordell had been told that departing soldiers hated the place so much that they had set it on fire to make certain they never had to return.

He had seen maps of this area. He tried to visualize them from memory and determine where he was in relation to the farm from which Buster had come. Unfortunately, he was stumped.

The sun was going down, and he was hungry, so he

decided to camp here. He could build a small campfire within one of the ruined buildings. The partially crumbled walls should protect the modest flames from view. He loosed an unwieldy bundle from behind the cantle, along with his rolled blanket. In the bundle were coffee beans from Irmadell's kitchen and part of a ham from Jedediah's smokehouse. He was glad he had had the foresight to take them. All that Galveston money in his saddlebags would do him no good if he starved.

He had found a stream below the hill and assumed it to be the Clear Fork of the Brazos. He could follow it and find Fort Griffin, but it was as crooked as a snake's track. It stood to reason that he had bypassed Griffin and now was to the west or southwest of it. After the mare had drunk her fill, he staked her where he found the grass tall and moderately green for this part of the country. Here rainfall was chancy, and grass had to be hardy to survive long periods of drought. But the struggle seemed to give the vegetation more strength than was common farther east. Animals thrived on it.

The ham, though good, was getting to be monotonous. Sitting beside the tiny campfire, he sipped from what was left of his coffee. He reflected darkly that he seemed to have spent most of his adult life like this, alone, hungry, sleeping with a single blanket on the hard ground. Usually, like tonight, he had wondered who might be coming behind him and how close they might be to catching up.

He thought about Son Dobson and how much he would give to trade places with the old farmer-fisherman, worried about nothing more than his noisy grandchildren. If they were Cordell's, they could make all the noise they wanted. That would be far preferable to the eerie silence of this old fort, where stone chimneys stood like tombstones over broken-down walls. The place was about as welcoming as a cemetery.

He dozed off, only to be awakened suddenly by the sound of horses moving through the grass. His heart hammered as he drew his pistol and sprinted out through an opening. He flattened himself against the highest part of the wall opposite the source of the sound.

Someone shouted, "Hello, the camp!"

Cordell remained silent. He heard a young voice say, "Told you I smelled smoke. There's a campfire in that old buildin'. What's left of one, anyway."

"Maybe they got some coffee," another replied.

Cordell held his breath. He heard the creak of leather as the riders dismounted on the far side of the ruined structure. The first voice said, "Don't seem to be anybody here. Must've fixed supper and left."

"Naw, there's a blanket yonder, and a saddle. And I seen a horse staked outside. Somebody's still around."

Cordell stepped back through the opening, pistol in his hand. "Somethin' I can do for you fellers?"

The pistol caught their immediate attention. Both men raised their hands to shoulder height. One stammered, "You don't need to point that thing at us, mister. We don't mean you no harm."

Cordell made his voice sound severe. "Did you come lookin' for me?"

"We don't even know who you are. We was just lookin' for some coffee, and maybe somethin' to eat."

Cordell placed several small pieces of dry wood on the fire to make it flare up. In its dancing light, he saw that both men were young, probably twenty years old or less. They looked like cowboys, possibly out of a job and riding the chuck line, depending upon others' hospitality. He lowered the pistol but did not immediately return it to its holster. Young or not, they could hurt a man. "Sorry if I gave you-all a fright, but you never know who might come ridin' in out of the night. Fort Griffin and the Clear Fork country have raised some hard characters."

"We're a ways past Griffin."

That told Cordell he had indeed ridden too far. It was by no means the first wrong guess he had made. In case someone should ask these two later, he decided to throw them off the track. "I know. Already been there. I'm headin' west, out to El Paso."

"They've got hard characters there, too."

Though not convinced, Cordell decided to give the pair the benefit of the doubt. He holstered the pistol but did not let his hand drift far from it. "The pot's empty, but you're welcome to boil some fresh coffee if you're of a mind to. Got smoked ham, too. Feel free to eat it all up. I'm tired of it."

He watched as they wolfed down what was left of his ham and drank coffee steaming hot. One had soft, patchy whiskers. He looked as if his next shave would be his first. The other's whiskers were just beginning to darken. Cordell asked, "You-all work around here?"

They looked at one another before the older of the two

answered. "We're drovers. Came up from south of San Antonio with a herd but got fired at Griffin. It wasn't our fault. We wasn't the ones started the fight."

"Anybody killed?"

"Not quite, but pert near. We decided not to stay around. Folks in Fort Griffin have been known to hang people."

Cordell noticed that the younger-looking one, who had spoken little, seemed to be studying Cordell's saddle with much interest. Perhaps he sensed that the bulging saddlebags held something more than grub.

"Much obliged for the supper," the older one said as he got to his feet. "If you don't mind, we'll stake our horses and camp the night here."

Reluctantly Cordell said, "It's a free country."

He watched them as they walked out to where they had tied their horses. The youngest seemed all of a sudden to be doing a lot of talking. The other nodded a couple of times and glanced back over his shoulder. Cordell wished he could hear what was being said. He had a hunch they were not discussing his health.

He knew he would not sleep tonight.

He spread his blanket outside the wall. They remained inside. While they settled in for the night, he kept watching them through an opening that had been a doorway. He waited until he heard snoring, then arose, rolled his blanket and tied it behind his saddle along with his little bit of camp equipment. So the pair would be less likely to hear, he led the mare out fifty yards or so before he saddled her. He circled back around and quietly untied the youths' horses. He led them westward about a mile before turning them loose. Not quite qualifying as horse theft, it was his favorite way of stalling pursuit.

By the time the pair found their mounts, he would be miles away.

He was still uncertain about their intentions. Odds were that they would have tried to rob him during the night. In that case he had no cause to regret setting them afoot. On the other hand there was a chance they were just what they appeared to be, a couple of luckless cowboys. If so, he had done them a wrong. But at least it was only a nuisance that would result in nothing worse than sore feet. Some people he had known, like Milt Hayward, would have shot them just to be safe.

He made little effort in the night to hide his tracks, for he could not see the terrain well enough to pick his ground. Much of it was sandy. Judging direction by the North Star, he kept riding west to confuse pursuers until he came into a dry wash with a gravel base. That ought to make him hard to track, he thought. He followed the wash in a northwesterly direction for several miles until it played out. He cut back to the northeast to compensate for the wide circle he had made.

At daylight he did not know where he was except in a general way. Far to the west stretched the rough breaks that led to the base of the high-plains escarpment. Somewhere to the east was notorious Fort Griffin, legendary first as a military post and buffalo hunters' rendezvous, then later as host to cattle drives on their way north to Kansas. He felt that its tales of violence had been exaggerated. Such stories almost always were, for most people were more interested in raw meat than in the facts. Still, there must be at least some fire to yield so much smoke. Perhaps in such an environment his past transgressions might be overlooked.

He was unaware of the half dozen riders until they topped a small rise in front of him, not fifty yards away. To run would be useless, for they had seen him. Dropping his hand to the grip of his pistol, he reined in the mare and waited. They had the grim and purposeful look of a posse. Had they come from behind him, he would not have been surprised, but their appearance head-on gave him a start. He resisted the temptation to draw the weapon. They could perforate him before he got off more than a shot or two.

The leader was a gaunt man with a severe expression and a black beard that hid his collar button, or would if he were wearing a collar. He said sternly, "I do wish you'd take your hand away from that six-shooter."

Cordell decided to try bluffing his way through. "Not till I know your intentions."

The leader beckoned to a rider whose hat was precariously perched atop a bandaged head. "Does he look like one of them, Hez?"

The little man called Hez gave Cordell only a brief inspection. "Naw, this feller is as big as the both of them put together. He don't look like no drover, and he sure as hell ain't no kid anymore."

"You're certain?"

"Damn right. They had their faces covered, but I could tell from their voices that they were a couple of young'uns. One of them no-good little bastards laid the barrel of a pistol upside my head. Like to've brained me."

The man with the beard turned apologetically to Cordell. "Sorry for the inconvenience, friend. We're lookin' for a couple of cowboys that robbed a saloon in Fort Griffin after closin' time the other night. Probably came off of a cattle drive and knew there'd be a lot of money in the saloon. Got themselves a road stake before they lit out for parts unknown."

Cordell knew whom he was talking about, but he saw no reason to say so. An honorable outlaw did not inform on others. It was a courtesy of the trade. He didn't see a badge among this bunch anyway. They looked more like a mob bent on vengeance. Citizens of Griffin had been known to mete out rough justice without waiting for the law. Waiting required patience.

He said, "I ain't seen anybody that fits your description. Fact is, I ain't seen anybody at all."

"They had a good head start. They're probably long gone." The bearded man frowned. "If you happen to run into a pair of that description, though, you'd better ride way around them. A young rattlesnake's bite is as danger- ous as an old one's. Hez's partner is laid up with a cracked skull. They're liable to kill somebody the next time."

Cordell said, "It's been some years since I was in Fort Griffin. What's it like these days?"

"It's seen better times. With railroads comin' across Texas, the trail drives are slowin' down. Since the Indians were put away, things are quiet up at the army post. Worst of all, Albany's the county seat now. Griffin ain't like it used to be, and sometimes I begin to wonder if it ever was."

Cordell had no interest in the fortunes or misfortunes of Fort Griffin except as they might apply to the Jackson family. He was doubly relieved when the posse rode on. First of all, they had not recognized him. Maybe the alarm hadn't reached this far west. Second, his suspicions about his visitors last night had proven well-founded. If he had relaxed his guard, he might be lying dead amid the ruins of Phantom Hill, and they might be marveling at their great luck in becoming suddenly rich.

Inasmuch as these possemen had looked him over without realizing who he was, he felt emboldened to visit Fort Griffin and ask about the Jacksons. He would finish his mission here, then move on. Perhaps that new life he had hoped for was finally within his reach.

Choctaw John chewed vigorously on a wad of tobacco as he squatted on his heels and studied the ground. "Ain't there been a storybook about a flyin' horse?"

Andy replied, "Can't say. I never read many storybooks."

"I'm afraid that's what we got here. For all the trace I can find, that horse just up and flew away."

John's tracking had led them to an abandoned military post, its walls crumbled, the brush growing up on what had been a parade ground. It was Phantom Hill, John said. Fresh ashes and charred wood showed that someone had built a campfire. Boot tracks were still visible where remnants of old walls had protected them from wind.

John said, "Looks like your man met up with two others here. Hard to figure what happened. All three horses started off together. Looks like somebody was followin' after them afoot. Damned peculiar."

A mile or so from the post, two horses had split off and headed north. The third, its tracks the same ones Andy and John had followed all along, had continued westward for a short time, then suddenly vanished. John and Andy spent several hours circling and searching but found no more sign.

Andy had heard stories among the Comanches about medicine men supposedly able to transform themselves into birds and fly to distant places. He had never believed those tales. Anyway, Cordell was no medicine man, but years of experience in escaping from the law appeared to have made him part coyote.

John said, "Maybe your Cordell is usin' an old Choctaw trick, wrappin' his horse's feet with leather so the hoofs don't cut deep."

Andy could not leave unanswered the implication that Choctaws were smarter. "Comanches did it, too."

He thought it more likely that Cordell simply had a strong instinct for finding ground where he would not leave a trail. Andy had developed a grudging respect for the fugitive's perverse ability to evade pursuit.

John said, "If you ever capture this one, they ought to promote you. He's about as slippery as I've ever seen not to have some Choctaw blood in him."

"That wouldn't surprise me. I don't know a lot about him except he's slicker than a greased pig."

John arose to a stand and leaned against his horse. "I'm afraid we've lost him for good. He'll eventually come to ground in one place or another, and some sheriff will grab him."

"I've been on his trail too long to quit. I couldn't go back and look at Tom Blessing's grave, knowin' I'd failed him. I wish you'd stay with me awhile longer."

John shrugged. "I hate to take money under false pretenses, except when it belongs to Thaddeus Hunnicutt. I get a kick out of aggravatin' that old skinflint."

"What if I offered you three dollars a day instead of two?"

John brightened. "Now, Ranger, you're speakin' the Choctaw language. But you know there ain't a Chinaman's chance I'll pick up that trail again."

"At least it's a chance, no matter how small."

"I like a man who makes up his mind to do a job and sticks with it even when it goes to hell. Must be the Comanche in you. They're the stubbornest damned people I ever knew."

"You might be right."

"As I remember it, though, every time us Choctaws had a fight with the Comanches, we won."

Andy grinned. "Like hell you did."

He knew that by tradition a Ranger was always supposed to be sure of himself, but he was undecided about what to do next. All he could think of was to keep going in a westerly direction and hope. Maybe they would get lucky and cut into Cordell's trail. Andy had a general sense of where he and John were. He had passed through this region during his time with the nomadic Comanches and later in his growing-up years. This was a transition area where the Cross Timbers yielded to the rolling plains.

Somewhere back to the northeast would be Fort Griffin. The town and the army post for which it was named lay along the south side of a Brazos River tributary known as the Clear Fork. It had been a favorite hunting ground for the Comanches before they were driven north of the Red River. Cattlemen had brought in their herds after hide hunters had killed off the buffalo. Now farmers were taking up the more arable portions, turning the native sod under. He had heard rumors of plans for a railroad.

Cordell had avoided towns for the most part, so Andy thought it unlikely he would go to Griffin and risk being recognized. More likely he would continue west, up over the caprock and out onto the open plains. On the vast Llano Estacado, Indian raiders had usually been able simply to disappear, confounding those who pursued them. Andy decided to keep moving that way and hope.

He saw half a dozen riders ahead, coming from the direction of the distant caprock. They slouched in their saddles as if they had almost reached the end of their endurance. He said, "Let's wait and see who they are. Maybe they've seen somebody."

The apparent leader was a man with a black beard not unlike the one Andy remembered seeing on Cordell, though this beard was better trimmed. The man gave Andy and John a quick but critical study, then asked, "Mind tellin' me who you-all are?"

"I'm Andy Pickard, Texas Ranger. John's my tracker."

"A Ranger?" The man looked frustrated. "We could've sure used you yesterday. I reckon now it's too late. They've given us the slip."

"They?"

"Two men, probably drovers. Robbed a saloon in Fort Griffin, pistol-whipped the owner and the bartender. Come nigh killin' them."

Andy's hopes surged. "Was one of them a big feller, forty or so?"

"No, these were young. Not much more than kids, the way the bartender told it."

Andy's hopes sagged.

The leader asked, "You're lookin' for a big man?"

"A man named Cordell. I've been on his trail all the way from southeast Texas."

The leader stroked his beard. "We may have seen him. We came upon a big feller yesterday and asked if he'd crossed trails with the two we're after. He said he hadn't."

"Was he ridin' a bay mare?"

"Sure was. What's he done?"

"It'd take an hour to tell you what all. Which way was he travelin'?"

"West." The posse leader frowned. "If you was to chance upon those two young scoundrels, we'd appreciate you puttin' them under arrest and bringin' them to Fort Griffin. We'd see that they never rob anybody again."

"I couldn't stand still for a hangin', if that's what you've got in mind."

"You ain't likely to see them anyhow. They're probably halfway across the plains by now, to Mobeetie or Tascosa."

Andy said, "I don't think so." He told how John had read the tracks. "Two riders turned north. I'll bet they're the ones you're lookin' for."

The leader looked puzzled. "We missed that. But why would they turn north after comin' so far west?"

"Maybe they figured to circle around and throw you off."

One of the possemen said worriedly, "They could be back in Fort Griffin right now, robbin' somebody else. They had their faces covered. Nobody would know them."

The leader said, "Then we'd better use our spurs and get back. Comin' with us, Ranger?"

"No. We've got our own job to do."

Andy strongly suspected that the posse had unknowingly come upon Cordell. Living up to the outlaw fraternity's code of ethics, he had lied when he told them he had not seen the young riders.

The riders pushed their horses into a reluctant trot. Andy and John continued in their westward direction. Late in the afternoon Andy noticed that John kept looking back. Andy saw nothing behind him. Finally John said, "I thought you Comanches had a guardian spirit to tell you about things you can't see."

"It doesn't always work. Choctaws are supposed to have one, too."

"I don't need any spirit to talk to me. My eyesight's good enough. I'll bet you hadn't noticed there's somebody followin' us."

Andy's first thought was of Cordell, but that made no sense. "If there is, how do you know he's followin' us? He might have a good reason to be travelin' in the same direction that we are."

"We can find out. Let's jog to the north and see if he keeps on comin'."

John's uneasiness was contagious. Andy had still not seen anyone, but he knew John's eyesight was sharp. Perhaps he had a sixth sense as well. "We'll try it. I hope you're wrong."

They made a sharp change in direction and rode on for a mile or so. John said, "Like I figured, he's trailin' us."

Andy had hoped it would not happen. He said, "There's brush up ahead. We can pull up there and lay for him."

"What'll we do with him when we get him?"

"Unless he's Cordell, I've got no idea."

Showing caution, the rider slowed as he approached the brushy draw where Andy and John had concealed themselves. He stopped to study the way ahead. By this time Andy could see that the man was large, somewhat as he remembered Cordell. But Cordell should be somewhere ahead of them. It made no sense for him to have fallen behind.

The rider overcame his doubts and came on. Pistols drawn, Andy and John rode out to confront him. Andy said, "Keep those hands up where we can see them."

Startled, the man instinctively reached for his pistol but saw he was covered. He raised his hands to shoulder height and blurted, "What the hell?"

"That's what we want to know. How come you're trailin' us?"

The rider shook his head. "I ain't trailin' you. I don't even know who you are. If you figure to rob me, you won't get much."

"We're not robbers. I'm a Ranger. Now, who are you?"

The man looked around as if gauging his chance of breaking away. "Name's Smith. John Smith."

Andy said, "My horse could come up with a better name than that." He saw that the man had a sizable blanket roll tied behind his saddle, as if he were traveling far. He probably had camp supplies bundled in it. His saddlebags bulged. "You're pretty well fixed for travelin'."

The man's eyes had a hard and defiant look. "It's a long ways between towns."

Andy said, "I wouldn't be surprised to find you in my fugitive book. Keep him covered, John."

Andy holstered his pistol and reached into his saddlebag, where he kept Len's list of wanted men. He cut his gaze away from the stranger for a moment. The stranger sank spurs into his horse and rammed into John, throwing him off-balance. John grabbed for the saddle horn, dropping his pistol. In an instant the rider had his own pistol out. He snapped off a shot at John and swung the muzzle around. For a couple of seconds he aimed point-blank at Andy. For some reason he did not squeeze the trigger.

Startled by the shot, Andy's horse danced in confusion. Andy drew his pistol but was unable to steady it enough for a clean shot. The shooter wheeled his horse around and quickly vanished from sight in the thick brush. Andy was about to spur after him when he saw that John was on the ground. Fearfully he swung out of the saddle and dropped to one knee. "Are you hit?"

John pressed his hand against his side, then raised it for Andy to see the blood. "Damn right I'm hit." He sucked in a sharp breath, his face twisting. "Feels like I've got a broke rib. Maybe a bunch of them."

The two horses ran off a short way, then stopped to look

back. The little pack mule followed them. Andy hoped that was as far as they would go, but he could not take time to catch them now. He had to see about John. Kneeling at the tracker's side, he pulled John's shirt open. The wound was bleeding.

After a brisk examination he said, "Looks like that bullet glanced off of your ribs and went on. Probably broke one or two."

John wheezed, "Hell of a way to earn three dollars."

"Think you can ride?"

John pressed his hand against his ribs and tried, with Andy's help, to get to his feet. He groaned and settled back down to a sitting position. "I don't think so."

It occurred to Andy that if one or two ribs were broken, which appeared likely, a sharp edge could puncture John's lung. He said, "I can't just leave you out here and ride for help. No tellin' how far it'd be or how long it'd take."

"There ain't no way in hell that I can ride a horse."

Andy weighed another possibility. "Maybe I can rig a travois like the Indians used."

John considered. "Sounds like a Comanche torture trick, but I don't want to stay here."

Andy rolled John's shirt and used it to bind the ribs as best he could. John grunted when Andy drew the makeshift wrapping tight. Face pinched with pain, he asked, "Who do you reckon that was?"

"Somebody who was afraid I'd find him listed in the book, I guess. It was just chance that we ran into each other."

"But he *was* followin' us."

"That I can't explain." There was something else Andy could not explain. "He drew a perfect bead on me but didn't shoot."

"I wish he hadn't shot at me either."

"He could've killed me, but he didn't."

"Count your blessin's. Anyway, I'm afraid I've cost you any chance to catch up with Cordell."

"It appears we'd lost him anyway."

Andy slowly approached the horses, talking gently in hope they would not run away. He caught his own, then John's. It took a while to find two branches long enough and strong enough to carry John's weight. He ran them through his stirrups and tied them, then secured shorter pieces as cross braces behind the horse. He placed his and John's blankets on as padding. "It's a long ways from a feather bed," he said.

Slowly and cautiously he eased John onto this awkward conveyance. Hurting, John said, "Don't you bounce me off of this thing."

Andy tied John's horse to the pack mule, knowing the mule would follow like a dog. He asked, "Are you ready?"

"No, but let's go anyway."

Andy sensed that his horse was uneasy. Allowing it time to accept this odd attachment it was expected to drag, he started in a slow walk. The horse kept looking back at first. Andy feared it might kick at the travois. But the animal calmed, and Andy felt secure enough to pick up the pace.

It was going to be a rough ride for John. Andy could only guess how far it was to Fort Griffin.

CHAPTER

13

Cordell was skittish about riding into Fort Griffin in broad daylight. He staked the mare to graze near the narrow river and took his ease beneath the shade of heavy trees while he waited for darkness. Three people rode by but gave him no more than a glance. He took that for a favorable sign. Maybe this town was not given to asking a lot of questions.

At dark he rode down the dirt street, looking first of all for a place to eat, one not crowded with customers. He found a small joint that seemed to have no business at all. The cook was the only person in the place, and he was skinny as a snake. That should have been a warning about the food, Cordell decided once he bit into the steak. It must have come from a tough, old bull, and the biscuits were hard enough to hurt his teeth. But it was the first time in a while that he ate his fill.

Carrying his saddlebags, he walked down a couple of doors to a saloon that suffered the same lack of customers and decided to give it a little of his business. Two men stood at the bar. More accurately, they leaned on it and gave every appearance of having been there too long. Cordell walked to a dark corner well away from the kerosene lamp that sat on the bar. He intended to have a quiet drink or two and, when nobody was close enough to hear and remember, to ask the bartender about the Jackson family.

The barkeep brought Cordell a drink. Cordell said, "Kind of quiet here tonight."

"Yeah, been a couple of days since a trail herd hit town. There's several just south of here, though. It'll get busier in a night or two."

Bits and pieces of the two drunks' conversation came to Cordell, but he could not hear enough to piece together any meaning, not that it mattered. They became louder when they argued over which had the fastest horse.

Their voices were drowned out by boisterous laughter from the street. Three young men pushed through the door, two jamming shoulders together as they tried to enter at the same time. A third trailed a couple of steps behind, dragging his feet. He looked to be the youngest, perhaps seventeen or eighteen. As the three approached the lamp and its full light shone on their faces, Cordell was startled. The two in the lead were the ones he had encountered at Phantom Hill. He remembered that their tracks had veered north a mile or so from the abandoned post. The posse had been wrong in assuming they went on west. They had circled and taken a roundabout way back to Griffin.

The third youth remained in a dim area well away from the lamplight. Cordell could not see his face clearly.

The oldest of the youths began to harass the two drunks. "How long has it been since you old farts took a bath? You stink."

The older men tried to ignore him. The one who had spoken grabbed the nearest drunk by the shoulder and turned him half around. "It'd be a service to the town if we was to drag you down to the river and throw you in. A soakin' would do you both a world of good."

The other youth shouted in gleeful agreement. The pair grabbed the two men by their arms and pulled them toward the door.

The bartender's face darkened. He slammed both hands down on the bar to get their attention. It sounded almost like a pistol shot. "Boys, I won't have you manhandlin' my customers. If you want a drink and have the money to pay for it, put it here where I can see it. Otherwise, go back outside and get you some fresh air."

The oldest of the three said, "Now, Oscar, you better be careful what you say. You just might get a bath yourself." He made a move as if to grab the bartender by the collar. Oscar stepped back out of reach, bent down, and came up with a double-barreled shotgun. His voice was angry. "Like I said, the air's fresher outside."

The challenger stared at the weapon but did not back away. Cordell had not intended to meddle, but he thought he saw serious intention in the bartender's face. If someone didn't yield, there was about to be a mess of blood on the floor and all kinds of people rushing in here to see what happened. A crowd like that was the last thing he wanted.

He said sternly, "Son, maybe you've never seen what a shotgun blast can do to a man."

The youths' attention shifted. The one who had challenged

the bartender took a step toward Cordell's table. "Ain't I seen you somewhere?"

The two drunks took advantage of the distraction to stumble out through the door.

Cordell laid his pistol on the table, where it immediately gained the youths' full attention. "Not as I recall."

The second young man said, "Sully, ain't he the one that—"

"Shut up, Finn," the older one snapped.

Cordell said, "I believe it'll be better all around if you take your business down the street. The whiskey here ain't that good anyway."

The youngest of the three said, "I never did like this joint. Let's git."

Sully said grudgingly, "All right. I don't care to spend my money where it ain't appreciated." To the bartender he said, "We heard what happened to Old Shep at his bar the other night, him and Hez. You might want to be careful how you talk to people, Oscar. It could happen to you." He turned. The other two followed him out.

The bartender waited to be sure they were gone, then placed the shotgun back beneath the bar. Bringing a bottle and a glass, he sat down at the table, refilled Cordell's drink, and downed one himself. "You said my whiskey ain't very good. What's wrong with it?"

"Nothin'. I had to say somethin'. It was about to get serious."

"We got some wild kids around here."

Cordell knew better, but he said, "Maybe they were just funnin'."

"Their kind of fun ain't funny. Sooner or later it'll get somebody hurt."

"Who are they?"

"The oldest two are the Keeler brothers. Got no mother, and their old daddy is too busy stayin' drunk to pay them much mind. They're like two young studs that nobody's managed to put a saddle on."

The Keelers were the ones Cordell had left afoot. "And the other?"

"Name's Dobie Jackson. Got no daddy, just a widowed mother. She's workin' herself into the grave to keep the farm goin'. That boy needs a quirt taken to him. If he keeps runnin' with them Keeler brothers, he'll end up dead or killin' somebody."

Jackson! Cordell had found out most of what he wanted without having to ask for it. He hoped it was the right family. Trying to be casual, he said, "Ain't she got any other sons to help her?"

"She used to have. She's afraid Dobie's liable to up and leave like her other boy did. If he keeps lettin' them Keelers lead him around, he may *have* to."

"What about that other son?"

"Name's David. He hung around with the Keelers too much, too. Got in a little trouble and took to the brush. Aurelia has no idea where he's at."

Cordell felt a wrenching in his gut. Probably the whiskey, he tried to tell himself, but he knew the cause.

Oscar said, "It's a damned shame to see a boy throw his life away. Like as not, David is in jail someplace. The way he's goin', Dobie is apt to follow right after him."

The bartender leaned forward, lowering his voice. "I got a strong suspicion it wasn't no drovers that robbed Old Shep's bar. Wouldn't surprise me none if it was them Keeler boys."

"They can't be very smart if they think they can pull a stunt like that in their own town and not be recognized."

"They covered their faces with sacks, but they ain't half as smart as they think they are. If they was to try that trick on me, I'd know them. They wouldn't get six feet inside the door."

Cordell swallowed another drink, emptying the bottle. He tried in vain to drive away the image of Buster lying dead in a doctor's office, taken down by a lawman's bullet.

Oscar said, "All of a sudden you don't look so good."

"Somethin' I ate."

"Must've been in that joint down the street. I ain't surprised. I wouldn't let my dog eat what comes out of that kitchen."

"I think I'd better go out and get me some air." Cordell thought of a way around having to ask the question directly. "I wouldn't want to run into those boys and have trouble with them. Whichaway will they be goin' home?"

"East, down the river. The Jackson farm is three or four miles, the Keeler place a ways further. But they won't be leavin' town till they run out of money or they're fallin'-down drunk." Oscar picked up Cordell's empty bottle from the table. "I wish we had chain gangs here like we had back home in Alabama. It'd do them boys a heap of good to work on the roads awhile. Maybe it'd sweat some of the meanness out of them. You ever see a chain gang?"

Suppressed memories and old emotions enveloped Cordell like a malevolent dark cloud. He winced. "Once."

He felt unsteady, making his way out the door. He leaned on the outside wall until he had his feet under him. He knew he had drunk too much. That was dangerous for a man on the dodge. He would be an easy catch should a lawman show up, or a thief coveting what he carried in his saddlebags. He found a wooden bench in front of a darkened store and slumped there, hoping the effects of the whiskey would soon pass. He dozed off, wakened when the saddlebags slipped from his lap, then dozed again.

His sleep was again interrupted by loud talking and a voice raised in what was meant to be a song. Down the street he saw three shadowy figures stumbling around a hitching rail. Trying to mount his horse, one let his foot slip from the stirrup. He fell on his back while the other two laughed. Though he could not see them clearly, their voices told him that they were the Keeler brothers and Dobie Jackson.

A thought penetrated the fog that had enveloped his brain. He had wanted to know where the Jackson family lived without having to ask directly. All he had to do was follow these three. He hoped they were on their way home and not simply looking for another place to carouse.

The mare snorted as he untied her. She probably did not like the awkward way he approached her, or perhaps it was the smell of the whiskey. "You're right, old girl," he muttered. "I don't like myself very much right now either." He managed to get into the saddle on the first try. He had the presence of mind to be sure he had tied the saddlebags down securely. As the three riders pulled away from town, he put the mare into a walk. They sometimes moved out of sight despite the full moon, but he could follow the sound of their voices. They talked and laughed and sang. They occasionally stopped, passing a bottle around. As he gradually sobered, he felt some concern that they might not make it home.

Eventually he saw light ahead. A lantern was suspended from the roof of a farmhouse porch. It was a mother's way of helping her boy find his way home, he supposed. He reined up to prevent overtaking the three. They stopped and talked a few minutes before two rode on. One made his way to a barn and started to dismount, then fell like a sack of grain. He lay on the ground a minute or two before he pushed shakily to his feet and removed the saddle, blanket, and bridle. Slapping his horse on the rump, he dragged his tack into the barn. He did not come out. Cordell suspected he had collapsed on the floor. He would probably spend the night there without going to the house.

Damned fool kid, Cordell thought. He remembered what the barkeep had said. *Ought to have a quirt taken to him.*

Now he knew where the Jackson family lived. He would retreat a little way and finish the night sleeping on the ground. Ever since Buster had died, he had tried to decide how to go about what had to be done. Now that he was here, all the options he had considered seemed to have evaporated. Maybe the morning sun would clear his head. Then he could make up his mind what to do next.

He slept fitfully, his stomach not taking kindly to the

abuse he had given it. *It's bad enough when some chuckle-headed kid drinks too much, but a man my age ought to know better,* he thought. After sunup he boiled coffee. It helped clear his head but did nothing for his stomach. His whiskers had been allowed to grow for several days. He feared his appearance might frighten Buster's mother, so he took time to boil river water and shave. He knew he was still a long way from handsome, but he had done the best he could.

If he betrayed his true identity immediately, he might not be allowed to enter the house. Buster's mother would have every right to blame him for losing her son, though the bartender had said the boy was already under a cloud when he left here. Cordell decided to play his cards close to the vest until the time felt right for showing his hand.

Riding toward the unpainted frame farmhouse, he could see that it was badly in need of work. A side window was broken out, a piece of cardboard put up in its place. Some roof shingles were broken, probably by a hailstorm. Out back, at the barn, a door hung by a single hinge. These were all things her son Dobie could repair if he were more inclined toward work.

Buster's rightful share of the bank money would come to just over three thousand dollars. Cordell could see that the farm badly needed patching up, starting with the unpainted frame house. That kind of money could do this place a world of good. He wondered about Mrs. Jackson's reaction. Would she eagerly grab the cash, as Irmadell almost certainly would, or coldly reject both it and him? He halfway hoped she would turn it down. He admired honesty and courage wherever he saw them. In that case, he would hide the money so she would find it later, after he was gone. A debt of honor had to be paid whatever the cost.

A picket fence surrounded the house, though like everything else around here, it needed work. He tied his horse and walked up to the front door. It was open, but it would be rude to enter without invitation, especially with the knowledge that a woman was inside. He knocked on the doorframe. He could hear the wooden floor creak as someone walked across it. A woman appeared at the door, wiping her hands on an apron. She said, "Yes?"

Taking off his hat, he had to look at her a moment before he could say anything. She was in her forties but by his estimation was still a handsome woman despite worry tracks around her tired eyes and gray beginning to streak the hair tied in a bun at the back of her head. "Ma'am," he said, "my name is . . . Walter Goodson. I'm lookin' for work, and I see your place could stand some fixin' up."

She gave him as intense a looking-over as he had given her. "That it does, but I can't afford to hire anybody."

He said, "That don't need to stand in the way. I've been hungry awhile. I'd work for meals and a place to sleep out of the rain."

He could see her struggling over the proposition. She said, "I wouldn't want to take advantage of you, asking you to work for nothing."

"It wouldn't be for nothin', ma'am. I'm takin' it on faith that you're a good cook."

"Fair to middling, but you won't see any fat people around here."

"I'd regard it as a real favor if you'd let me stay at least a little while. I promise you I'd earn my keep."

She was weakening. "I never like to turn anybody away from the door hungry, and it's a fact that we could use some help." She smiled. It was just a half smile, but it was a pleasant one. "All right, for a little while. And if there's any way I can do it, I'll pay you. I warn you, it may not be much."

"I don't need for much."

"You'll find hay in the shed for your mare. You can turn her loose in the corral. And there's an old cot in the barn where you can lay out your bedding. It'll still be a while before dinner."

"I'll find somethin' useful to do till then." He put his hat back on. "I thank you, ma'am."

"By the way, my name is Aurelia Jackson."

"Mighty pleased to know you, ma'am." He took the hat off again.

He noticed a large woodpile in back of the house, but only a small stack had been chopped into the right length for a cookstove. He turned the bay mare into the corral and put out some hay for her. He found a folding steel cot and dropped his blanket roll on it. He hid his saddlebags beneath the pile of hay, then returned to the woodpile and began swinging the ax. His hands were tender, not used to hard manual labor. They soon became sore. He could feel a blister rising, but he was determined to get himself into the widow's good graces. Then, at the proper time, he would tell her why he was here.

He became so absorbed in the work that he did not hear

someone walk up behind him until he saw a shadow. He whirled, dropping his hand to his hip.

Dobie Jackson stood there, looking considerably less cheerful than in the saloon last night. His eyes were bloodshot. He sweated profusely though the day had not turned more than moderately warm. He demanded, "Who the hell are you, and what're you doin' here?"

"My name's Walter Goodson, and I've hired on to work." Though he knew, he asked, "And who are you?"

"I'm Dobie." The youth frowned darkly, squinting one eye. "Ain't I seen you someplace?"

"Maybe. I've been lots of places."

"You wasn't in Oscar's place last night, was you?"

"I believe I was. And I believe I saw you there, too."

Dobie's voice carried a bit of resentment. "You busted up a little innocent fun. Me and the Keeler boys wasn't really goin' to throw anybody in the river. We were just hoorawin' a couple of drunks."

"It looked to me like you were a little drunk yourself."

Concern crept into Dobie's eyes. "You won't tell Maw about that, will you?"

"I won't tell her about you if you won't tell her about me."

"Fair deal." Dobie started toward the house, then turned back. "What did you say you're doin' here?"

"Just hired on to do some fixin' up. The place needs it." Accusation slipped into his voice. "Been needin' it for some time, looks like."

"Yeah. I been meanin' to get around to it."

Cordell leaned on the ax. "Who are those Keeler boys?"

"They're neighbors." Dobie jerked his thumb toward the east. "We used to go to school together till we all decided to quit. Got tired of teachers tryin' to tell us what to do."

"Do those Keelers tell *you* what to do?"

"Nobody tells me what to do. I do my own thinkin'."

And a damned poor job of it, Cordell thought. *Well, you're none of my worry. But I feel sorry for your mother.*

He chopped what he thought would be enough wood for at least four or five days, then drove the blade of the ax into a log he had used for a chopping block. He picked up an armload and carried it into the kitchen to replenish the woodbox beside the hot cast-iron range. He could smell bread baking in the oven.

Aurelia Jackson poked a couple of sticks of wood into the stove and said, "You'd just as well quit and wash up. Dinner'll be ready pretty soon. I expect you're hungry."

He breathed a bit heavily from the exertion. "Yes, ma'am, I sure am."

"I wish you'd call my son. He's workin' at the barn, I think."

Cordell saw no reason to tell her that Dobie was slumped on a bench in the shade at the side of the house. "I'll fetch him."

He told Dobie what she had said. He did not look up but said, "I don't know as I can eat anything. My stomach is all tore up."

"Whiskey'll do that to you every time. What you need is good hard work to sweat it out of your blood. I saw a stack of shingles out yonder. After dinner we'll climb up and patch your mother's roof."

"It don't rain here all that much."

"We'll fix it just the same." Cordell's own hangover made him short of patience. "Get off your butt and wash for dinner."

"Who do you think you are, orderin' me around?"

"I'm a man who can kick you from here to Fort Griffin. Now go wash up for dinner."

Resentfully Dobie left the bench and walked to a small back porch where a bucket of water and a basin sat on a waist-high shelf. He glared at Cordell as he washed his hands, then splashed his face with water.

Cordell said, "Wouldn't hurt none if you combed your hair. You look like a woolly booger."

"You ain't no rose yourself."

Cordell washed up and went into the kitchen. He was greeted by the smell of fresh bread and roast pork. He had already noted a pen of hogs out back of the barn.

Mrs. Jackson said, "It's a rare thing when we have beef around here, but hog meat is plentiful enough."

Cordell had eaten his fill of ham out of the Fergus smokehouse. Roast, however, was a different matter. "It looks mighty good," he said.

He was pleased to see Dobie walk into the kitchen with his hair combed. The youth flashed him a quick frown, then glanced away. Cordell said, "Me and your son are goin' to work on your roof after dinner. Looks like it might have a few leaks in it."

"That it does," she agreed. "I'd be much obliged if you'd show Dobie how it's done. Since his daddy died, there hasn't been anybody here to teach him things like that."

"We'll get along just fine, him and me." He gave Dobie a hard glance that told him there would be no argument.

He started to reach for the biscuits but saw Mrs. Jackson bow her head and begin giving thanks. That caught him off guard. It had been a long time since he had given the blessing or even heard someone else do it. Flustered, he looked down at the table and followed her "Amen" with a barely audible one of his own.

She said, "Dobie doesn't know how fortunate he is to have someone show him how to do things. I wish there had been somebody here for David."

Cordell felt a jolt but tried not to show it. "David?"

"My older son. He went kind of wild after he lost his father. Then one day he just up and rode away. We had a couple of short letters from him, but that was all. I wish I knew where he is."

Cordell could not look at her.

She said, "I keep hopin' he'll come ridin' in here someday, all grown-up, ready to settle down and start a family. That dream is about all that keeps me goin'."

Cordell lost his taste for biscuits and roast pork.

CHAPTER

14

Andy wondered how Choctaw John kept from crying out as the crude travois bumped along the broken ground. He tried to avoid the rougher places, but the uneven terrain was a constant challenge. He stopped from time to time, dismounted, and went back to make sure John was still breathing. A punctured lung, should that come to pass, might well kill him.

He said, "Maybe we'd better stop awhile and let you rest."

John's face had paled. His eyes were pinched in pain, or perhaps from the burning of sweat that ran down his forehead. "The sooner we get to where we're goin', the sooner I can get off of this devilish drag."

Andy could only guess the distance to Fort Griffin. At this slow rate, it was a cinch they would not reach there before sometime tomorrow, if then.

John asked, "Are you sure they got a doctor in that town?"

"I'm not sure of anything except that it's a long way."

"They've probably got an undertaker. That may be what I need by the time we get there."

"Don't talk about dyin'. You haven't earned your money yet."

"I've got no interest in dyin'. I wouldn't give Thaddeus that satisfaction."

At least John had not lost his sardonic sense of humor. Andy took comfort in that.

Toward sundown he decided John had had about all he should have to stand for one day. They had enough canteen water that they could camp without traveling farther to find a creek.

John protested, "The day ain't finished yet."

"No, but you are, just about." Andy helped him off the travois and spread his blanket in the shade of a tree. "I'll try to whip up a little supper."

"I doubt I can eat much. Lord, but these ribs do hurt." John stretched himself slowly and carefully on the doubled blanket. He let out a long breath as if he had been holding it all day. He closed his eyes and said, "I almost wish that jay-bird was a better shot. I wouldn't be feelin' anything now."

"Think about the money," Andy suggested. "Three dollars a day."

"Money's good for nothin' except gettin' you things you want, and I don't want much. I'd give up the wages just to get my ribs fixed back the way they was. Hell, I'd even kiss Thaddeus Hunnicutt."

"I'd give ten dollars to see that. He'd fall down in a dead faint."

"If I didn't beat him to it." John squinted one eye. "Who's goin' to foot my doctor bill?"

Andy said, "Me, like as not. You know how the state hates to pay up. The politicians get their hands into the pot first, and they don't leave much."

"I wish it was them ridin' on that drag instead of me."

Pain kept John awake most of the night, so Andy did not sleep much either. At sunup he boiled coffee and fried bacon. He could persuade John to eat only a little. John said, "It tastes better when a woman fixes it."

"You've got no woman."

"Now and again I do. They stay till we can't stand one another. That don't generally take long."

Andy caught up the horses, packed the mule, and helped John settle onto the travois. The second-day hurting was more severe than the first. His face contorted, John said, "Next time I get shot, I'll try to be closer to town."

Andy felt like groaning with John as the travois dragged across rough ground. About midmorning he saw a wagon moving eastward on a path parallel to his own. Its hoops were partially covered by canvas. A milk cow plodded along behind at the end of a short rope.

He said, "Hold on tight, John. We may get you a better ride."

The people with the wagon gave no sign that they had seen this makeshift procession. Andy realized they were going to outdistance him. He drew his pistol and fired a couple of shots into the air. The wagon stopped. People who had walked alongside quickly disappeared behind it.

John muttered, "They may think we're Indians."

Andy said, "We are, aren't we? You anyway."

"Just half. We better move up slow, or they're liable to shoot us both. I don't need any more of that."

Andy tied a handkerchief to his rifle barrel and waved it over his head. He heard a faint shout from the wagon but could not decipher the words. He assumed they meant for him to come on in but do nothing sudden. Moving closer, he saw a man half hidden behind the rear of the wagon, his rifle aimed and ready. The voice was clearer now. "That's close enough. State your business."

"I'm a Ranger," Andy shouted back. "Got a wounded man here. He needs help."

The man beckoned him to move closer, but he held the rifle steady. "You got anything to show that you're a Ranger?"

"Just my word."

The man stepped hesitantly into plain view. He appeared to be in early middle age, wearing an untrimmed salt-and-pepper beard, a plain cotton shirt without a collar, and faded bib overalls. He lowered the rifle. "I'm takin' you at your word. Just be careful that whatever you're draggin' don't booger my team. Got my wife and youngest baby in the wagon."

"Would you be headin' for Fort Griffin?"

"I'm sorry to say that we are. We'd prefer to go around that Sodom and Gomorrah, but we've got to pick up a few provisions to carry us back to East Texas."

Andy thought the description of the town was exaggerated, but this was not the time to argue the point. "Have you got room to carry this man? The travois is about to kill him."

The farmer frowned. "Is he a prisoner?"

"No, he's been helpin' me. Got shot in the line of duty."

Easing, the farmer said, "I reckon we could shuffle things around and make room."

Three pairs of young eyes peered with great curiosity from beneath the wagon bed. A boy of about twelve stepped out and asked, "Are you really and truly a Ranger? We never seen a Ranger before."

"Yes, and there's no need for you to be scared. Me and John don't have any horns."

The farmer said, "I'm Henry Orville. My wife Hannalee is in the wagon." A bonneted woman looked out from beneath the canvas cover. Orville climbed into the wagon. Andy could hear the pair moving things around. The farmer finished tying the cover down over the hoops so the entire wagon was covered. He said, "We've got a bed of sorts fixed for your deputy."

He helped Andy lift John up over the end gate. John winced but did not cry out. Andy could hear Mrs. Orville beneath the canvas, telling him to lie down gently. "Poor man," she said. "Seems like there's no end of misfortune in this godforsaken part of the world."

It was obvious the family was moving. Belongings of various kinds were tied to the sides of the wagon and even beneath its bed, including two crude coops containing several chickens. Andy said, "Most people these days are movin' west. How come you're goin' east?"

"We already been west," Orville said, frowning as if he had bitten into something sour. "Out on them plains yonder, up over the caprock. A new land, they said. A new start. A barren desert, I call it. Fit only for Indians, and I doubt even they would want it back."

Andy could argue about that, but he had more important things on his mind.

Orville said, "We had us a few cattle. What the four-legged wolves didn't kill, the two-legged ones stole. We tried to farm, but the wheat was so short I'd've had to lather it before I could cut it. We had to dig for our water. And trees? There wasn't none, just wide-open plains for miles in every direction. Made a man feel buck naked in front of the world."

"Henry," his wife admonished. "The children . . ."

"I'm just tellin' it the way it is. We're goin' back to where it knows how to rain once in a while, where a man can raise a garden and rest in the shade of a tree when he's tired from his labor."

Andy had strong memories of the plains from his years with the Comanches. They differed from this disheartened farmer's description. There had been water if one knew where to look for it. Game had been plentiful most of the time, so meat had seldom been short. Bushes and shrubs in the canyons and draws offered wild berries and nuts of many varieties. The strong grass supported not only the buffalo but vast numbers of horses, both wild and tame. These people who came from a much different environment did not recognize the bounty nature placed there for the taking. The Indian had known, and it had served him well. Andy feared white men had already begun to spoil it, trying to turn it into the image of what they had left behind.

The two oldest children stared at him openly and without reserve. A little girl of four or five years stayed hidden behind a wheel, peeking out with one eye.

Andy beckoned the oldest boy. "Would you like to ride my deputy's horse so I don't have to lead him?"

The boy agreed with a broad grin. He quickly climbed into the saddle as if he feared Andy might change his mind. Orville returned to the wagon seat. "You young'uns stay clear of the wagon now. Everybody set? Here we go." The first forward movement caught the milk cow unprepared and almost jerked her off her feet. The two younger children walked alongside the wagon. The pack mule followed.

Orville's wife sat beside him on the wagon seat, the baby in her lap. Andy pulled his horse up beside them. He asked, "Where did you-all live before you came out here?"

Orville said, "The piney woods, over by Nacogdoches. I reckon that's why we couldn't find comfort out on that open prairie. You could see for ten miles in any direction, only there wasn't nothin' to look at. Had to hunt high and low for firewood. And lonesome? Now and then some cowboy came by, was all. Hannalee went for four months once without seein' another woman."

She nodded grimly.

Orville continued, "Folks weren't meant to live like that, white folks anyway. Hannalee was always afraid the Indians might show up, and I wasn't none too sure myself."

"They've been on the reservation for years now."

"They might decide to come back, though for the life of me I can't see why." Orville glanced at the sleeping baby in its mother's lap. "We decided to go home to East Texas and raise our young'uns in a civilized country." He rode in silence awhile, then asked, "How did your helper come to get hisself shot?"

Andy explained the circumstances without going into detail.

Orville said, "You never saw the shooter before?"

"Not that I know of. Odd thing, though, he seemed to be followin' us."

"He probably thought you were lookin' for *him,* and he decided to get you first."

"After he shot John, he was all set to shoot me between the eyes, but he didn't do it. I've got no idea why."

"There's no way of knowin' what goes on in the minds of men like that. They ain't normal."

Andy had searched the fugitive book, but the physical descriptions in it were sometimes vague. Besides, he had seen the outlaw close up for only a few wild and confused moments. The man could have been any one of fifty on the list.

Orville said, "That's another good reason for us to leave. Too many wild and lawless heathens out this way."

"There's good people here, too."

"Maybe so, but they're scattered too thin for my taste."

Andy was disappointed that Fort Griffin was still not in sight at dusk. The Orvilles made camp. Andy spread blankets on the ground for John and helped him down from the wagon. He had seen at noon that the family did not carry much food with them, certainly none to waste. He said, "Maybe the deer will come out in the cool of the evenin'. I'll see if I can get us some fresh meat."

He had not ridden far before he spotted three does easing warily into the open. They reached down to graze a patch of weeds, then jerked their heads up, chewing while they watched for danger. Andy knelt with his rifle, steadying one elbow on his knee. He aimed at the fattest of the three and fired. All the does jumped, but one fell kicking while the other two sprinted back into the brush. Andy gutted her on the ground, then tried to lift her up in front of his saddle. The horse shied away, spooking at the smell of fresh blood. Andy kept trying until he managed to get her into place and swing into the saddle. He feared for a while that the horse would pitch, throwing both him and the doe. Holding a tight rein, he reached camp just before dark.

The family welcomed the venison as a change from their meager fare on the trail. John had recovered his appetite, asking for a second helping. Andy took that for a good sign. John walked around a little, easing the stiffness in his legs, though he kept one hand pressed against his ribs. He coughed a few times. Andy hoped the cough was just caused by dust.

He asked, "How's the wagon ride?"

John considered his answer. "Better than that damned travois, but it's still hard on the constitution. How much further do you suppose we have to go?"

"We ought to be in Griffin tomorrow."

"It's damned sure time."

The next morning they moved along the upwind side of a trail herd, keeping away from dust stirred by the cattle. The trail boss was a young man of barely more than twenty, but he had already made two trips up the trail. He told Andy the wagon should reach Griffin by afternoon.

He turned out to be right. Reaching town, Andy inquired about a doctor and was pointed toward an upstairs office. Orville pulled the wagon as close as he could. Andy helped John up the steps, taking them one at a time. The doctor was an all-business little man wearing an old gray vest with tiny holes burned in front, indicating carelessness with his smoking. He gave John a thorough feeling-over without regard to the pain he caused.

His voice sounded critical. "Who wrapped you up so tight?"

Andy dreaded the lecture he was sure was coming, but he said, "I did."

"It's a good thing. He's just got one broken rib," the doctor declared, "but it's enough." He said to John, "If the Ranger hadn't taken good care of you, you could be hammering on the pearly gates by now because of a punctured lung. Or you could be dead of blood poisoning from the wound. Either way, you'd be trying to look up through six feet of dirt."

Andy asked, "What should I do with him now?"

"There's a hotel down the street. It's not the Brown Palace, but it's got no bedbugs as far as I know. Put him there where I can keep looking in on him for a few days."

"A few days?" Andy had not counted on such a delay.

"A broken rib is not like a broken spoke in a wheel. It can't be fixed in an hour."

Andy knew the state office would complain about paying for the doctor, much less the hotel, especially inasmuch as John was not a state employee. If it came to that, Andy would pay the bills out of his own pocket. He owed John that much for getting him into this fix. To make things worse, he had lost all track of Luther Cordell.

The family wasted no time in buying the supplies they needed and preparing to get under way. Orville said, "I'd like to put this town several miles behind us before we stop for the night. I want none of its corruption rubbin' off on the children."

Andy had seen no corruption yet, but he supposed if he were a family man, his viewpoint might be more critical. He felt that the Orvilles had given up their farm too soon, but perhaps it was for the best. Some people would never adapt to the dry and open plains. He bade the family goodbye and good luck, then watched their wagon pull out toward the east. The milk cow struggled against the rope that forced her to follow.

The hotel manager moved a cot into John's room for Andy. "Nothing is too good for the Rangers," he said. "It will be good, having you here in case some of the drovers stay too long in the barroom. We had a bad robbery in one of the saloons a few nights ago."

Andy said, "I heard about that. Folks seem to think a couple of drovers did it."

"Maybe yes, maybe no. There are some suspicions about that. Cowboys are free spenders. That money is a temptation to vultures who hover about, looking to reap where they have not sown."

"It takes a low class of criminal to hold up a saloon."

"The petty criminal will settle for less if he can get it with little risk. You say you have been hunting for a man who robbed a bank?"

Andy nodded. "I guess you could consider him a higher class of criminal. Not only was it a bank, but it was in one of the biggest towns in Texas."

"A man of high ambition."

"It's my ambition to catch him."

Andy was hard put to decide what to do. Loyalty to Choctaw John would require him to remain here at least until he knew John was going to recover without complications. Loyalty to the Rangers, on the other hand, would require him to go back where they had lost Cordell's trail and try again to discover some trace.

John had found that Cordell turned northward a while after leaving the ruins of Phantom Hill. It might have been only a temporary change of direction in an effort to throw off pursuit, or it could mean Cordell had not meant to travel farther west in the first place. It could mean he had circled back around, that he could even be here in Fort Griffin. It was a long shot, about as likely as Andy's getting an apology from Farley Brackett. Still, it was an intriguing possibility, enough to argue for his staying around at least a few days should the state office question his decision. He might see or hear something.

His first order of business, after seeing to John's needs, was to visit the local law. He found that the sheriff's office was in Albany, but a deputy was assigned to Fort Griffin. He introduced himself and told about his search.

The deputy gave him scant comfort. He said, "Sure, I could've seen your man. In the last couple of weeks, with the cattle herds comin' through, I've probably seen twenty that would match your description. Been a lot of strangers passed this way. As long as they haven't caused a row, I haven't paid much attention. Except for a pair that robbed Old Shep's saloon the other night, there hasn't been much excitement. In spite of the stories people tell about us, we're pretty good folks here in Griffin Town."

Andy told about meeting an impromptu posse on the trail of the two. The deputy grunted. "They were a hangin' party. They didn't have any authority from me or the sheriff. It's probably a good thing they didn't find those men. Somebody would've gotten killed, and it wouldn't have been just the robbers."

Andy agreed. A group of gun-toting citizens on the hunt could be more danger to themselves than to their quarry. "I'll probably hang around a few days," he said. "If you see or hear anything suspicious, I hope you'll let me know."

"Sure 'nuff. And if you spot your man and need help, all you've got to do is holler."

CHAPTER

15

Cordell felt satisfaction in a job well done as he looked at the repaired corral fence. Only the blind would call it pretty, but it was strong, and it would hold just about any animal bigger than a house cat.

Dobie Jackson leaned on a shovel, sleeves rolled up and shirt stained with sweat. His voice was antagonistic. "I hope you're satisfied now. I don't see why we had to build the whole thing over. A little patchin' would've done it."

Cordell said, "A job worth doin' at all is worth doin' right. It's too bad we had to use old lumber, but at least you won't have to be ashamed of it now."

"I wasn't ashamed of it in the first place."

"It ought to give you a warm feelin', knowin' you've finished a good piece of work."

"All I feel is tired."

Cordell's good mood began to sour. He didn't know what it would take to straighten this boy out. Maybe a roof needed to fall in on him, or something. *His paw ought to've taken a razor strap to him a long time ago,* he thought. But he remembered that Dobie's father had been dead for some years. *He's too big for his maw to whip him, and it's not my place to do it, bad as I'd like to.* It bothered him that Dobie looked a little like his brother,

and he was showing signs of following in Buster's way-
ward footsteps.

Cordell had not found a way to tell Aurelia Jackson that
her oldest son was dead. He had meant every day to do it,
but every day he had put it off, dreading the pain it would
cause her. He had immersed himself in work, repairing
much around here that had long needed fixing. He had bul-
lied Dobie into helping him, hoping some healthy sweat
would bring the youngster around to a greater appreciation
for the home he had. Dobie had been a competent worker,
though not an eager one. He took no initiative. He had to
be told what to do, and sometimes how to do it.

Cordell liked this farm. It stirred up half-forgotten memories of one long ago in Louisiana. What he would give, he
thought, if he could turn back the years and start over. Seeing Mrs. Jackson every day made him think of the wife he
had lost by going off to war, and the empty years he had
spent alone. He barely remembered anymore what she had
looked like. It had been a long time since he had been able
to conjure up a clear vision of her as she had been the last
time they were together. But he remembered well the long
and futile search he had made for her and their son.

If he still lived, that boy would be fully grown now,
older than Dobie. Cordell had often tried to imagine what
he would look like, what kind of man he would be. A better man, surely, than his father. It was just as well that the
boy never got to know him, or to know what his father had
become. Even if he chanced to hear the name Cordell, he
would not recognize it, for that was not the name he had
been born with.

So far he had not felt comfortable enough to use Aurelia's given name, though she had indicated that he need not continue being formal. He was hesitant to call her anything except Mrs. Jackson. Buster still haunted him, especially here where the boy had once been at home. He was sure that when he finally told Aurelia what had happened, she would hate him.

He said, "We'd just as well go to the house. I expect supper will be ready before long."

"No readier than I am," Dobie replied.

"Nothin' like hard work to give you an appetite."

"Or blisters." Dobie looked at his hands and frowned. "Before the war, did you have any slaves?"

"I never had money enough."

"Too bad. You'd've been a good slave driver."

Cordell pretended to take that for a joke, though he knew it was not meant to be. He had suffered about as much of Dobie's attitude as his patience would endure. He felt a strong urge to tell Mrs. Jackson about Buster, then ride on. Any day now, a Ranger or other lawman might show up at the door. Though he had seen no sign of pursuit, he had a nagging feeling that it was there, somewhere. It was time he headed west again, or he might become so attached to this place that he would stay and let himself be captured.

Halfway to the house, he heard a holler. Two horsemen approached from the east. He recognized them as the Keeler brothers. One shouted, "Hey, Dobie, wait up."

Dobie grinned and turned to face the pair. Cordell felt his stomach draw into a knot. He had seen the brothers twice before, and they had given him indigestion both times.

Keeler said, "Come and go with us to town. We'll have us a time."

Cordell did not give Dobie a chance to accept. He said, "Dobie ain't had his supper."

Keeler gave Cordell a hard look. "He can eat supper in town."

"Costs too much. He'll stay here."

Dobie turned hostile eyes on him. "Who are you to tell me what I can't do? You're not my daddy."

Keeler asked Dobie, "Is this old man kin to you?"

"Not kin to me or to anybody else I know of. He just came here to bum a meal and decided to stay."

Keeler demanded of Cordell, "Who the hell are you, anyway?"

Cordell clenched his big fists and rested them on his hips. "It don't matter who I am. Just know that I'm a man who can whip the both of you." He glanced at Dobie. "Three of you, if it comes to that."

The three young men tried to stare him down, but they could not hold their gaze long. They all cut their eyes away.

Keeler said, "We're goin' on, Dobie, with or without you."

Cordell said, "It'll be without him."

As the brothers rode away, Cordell said, "You ought to steer clear of people like that. They'll do nothin' but get you in trouble."

"Who I choose for friends is none of your business. I'm a grown man."

"Lackin' a few years."

"We wouldn't do anything but have a little fun. Ain't been much fun around here lately with all the work you've found to do."

"There's nothin' wrong with a little fun as long as it's the right kind. But people like those Keelers, they've got peculiar ideas about what that is." He was convinced the two brothers had held up and pistol-whipped the saloon-keeper in town. "Let yourself step onto the outlaw trail, and pretty soon you find you can't get off of it. You're trapped there, like . . ." Catching himself, he broke off. He had been about to blurt *like your brother.*

For a moment he hoped he was beginning to get through to Dobie, but the young man asked, "How much longer do you figure to stay here?"

"I haven't decided."

Eyes narrowed, Dobie said, "Maybe you figure to stay from now on. Maybe you think you'll smooth-talk my mother till she decides to marry you, and you'll have this farm real cheap."

Heat rose in Cordell's face. "I've got no such notion. You have a dirty mind, boy. And a dirty mouth."

Dobie's eyes blazed with defiance. "You goin' to try to wash it out with soap?"

"Not even lye soap would be strong enough. Your mother is wavin' us in for supper. Get yourself into the house."

They ate supper in strained silence. Aurelia looked from her son to Cordell and back again. It was clear that she felt the tension between them. Dobie left some of the food on his plate and strode out onto the front porch to flop in an old wooden chair and sulk.

Worriedly Aurelia said, "I saw the Keeler boys ride up to talk to Dobie. What did they want?"

"Wanted him to go to town with them."

"I have a feeling he would have gone had it not been for you. What did you say to him?"

Cordell felt as if he were trapped in a narrow chute. "Just told him it wouldn't be a good idea. Those boys are no-account."

"I know. I've tried to talk to Dobie, but he's drawn to them somehow. He doesn't want to listen to what I say. I'm glad you're here, Mr. Goodson. You can talk to him better than I can."

"It's not because he likes what I tell him, but because he's half-afraid of me."

"He's still more a boy than a man. He'll come around when he gets a little older and has more experience."

He may not last that long, Cordell thought. *Buster didn't.*

Aurelia sipped a little coffee and put down the cup. "Cold," she said, her face twisting a little.

She probably meant the coffee, but she could have meant her son, Cordell thought.

She said, "I'm glad you're here to keep him away from trouble."

"There's reasons why I'll have to be movin' on pretty soon. I may have stayed too long already."

He had noticed her dark brown eyes the first time he saw her. Now they looked even darker, and much troubled. She said, "Whatever your reasons, can't they wait? I need you here. Dobie needs you."

He felt himself melting under her steady gaze. He knew he should end it right here. He should saddle up and leave without spending another night in the barn. He knew also that he would not.

He said, "I believe I'll have another cup of coffee. Can I bring you one?"

A few nights later he sat on the edge of his cot in the barn, yawning as he mended harness by lantern light. He heard horses approaching the corral, and the low murmur of voices. He put out the light and stepped through the open barn door into the darkness. He recognized Dobie by the way he moved, catching and saddling his horse. Two other men on horseback waited outside the corral. He could not see their features, but he sensed that they were the Keeler brothers. Unable to make out what they were saying, he moved closer, careful that his footsteps not be heard.

Dobie was saying, "Good thing Maw went to bed early. Otherwise I couldn't have slipped out of the house. She'll raise hell when I come home."

One of the Keelers said, "You'll be back before daylight. It's time you cut loose from the apron strings anyway. You're a man, ain't you?"

The other said, "You'll come back with your pockets full. We figure there's a lot of drover money piled up in old Oscar Counts's saloon. He was pretty snotty to us the last time we was in his joint. We'll pay him a visit as he closes up."

"You meanin' to rob him?"

"Let's don't say *rob*. Let's just say we don't like to see an old man havin' to tote all that extra weight around. We'll lighten his load."

Dobie argued, "People in town know us too well. They'll be comin' to get us."

"Not if we cover our faces, like before." One of the Keelers pulled a small cloth sack from his pocket. It had slits cut for the eyes. "Oscar'll think we're some of them drovers, takin' their money back."

The second Keeler said, "You like money, don't you?"

"Sure, I do. But . . ."

"But nothin'. All you'll have to do is stay outside and hold the horses for us. Now git in the saddle and let's be movin'."

Dobie took the reins and started to mount. Cordell saw that he had made up his mind. He shouted, "Dobie, you get down from there. You're not goin' anyplace." He ran to stop the boy.

One of the Keelers jumped his horse out in front of him. "Where did he come from?" he demanded. Cordell's first reflex was to dodge the horse. Before he could do anything else, Keeler swung a pistol barrel and struck a glancing blow to the side of his head. Cordell staggered and went down.

He heard Dobie say anxiously, "You didn't kill him, did you?"

Keeler replied, "His head is too hard. I just dizzied him a little. Let's go."

Cordell pushed to his knees, choking on the dust the

horses raised as they loped away. He saw Aurelia step out onto the porch in her nightgown. She looked in the direction the three young men had gone. Then she saw Cordell, bracing himself against the fence. She ran toward him. "Mr. Goodson! What happened?"

Cordell rubbed his pounding head. He felt a small tickle of sticky blood where the pistol had struck. "Those Keelers." His voice sounded raspy.

"Dobie went with them, didn't he?" she demanded.

Reluctantly he said, "I'm afraid he did."

"They'll be the death of him one of these days."

And this could be that day, he thought. "I'll saddle my horse and go fetch him back." He stepped away from the fence and almost fell. She grabbed his arm and steadied him. "I don't think you're in any condition to ride. I'll hitch up the wagon and go myself."

He helped her with the team, then went into the barn. He had not worn his pistol since he had come here, but he buckled his gun belt around his waist and climbed up into the wagon. "We'll both go," he said. He let her take the reins. He held on to the seat the first mile or so until he felt steady enough not to fall.

She said, "You find him for me. I'll take him by the ear and drag him out. Maybe that'll shame him enough to bring him to his senses."

"Or make him run away for good," he cautioned her.

"What else can we do?"

"I don't know. I'll figure it out when the time comes."

Approaching town, they circled around a trail herd bedded down for the night. Cordell saw what appeared to be the chuck wagon, a lighted lantern atop the box, like a beacon to guide the cowboys to camp. They passed a festive group of riders who had evidently finished their evening in town and were returning to the herd.

"Cowboys," she said. "Most of them aren't much older than Dobie. They're David's age, a lot of them." She became pensive. "I wish I could hear from David. You don't know how hard it is, not knowing where your son has gone."

Cordell knew. He had done a lot of thinking about his own lost son, especially since Buster's death. He felt that it would ease his pain a little if he could talk to her about it, but he did not want to burden this good woman with his problem. She had too many of her own.

Most of the town was dark. The streets were almost deserted. A few horses were still tied in front of the saloons, but Cordell figured most of the visiting drovers had quit for the night and returned to their herds. The last stragglers would soon give up and allow the saloons to close. That, he knew, was when the Keelers would strike.

"Pull in at the wagon yard," he said, "but leave the team hitched. We may want to leave town kind of quick."

She did as he directed. "What do we do now?" she asked.

"I'll see if I can find Dobie. You wait right here. It may take a while."

"He won't want to come with you."

"I know. But he'll come." He climbed down from the wagon and tested his balance. His head still hurt a little, but his legs were steady.

He thought it unlikely that the Keelers would enter Oscar's place until they were ready to rob him, for he would remember them by the way they were dressed, even if they covered their faces. If they were smart, they would not be drinking at all tonight. Whiskey was dangerous when a man set out to do a job that was risky even for somebody cold sober. Whiskey had allowed Sheriff Tom Blessing to capture Cordell after that Galveston bank job.

No, if the boys had the judgment God gave a jackrabbit, they would be lurking in the dark, waiting for Oscar to close up. Still, Cordell had not figured them for high intelligence. Most criminals he had known were longer on nerve than on brains. He stopped in front of the first saloon he came to and peered through the door. He counted two customers he surmised were drovers. The bartender was watching them impatiently, evidently hoping they were about ready to call it a night. A small white bandage on the side of his head told Cordell he was the one the Keelers had robbed sometime back. When he stepped out from behind the bar, Cordell saw that he had a pistol belt strapped around his waist. He was not going to accept a second robbery without a fight.

Cordell remembered that Oscar kept a shotgun within easy reach behind his bar. The Keelers might not find him to be easy pickings.

He walked past several darkened buildings until he reached Oscar's place. A lighted lantern hung beneath the porch roof. As before, a lamp stood on the bar. It furnished the only light inside the saloon. Cordell eased up to the window and looked through. He did not expect to see the Keelers and Dobie there, but he had to be sure. He saw

only two customers, sitting at a table halfway toward the
back door. Cordell gave them a cursory glance, then felt a
sudden alarm and looked again. One face was vaguely familiar. Cordell searched his memory. He had seen it somewhere weeks ago. But where?

Realization struck him like the kick of a mule. This man
had visited Tom Blessing in the jail just before Blessing
was killed. Cordell was not certain, but this could have
been one of those shooting at him during the jailbreak. He
could even be the one whose bullet struck Buster. He must
be a lawman of some kind, perhaps a Ranger.

Cordell's first instinct was to grab a horse and run. He
went so far as to survey the few horses that remained tied
on the street, wondering which he should take. But he hes-
itated, his mind going back to that woman waiting at the
wagon yard. She depended on him to save her son from
himself. He could not leave until he fulfilled his obligation
to her. He retreated to a dark space between two buildings
and waited, his stomach in turmoil as he rethought his options: to run or to stay.

The two customers left the saloon. Oscar came onto the
narrow porch and blew out the lantern. The lamp on the
bar still burned. Cordell heard horses and saw three riders
coming down the dark street in a walk. Two, wearing sacks
for masks, dismounted in front of the saloon and handed
their reins to the third. Cordell knew that would be Dobie.

He waited until the two Keelers entered the saloon, then
stepped out into the street. He swung up onto one of the
Keelers' horses while Dobie froze in astonishment. He
said, "Come on, boy, we're gettin' away from here."

Dobie started to protest. Cordell swung his fist with all the strength he could muster and connected with Dobie's chin. He held Dobie to prevent him from falling, though the boy lost his hat and the mask. Cordell grabbed Dobie's reins and moved into a run back up the street. Behind him, he heard a shotgun blast and a scream. Pistol shots quickly followed.

By the time he reached the wagon yard, people were spilling out onto the street. He led Dobie's horse up against the wagon and gave the stunned boy a shove that tumbled him out of the saddle and into the wagon bed. He swung to the ground and gave the Keeler horse a slap on the rump. It trotted down the street. He tied Dobie's to the tailgate and climbed up beside Aurelia.

Wide-eyed, she said, "I heard shooting. Is he . . . ?"

"He's not shot. I hit him with my fist because he was fixin' to get himself into bad trouble, and I didn't have time for argument."

"It sounded like *somebody* got shot."

Grimly he said, "Them Keeler boys, I expect. But as far as anybody needs to know, Dobie never came to town. Us neither."

"Thank God." She laid her head against his arm. "And thank you too, Mr. Goodson. I'll always owe you for this."

"You don't owe me nothin'." He flipped the reins to put the team into a trot. "I had a boy once, but I lost him. You lost a boy, too. I didn't want to see you lose another."

The wagon bumped along the road. As they neared the house, she broke a long silence. "You don't have a home, do you, Mr. Goodson?"

"I used to have, a long time ago."

"Since you've been here, a lot of things have changed for the better. I do wish you'd stay."

He felt his throat tighten. Regret weighed on him like a stone. "Aurelia, there's no place I'd rather be than right here. It's like I've found what I've been lookin' for the last twenty-thirty years. There's reasons I can't stay, but this isn't the time to talk about them. Right now let's get Dobie home. If somebody comes askin' after him, we can say he's been there all night."

CHAPTER

16

Andy was itching to leave town. Choctaw John said he was not sure he was healed enough to ride, though Andy suspected he simply liked the wages. He was walking around on his own and had discovered Oscar Counts's saloon without help from Andy. He claimed whiskey eased the pain.

Andy said, "I thought it was against the law to sell liquor to Indians."

"I ain't but half of one. It's the other half that drinks."

With aid of the deputy sheriff, Andy had contacted other lawmen in the region, alerting them to be on the lookout for Cordell. He decided Griffin was as good a place as any to await developments. He passed the time by visiting drovers who came by with northbound herds, learning about the areas from which they had started, the chances of going into ranching for himself. Perhaps if he found the right place, he could wean Bethel away from the family farm and shed himself of Farley Brackett for once and for all.

Oscar was a flowing fountain of information, though little of it was of help to Andy. He had been in Fort Griffin since buffalo-hunting days. He told Andy and John, "You ain't smelled smells till you've smelled a big stack of buffalo hides from the downwind side. They'd blister your nose. And flies? They'd swarm to where you couldn't see the sun, hardly. There wasn't but one savin' grace to the buffalo trade. That was the money. We had flush times here while they lasted."

Andy observed, "Looks like you've been doin' pretty good with the trail herds comin' by."

"Durin' spring and part of the summer. It shuts off then because they want to get to Kansas before the snow flies. Them South Texas cattle don't take kindly to a blizzard, and neither do South Texas cowboys. So I've got to make hay while the sun shines." He frowned. "I'm afraid it ain't goin' to shine much longer here. The railroads are soon goin' to finish the trail drives."

"We've heard about the robbery that took place some nights ago. Have you taken precautions?"

Oscar stepped behind the bar and brought up a double-barreled shotgun. "I've got old Chickamauga here. Kicks like a mule, but it blows a hole big enough to drive a wagon through."

"If they give you a chance to use it."

"I never get far from it when there's suspicious-lookin' characters in here."

Andy described Cordell as best he could. "Been anybody in here who looked like that?"

Oscar shrugged. "There's half a dozen of them any night. Hell, you've come close to describin' me, except I'm too old to fit." He considered for a moment. "Come to think of it, I remember one man in particular. He was sittin' back yonder mindin' his own business when them

Keeler boys come in one night and started hoorawin' a couple of my customers. Me and him, we set them straight. He looked like he could chew them up and spit them out. I think he put the Indian sign on them, because they ain't been back."

Andy sat up straight. "What did he look like?"

"About the way you described, only he didn't have no beard. Just a few days' whiskers, was all. He put away enough whiskey to bring a mule to its knees, but it didn't faze him none that I could see."

"Do you know where he came from, or where he went?"

"Never seen him before or since. I judged that he might be bossin' a trail herd. He looked like one of them tough cowmen from down in the brush country. If so, he's close to the Red River by now, or across it."

Andy eased. It seemed unlikely that Cordell would be with a trail drive. Cattle herds traveled no more than about ten miles a day, and that only on the good days. Cordell would want to move faster.

Oscar brought Andy a beer and filled John's whiskey glass. "You fellers are welcome to sit here as long as you like. It's on the house. If they hear there's a Ranger and his helper around, them robbers are apt to steer clear of Griffin."

Andy said, "I can't stay in town much longer. I've got to get out and look for Cordell."

"You don't have any idea where he's at, do you?"

"No."

"So any direction you go, you're apt to be movin' farther away from him instead of closer. Ain't that right?"

"That's a way of lookin' at it."

"So, if I was you, I'd stay right here till I heard somethin'. That makes sense, don't it?"

Andy knew it made sense to Oscar, but he had a vested interest in keeping a Ranger here. The state office might not feel the same way. "Well, maybe just a little bit longer."

Andy had about made up his mind to leave town. He had received a wire from Austin telling him to continue the search for Cordell at his own discretion, though the state office offered no new leads to help him. He had satisfied himself that Cordell was not in Fort Griffin. He was undecided where to go from here. He told John, "I'll write a voucher for what the state owes you. You can submit it from back home."

John took the news in good nature. "I guess my vacation is over, and so is Thaddeus's. I've missed bein' able to wart that old skinflint. How about we go down to Oscar's place and have a last drink together? Or maybe two."

By the time Andy had finished one beer and John had downed three whiskeys, the evening's cowboy crowd was gone. A local citizen came in and visited with Oscar a couple of minutes, his expression grim. He spoke in a voice so low that Andy could not make out what he was saying. Oscar came to Andy, his face troubled. "I hope you-all ain't in a hurry to go to bed."

Andy asked, "What's the trouble?"

"None yet, but a friend of mine just told me he saw them Keeler boys down by the river."

Andy remembered Oscar talking about the Keelers before. "You think they may be up to no good?"

"I never seen them when they wasn't. And I hear there's another one with them. Probably that Jackson kid."

Jackson. Andy wondered why that name sounded familiar. He tried to remember where he had heard it.

Oscar said, "I've suspicioned all along that it wasn't no drovers that pistol-whipped and robbed Old Shep. I believe it was them Keelers. I suspect they've held a grudge agin me since the night me and that stranger ran them out of here."

"Have you got your money in a safe place?"

"I keep enough behind the bar to make change. The rest is in a steel box under a trapdoor back here. Ain't but three or four people besides me know that."

Andy considered. "If they're plannin' to rob you, they probably figure to do it as you close up, when you're by yourself. So me and John will let them see us leave, but we won't go far."

Oscar checked the shotgun. "This town has put up with their shenanigans long enough. If they come here on mischief, they've got a surprise waitin', and it ain't a birthday present."

Andy said, "Just be sure you don't shoot me or John." He moved to the door. He told John quietly, "You cut around and cover the back door in case they try to go in that way. I'll watch the front."

John said, "This sounds a little dangerous. Reckon you can get me extra pay for it?"

"Just remember how many free drinks Oscar has given you."

They turned into the darkness at the side of Oscar's

saloon. John walked down to the far end, near the back door. Andy saw Oscar blow out the lantern that hung on the front porch. That threw the area outside the saloon into near darkness, compromised only by a pale light from the lamp on the bar.

Andy found himself sweating. He usually did when he faced the probability of a fight. It was something he had never talked to other Rangers about. He feared they would take it as a sign of weakness and have less confidence in him. He rubbed a clammy hand on a trouser leg and concentrated on the street.

He did not wait long. He saw three horsemen moving in the darkness. In front of the saloon, two with faces covered dismounted and handed their bridle reins to the third rider. His face was masked, but his wiry form indicated he was young. The two stepped up onto Oscar's porch, paused a moment as if summoning their nerve, and walked through the door.

Seemingly from nowhere, a large man appeared on foot, grabbed the reins to one of the horses and swung quickly into the saddle. He said something sharp, then drove a hard fist against the rider's jaw. He grabbed the young man to keep him from falling, then set both horses into a run back up the street.

Andy froze. He could almost swear he had seen Cordell. It was like reliving the jailbreak.

Oscar's shotgun blast reverberated like a cannon inside the saloon. An agonized scream followed the shot. One of the robbers rushed out the door and turned to fire his pistol back into the saloon.

Andy shouted, "Halt! Drop the gun!"

Instead, the man whirled and triggered a quick shot in Andy's direction. Andy fired. The man doubled over, staggered, then sprawled on the porch.

Oscar yelled from inside, "Everything all right out there?"

His body shaking, Andy answered, "It's over with." John came running around the corner, pistol in his hand. He stopped when he saw the would-be robber lying on his stomach. The man groaned. Andy turned him over and pulled off the sack that had hidden his face. The robber was young, his eyes full of terror. Spitting blood, he spoke in a raspy voice Andy could barely hear. "It wasn't supposed . . . to happen like this." He cried in desperation, "Somebody help me!" He reached out a hand, then let it drop. He trembled and went still.

Andy shuddered. Rusty Shannon had told him he should never become so hardened that it did not disturb him to kill someone, even in self-defense. He doubted that he ever would. He *hoped* he never would.

Oscar came onto the porch, holding the bar lamp. Shaken, he said, "It was the Keelers, all right. But where's Dobie Jackson? I figured he was with them."

Andy considered telling what he had seen, but instinct told him to wait. The name Jackson nagged at him until he remembered where he had heard it. That was the name of the young outlaw he had shot when Cordell was being broken out of jail. Andy had helped bury him. The pieces began coming together.

He said, "Looks like you might've figured wrong."

Oscar replied, "I suppose I did. These two were all that I saw. But it wouldn't hurt to talk to Dobie. He might know somethin' about this."

"I'll talk to him. Where does he live?"

Oscar said Jackson and his mother lived east of town, on the river. "A widow. Nice woman, but she raised two wild sons. The older one ran away from home. I been expecting the younger one to do the same thing."

"The older one . . . what was his name?"

"David. Seemed like a decent kid till he took to the wild bunch. Why, do you know somethin' about him?"

"Just curious."

By this time an excited crowd had gathered, including the grim-faced deputy. Oscar explained to him what had happened. The lawman said, "Too bad, but those boys've been tryin' to get through the penitentiary gates for a long time. Or the gates of hell. There wasn't anybody with them?"

"I just saw these two," Oscar said. "Soon as they came in with their faces covered, I knew what they was fixin' to do. I let go with old Chickamauga. Cut the first one in two. The other one turned and ran, but he taken a shot at the Ranger. Worst mistake he ever made."

The deputy turned to Andy. "Lucky thing you were close by."

Andy looked down at the body on the porch. "Not for this boy." He shuddered again. He felt as if he might throw up, and he fought to bring the nausea under control.

The deputy shook his head. "I dread ridin' out to tell old man Keeler. He'll just sink deeper into the bottle after this."

Oscar said with some bitterness, "That boy died callin' for help. He needed it a long time ago, him and his brother both. Damned little they got from the old man."

Andy beckoned to John. "We've got to take us a ride."

"Right now?"

"We won't sleep tonight anyway, not after this. Let's go saddle up."

Lamplight shone through the farmhouse window. Approaching it, Andy said, "No respectable farmer is awake this long after midnight unless somebody's sick."

John remained skeptical. "Maybe you've been huntin' Cordell so long that everybody has started to look like him."

"Maybe. We're fixin' to find out." Andy moved up to a window propped open with a stick. In the dull light of a lamp he saw a woman sitting with a young man at a kitchen table. He assumed from what Oscar had told him that they were Mrs. Jackson and her son Dobie. A large man stood nearby, turned away so that Andy could not see his face.

The young man was complaining, "But they'll think I went coward and ran out on them."

The woman said, "Son, those Keelers are of bad blood. It makes no difference what they think. The main thing is that Mr. Goodson probably saved you from going to the penitentiary. Or to your grave."

Dobie cried, "Who is he to be runnin' my life? He ain't my paw, and he ain't your husband. He ain't nobody."

The man said gravely, "Boy, you were fixin' to set foot on the road to perdition."

Dobie shouted, "What would you know about it? Are you a preacher or somethin'?"

"I'm a long ways from bein' a preacher, but I know that road. I've been on it. I'm still on it. It's hard to get off of." He placed a hand on Dobie's shoulder. Dobie twisted away from him.

Mrs. Jackson told her son, "It was my doing as much as his. I asked Mr. Goodson to stop you."

Dobie lashed out at her, "Why don't you mind your own business? You're naggin' me like you nagged David. It was you that made him run away from home."

She said, "I was trying to keep him from making a bad mistake. The same kind you were about to make tonight."

"So he got a bellyful of it and left. Now you have no idea where he's at."

"I wish to God I did."

"I've had it in mind to go and find him. That's why I went with the Keelers, to get me some travelin' money."

Mrs. Jackson began to weep. The man stepped up closer and moved a hand as if to touch her, then changed his mind and drew it away. "Aurelia, there's somethin' I've got to tell you. I've been meanin' to from the first, but I couldn't bring myself to do it." He paused as if gathering courage. "Dobie, there's no use in you lookin' for David. He's dead."

Mrs. Jackson gasped. Dobie froze.

The man said, "David made the mistake of throwin' in with a bad man. That mistake got him killed."

Mrs. Jackson seemed too stunned to speak. Dobie demanded, "What bad man?"

"Me."

Andy had heard enough. Though he had not seen the face, he knew this was Cordell. Drawing his pistol, he motioned for John to follow him through the kitchen door. He declared, "Luther Cordell, I'm a Ranger, and you're under arrest."

Cordell turned slowly, raising his hands. Andy had not seen him without the dark beard he had worn in jail. Nothing in his face showed him to be the same man except perhaps the piercing dark eyes. Cordell appeared more resigned than surprised. He said, "You're that friend of Sheriff Blessing's."

"That's right. I am."

"You've been followin' me all along, ain't you?"

"I have." Andy wondered at Cordell's unflinching acceptance of his capture.

"I didn't know who it was, but I felt in my bones that somebody was doggin' me. I stayed on the move till I got to this place. I kept meanin' to go on, but I couldn't." Cordell looked regretfully at Mrs. Jackson. "The longer I stayed, the harder it was to do what I came for."

Her eyes were sad. "And what did you come for?"

"To tell you about your boy David. I owed it to you to tell you where he's buried. And I was goin' to give you the money that rightfully belonged to him."

Andy said, "If it's the Galveston money, it's not yours to give." He reached out and lifted Cordell's pistol from its holster.

Cordell said, "Don't worry. I won't try to get away. I won't bring trouble to this good lady's house. She's already had enough." He lowered his hands and sat down at the table. "Aurelia, I'm a wanted man. Been one for a long time. But I didn't lie to you about my name. It's really Walter Goodson. I borrowed the name Cordell from a man I knew that got killed in the war. I didn't figure it could hurt him none."

"What about David?" she asked anxiously.

"I called him Buster. Didn't even know his rightful name for a long time. He was pitiful as a lost pup, broke and hungry, lookin' for somebody to join up with. I fed him and tried to run him off, but he kept followin' me. I got to where I liked havin' him around. I've wished a thousand times that I'd turned him away. It would've been a kindness." Cordell looked at Dobie. "That's why I stopped you tonight. I didn't want you to end up like your brother."

Andy said, "I saw what you did in town. It was the right thing. The Keeler brothers are dead."

Dobie's jaw dropped. "Dead? Sully and Finn both?"

"Both of them."

Dobie seemed to wilt.

Cordell said, "You don't have to arrest Dobie, do you, Ranger? He never set foot in that saloon, and he was gone before the shootin' took place."

Andy saw grief and fear in Mrs. Jackson's eyes. His voice was severe as he spoke to Dobie. "Boy, you came within an inch of bein' killed. If it wasn't for Cordell, you'd likely be laid out at the undertaker's right now, alongside the Keelers."

Dobie was still stunned. In a breaking voice, he asked Cordell, "Do you know for sure that my brother is dead?"

Cordell said with regret, "I was with him when he died."

Andy said, "And I was there at his buryin'."

Dobie broke down and cried. His mother put her arms around his shoulders and cried with him.

Cordell's question was still unanswered. He said, "If you'll let the boy go, I promise I won't try to get away from you. Not now, and not later."

Andy said, "I don't see the harm. Maybe he's learned somethin', and I wouldn't want to see the lady lose another son."

Cordell attempted a smile, but it did not quite come off. "I'm much obliged. What do we do now?"

Andy snapped the cuffs over Cordell's wrists. "We get that Galveston money, and then we head east."

John asked, "What about me? Don't you think I ought to go along to help you guard him?"

Andy knew John was mainly interested in getting paid a while longer. "You heard him promise he won't try to get away."

"Ain't you ever had an outlaw lie to you?"

"All right, you're still on the payroll, even if it comes out of my pocket."

"Just till we get to my place. If you need help after that, you'll have to hire somebody else. I've got things of my own to do."

Mrs. Jackson took control of her emotions and set about making breakfast. "It'll be daylight pretty soon," she said. "You-all shouldn't start a long trip on an empty stomach." The way she looked at Cordell told Andy she wished he would never go.

Andy wondered again what it was about the man that drew so many people to him. He *was* an outlaw, after all, yet people instinctively liked him. Andy said, "Cordell, I can't figure you out. At the start, I took it for granted that you shot Tom Blessing. Now, the way folks keep takin' up for you, I wonder."

"Milt Hayward done it. I didn't intend for him and the boy to bust me loose. I've never seen a jail I couldn't get out of by myself. But Milt was anxious for his share of the Galveston take, and he never was one for waitin'. I cussed him good for shootin' the sheriff. There wasn't no need in it."

"Where do you suppose he is now?"

"With Milt, there's no tellin'. He could be anyplace."

"If I could catch him and make him talk, the law might go easier on you. As it is, all I've got is your word that you didn't shoot Tom."

"And I don't reckon my word is worth a plugged nickel."

Andy pondered, then admitted, "It is to me, but it might not be enough for a court."

"Looks like my goose is cooked."

Mrs. Jackson poured coffee and brought scrambled eggs and bacon to the table. She looked in the oven. "Biscuits are almost ready."

Andy noticed that her eyes were on Cordell except when she had to tend to her cooking. He saw there a look that he had sometimes seen in Bethel's.

He said to Cordell, "You look like a man who could do anything he wanted to. How did you come to get started on the wrong side of the law?"

"It was after the war. I'd lost everything that meant anything to me. Didn't have coin enough in my pocket to buy
coffee. I came onto this little old country bank just sittin'
there doin' nothin'. I thought about all the money in it just
sittin' there doin' nothin', and I decided to put it to work.
I'd've been happy to quit after that, but the law wouldn't let
me stop anywhere long enough to hold an honest job.
Pretty soon I was broke and hungry again, and I found me
another bank. It's been like that ever since."

"Think you could ever have got yourself straight?"

"I've wanted to. I'd do it in a minute if the law wasn't
crowdin' me. If I could start over fresh, I'd be the happiest
dirt farmer you ever saw." He turned to Dobie. "I've been
tryin' to tell you about the road to perdition. I've been on it
a long time and tryin' hard to get off."

Mrs. Jackson pleaded, "He means it, Ranger, can't you
see that?"

Andy felt himself caught in a bind. "I'm sorry, but I'm
honorbound to bring in Luther Cordell."

He and John had tied their horses thirty yards from the
house. John went out to fetch them while Andy and
Cordell walked to the barn. The sun was just coming up,
hitting Andy in the eyes. Cordell said, "That's my mare in
the pen. She won't leave the barn at night. The feed has got
her spoiled." He opened the gate. "Don't worry, I didn't
steal her. I bought her fair and square."

With stolen money, Andy thought. "I met the old man
you bought her from. He stood up for you, said you're on
the square."

"I've always tried to be, after my fashion. I never robbed

anybody that didn't have too much money for his own good."

Andy had holstered his pistol, but he kept his hand on the butt of it. Though Cordell had promised not to try to get away, Andy had observed that even the most honest of men would lie now and again if the stakes were high enough. "Get her saddled, then tell me where you hid the money."

Cordell said, "In the barn. I found a loose board under the saddle rack. Lift it up and there'll be my saddlebags." John had arrived, leading his and Andy's horses. Andy motioned to him, and John entered the barn. In a minute he was back with the saddlebags. He opened one and whistled in surprise. "I never saw so much money in all my life."

Cordell said, "It should be somethin' over nine thousand dollars. I've had to spend a little along the way. It costs a right smart to live nowadays. Have you seen the price of flour and coffee?"

John said, "Do we really have to turn it in? We could split it and say he spent it all. I'd be almost as rich as old Thaddeus."

Andy was not sure John was joking until he saw a boyish grin spread across the man's face. "Don't even talk about it unless you want to find out if a Comanche can whip a Choctaw."

Mrs. Jackson and Dobie came up together from the house. She had her hands clasped in front of her, and her eyes glistened. "Mr. Goodson, when you get free, you'll always be welcome here."

Cordell's expression was downcast. "Ranger, I owe her a decent good-bye."

Andy nodded. "Go ahead."

The outlaw walked to her, leading the mare. Despite the cuffs around his wrists, he took her hands in a tight grip. "Aurelia, I'd give anything . . ."

Her eyes filled with tears. She grasped his shoulders and kissed him. "I know."

Dobie watched with amazement. Cordell turned to him and said, "Remember what I told you about the road to perdition. And take good care of your mother. She needs you real bad."

Dobie looked dazed. He said nothing.

Cordell told Mrs. Jackson, "He's learned a lot today. Once he's sorted it all out, I believe he'll be all right."

A bewhiskered horseman rode out from behind the barn, taking Andy by surprise. Brandishing a pistol, he ordered, "Everybody raise your hands to where I can see them." He poked the muzzle in Andy's and John's direction. "You two, drop them guns on the ground. Do it with your left hands."

He was almost as large as Cordell. Andy recognized him.

John muttered, "That's the jaybird that busted my ribs."

The man said, "I'll do worse if anybody messes with me." He turned his attention to Cordell. "Howdy, Luther. I've wore out three horses tryin' to find you."

Cordell said sullenly, "Thought you ran off to Mexico, Milt."

Milt Hayward replied, "Started to, but I kept thinkin'

about the money you was supposed to hold for me. You still got it in them saddlebags?" He motioned toward the pouches Andy had just tied to his saddle.

Cordell said, "Except for what little I spent. How did you manage to trail me so far?"

"I couldn't. You were too slippery. But I figured the Ranger was trailin' you, so I followed *him*. I hoped he'd catch up to you sooner or later."

Andy realized why Hayward had avoided shooting him when he wounded John. He had needed Andy to lead him to Cordell.

Cordell said, "You left before we could make the split. I always intended to give you your share."

Hayward made a crooked smile. "I'll bet you did. Luther, I like the way them handcuffs fit you. As long as the law has got you, I don't have to worry about you comin' after me. And I don't have to settle for part of that money. I can take all of it."

Cordell's jaw tightened with anger.

Hayward said, "That woman'll be good insurance for me. I'm takin' her along. If anybody crowds me, she's dead."

Dobie shouted, "No." He moved protectively in front of his mother. "Take me if you need somebody, but leave her alone."

Hayward said, "You're a fool, kid. Move aside, or I'll have to shoot you."

Mrs. Jackson gently pushed her son away. "Do what he says."

Andy declared, "You're the man that shot Tom Blessing."

"You mean that clodhopper sheriff? Damn fool got in my way."

Andy trembled with anger. "You'd better ride far and fast, because I'll be comin' after you."

Hayward's eyes had a poisonous look. "There's one way to take care of that." He pointed the pistol into Andy's face.

Cordell took a quick step forward, placing himself between Andy and Hayward. "Killin' a Ranger will bring all the law in Texas down on us. Leave him to me. Let me pick up one of the guns, and I'll see that he gives you a long head start."

Hayward shook his head. "Or maybe you'd shoot me and him both and keep the money yourself. I ain't no tenderfoot. Step out of the way."

Cordell did not move. Hayward began to look flustered. He said, "All right, Luther, I won't shoot the Ranger. You can bring them saddlebags to me yourself. And woman, get on that mare."

Dobie again stepped in front of his mother. Cordell told him, "He means what he says. For your mother's sake, you'd better do it." Cordell's voice crackled with hatred as he warned Hayward, "Don't you hurt this woman, or I'll follow you to hell's far side."

Hayward grumbled, "Fetch me that money, or I *will* shoot somebody."

Hampered by the cuffs, Cordell fumbled in detaching the bags from Andy's saddle. He moved toward Hayward. "Here they are, and be damned."

As the outlaw reached for them, Cordell flung them at

the horse. The startled animal jumped, slinging its head and squealing. Almost unseated, Hayward cursed and grabbed at the saddle horn.

Cordell shouted, "Let's get him, Ranger!" He grabbed up the pistol John had dropped, but Hayward fired first. Cordell grunted at the impact.

Hayward's frightened horse kicked up clods of earth as it pitched out from under him. The outlaw fell heavily but kept his grip on the pistol. In the moment of confusion Andy retrieved his own weapon and fired. Hayward jerked as the bullet drove into his chest, but he did not drop the pistol. Andy fired again. Hayward pitched forward beside the saddlebags. Struggling for breath, he murmured, "Burn in hell, all of you." He reached for the bags, but his clawing fingers could not find them. A long sigh escaped from deep in his chest. He did not breathe again.

Andy felt no nausea this time. Instead, he felt satisfaction and a sense of closure. Now maybe Tom Blessing could rest easy.

He said, "Thanks, Cordell. You made a good try."

Aurelia Jackson grabbed her son and gave him a sweeping glance up and down. "Did he hit you, Son?"

Dobie's voice trembled. "No, but I think he got Mr. Goodson."

Andy had been too busy to see Cordell fall. He took two long strides, dropped to one knee, and turned Cordell over onto his back. Blood pumped from a wound in his shoulder. Andy said, "At least he missed the heart. John, you'd better hitch up the wagon. We have to get him to town pretty quick, or we'll lose him." He tried to stanch the blood with a handkerchief, but it was not enough.

Aurelia was on her knees, her arm around Cordell. Tears in her eyes, she said, "That might be better than spending the rest of his life in the penitentiary." Then she cried, "I didn't mean it. Hold on, Mr. Goodson. Please hold on."

Andy drew back, addled by the way a situation that seemed so simple and straightforward had taken such an unexpected turn.

Dobie hurried to the house and brought back a couple of towels. Andy tore Cordell's shirt open and pressed one against the wound. He told Mrs. Jackson, "Hold it tight so he won't bleed to death."

John brought up the wagon. He said, "Andy, if you know any Comanche medicine songs, this might be a good time to sing them."

"I don't remember one. You know any?"

"Us Choctaws don't believe in that foolishness."

Andy and John lifted Cordell into the bed of the wagon. The strain of the man's weight caused John to clutch at the side where his rib was still bandaged. Andy said, "Mrs. Jackson, you and Dobie get started. Me and John will be right behind you." He turned his attention to Hayward's still form. "We've got to take Cordell's body in to show the deputy."

John blinked. "What do you mean, Cordell's body? Cordell is in the wagon."

"No, that's Mr. Goodson." Andy pointed with his chin toward the man on the ground. "This is Cordell."

It took John a moment to absorb what Andy was saying.

"You went to a lot of trouble to find him. Now you're lettin' him go?"

"I was after the man who killed Tom Blessing. I got
him. That's as much as anybody needs to know."

"You're takin' a hell of a chance. If Cordell ever goes
outlaw again, they won't only be lookin' for him, they'll be
lookin' for you."

Andy watched the wagon move away, Dobie driving the
team. Aurelia Jackson sat in the wagon bed. The man she
knew as Goodson lay with his head in her lap. Andy said,
"The dead don't come back to life. Luther Cordell is dead,
and we'll give him a tombstone to prove it."

Judge Tompkins stood up from his paper-strewn desk and
took a half-smoked cigar from his mouth as Andy walked
into his office. "The prodigal has returned," he said, beam-
ing. "Ranger headquarters sent us a wire saying you got
your man."

Andy said, "Dead and buried. Anything new around
here?"

The judge said, "A little. You been out to the Brackett
farm yet?"

Andy shook his head. "No, I've been sort of dreadin' it."

"I suspect that little girl will be glad to see you."

"But her brother won't. I had one fistfight with him. I
left to keep from havin' another. I doubt his temperament
has changed much."

"He's got more things to worry about than a little argument with you. We've set the date for a special election to

fill Tom Blessing's job as sheriff. Farley Brackett was the first to file."

Andy grunted in resignation. "I figured as much."

"But he's got opposition. A group of us convinced Rusty Shannon that the county needs a better sheriff than Farley. From what I can tell, most people around here agree with us. On election day, Farley is going to feel like a cyclone hit him. I think he already senses it."

Andy took pleasure in the thought that Rusty would be the next sheriff. But defeat would probably make Farley even more antagonistic than he already was.

The judge fingered through several papers on his desk. "I've got a wire here from the state Ranger office. It's for you." He found it and handed it over. "They're pleased with what you've done. They're offering you a new station."

Andy read the wire. It should have been good news, but it left him feeling cold. "Kerrville's a long way from here. A long way from Bethel."

"And from Farley," the judge pointed out.

"That part I like."

"There's something else. Being gone, you couldn't have heard. Old Mrs. Brackett died a couple of days after you left. Bethel's feeling pretty low. She's lost her mother, and she figures she's lost you." He paused. "Has she?"

"Not if I can help it."

A dog met Andy a hundred yards from the Brackett farmhouse and escorted him in, barking an announcement all the way. Farley walked out onto the front porch and waited for him. Glum-faced, he grunted, "Back, are you?"

Andy tensed, half expecting Farley to order him off the place. "For just a little while."

Farley frowned. "I expect you came to see Bethel. She's inside."

Andy stepped down and tied his horse to a post.

Farley said, "I suppose you heard that your friend Rusty Shannon is runnin' against me."

"So I've been told."

"From everything I hear, I'd just as well withdraw. I can't understand what people around here have got against me." Farley stepped down from the porch and started toward the barn. He stopped and turned half around. "This county has got more sunshine, more sunflowers, and more sons of bitches than any place I've ever been." He stalked away, his shoulders hunched.

Bethel met Andy at the door. He thought he had remembered how beautiful she was, but she looked even better as she moved eagerly into his arms. He said, "I just now heard about your mother. I'm sorry."

A tear moved down Bethel's cheek. "It was her time. She was ready to go. Now it's just Farley and Teresa and me. And you."

He lifted the message from his shirt pocket and unfolded it. "I won't be here for long." He handed her the paper. "They're sendin' me way off to West Texas, to Kerrville."

"I've heard you talk a lot about the hill country. You loved it when you were stationed there."

"I always figured to have a place of my own someday. Maybe I'll find it out in the hills."

She read the wire and looked up at him. "When are we leaving?"

"We?"

"Farley can run the farm to suit himself. With Mother gone, there's nothing to keep me here."

"But what would people say, us goin' off together and not even married?"

She clasped her hands behind his neck, pulled him down, and kissed him. "That should be easy to fix."